It was said a man could travel the leng[th] touching the ground. Ahren had neve[r] occasions traveled the shingle highway escape the city guards. Other thieves ~~swore~~ within Lichthafen's vast sewers, but the dark and dangerous maze-work never appealed to him. Many of the daring souls who entered the tunnels never returned.

Following the easiest path between buildings, Ahren circled around the block before finally nearing the widow's house. Careful not to slip on loose shingles, he hopped onto one of the adjoining rooftops then froze.

Katze stood on the roof before him, her dark cloak blowing in the breeze. Smiling, she held up the vase in her hand.

Bitterly, he nodded back.

A shadow moved on the rooftop beside her. Marten stepped out from behind a chimney clutching a thick-bladed knife. Another man rose from behind a peaked rooftop holding a cudgel. Katze whistled and the two men charged toward him.

Spinning around, Ahren retreated in the other direction. Katze might have agreed not to kill him, but her thugs had made no promise. He raced down a steep rooftop and leaped across to the neighboring building.

Footsteps pounded wooden shingles behind him, racing to catch up. The heavy satchels jostled Ahren's hips as he ran. He jumped down onto a lower roof and hurried along the slender peak stretching to the neighboring block. A wide canyon opened before him, dropping four stories to the street below. He glanced back, finding his two pursuers not fifty feet behind him. Ahren took a breath, and leapt across.

MOUNTAIN OF DAGGERS

Tales of the Black Raven Book 1

by SETH SKORKOWSKY

MYSTIQUE PRESS

In memory of Austin Schaefers.

Contents

Birth of the Black Raven

Nobles and merchants laughed and talked amongst the chorus of clinking glasses and music echoing from the ballroom below. Ahren kept his eyes to the marble floor or on the bright tapestries to avoid attention. Adjusting his doublet, he wove his way up the crowded staircase. The coarse cloth of the server's uniform itched terribly. He wondered how anyone could ever get used to it. When the day came that he could have servants of his own, their uniforms would be more comfortable.

Earlier in the evening, he had thought the ruse over when an older gentleman had tried to speak with him. Presuming the man was ordering a drink or maybe food, Ahren had only nodded as a servant should, and melted into the crowd. It would only be a few minutes longer before he could spend the rest of the night in hiding; tomorrow he would be a rich man and on his way home, or at least to a coastal city where he spoke the language.

Leaving the party behind, he followed a long hallway. Stopping at the fourth door on the right, he looked around. No one was watching. Quickly, he opened it and stepped inside.

"Did you get it, thief?" Baron Krevnyet asked in Mordakish.

"Yeah. I got it." Ahren strained to see in the darkened room. He could barely make out a hint of light from between the window shutters.

"Where is it?" He heard the baron step closer.

"Right here." Ahren pulled the heavy brooch from under his doublet. He ran his thumb across the encrusted gold and the giant sapphire at its center.

"Give it here. Let me see it."

Ahren's eyes had adjusted enough to see the nobleman's extended palm. He handed it over.

The baron peered closely at the prize. "Magnificent, don't you think?"

"It is." Ahren nervously fingered the medallion underneath his shirt as he looked around the room. He could make out silhouettes of chairs and a large bed.

A dagger rasped from its sheath.

Seeing the baron pry the gem with the blade, he sighed. The man chuckled to himself as he pulled the inch-wide sapphire free from the prongs.

"Your pay," the baron said, handing back the brooch.

Even without the gem, the gold and diamonds were worth a small fortune. More than enough to pay for passage back to Mordakland. But why waste it? He could work a vessel, and when he made it home he could set himself up in style.

"Open the window a little," the baron said, still examining the stone. "I want to see it in the light."

Ahren cracked open the shutters slightly to avoid being noticed by any of the partygoers in the courtyard below. He turned to see the spacious bedroom. Several busts stared at him from atop short pedestals. A painting of the baron hung above the mantle beside a blue-canopied bed. Ahren's eyes stopped in the corner of the room.

The body of a woman lay on the floor in a pool of blood.

His mouth opened in horror. Then he saw the baron charging, the dagger clutched in his hand.

Ahren jumped back. The swinging blade still caught him. He felt the sting as the dagger sliced through his doublet and across his stomach. The baron pressed forward in another attack. Ahren back-stepped and fell, crashing through the open shutters and out the window with a cry of surprise. Crying out, he landed in a hedge, his foot twisted beneath him. The golden brooch dropped from his hand and bounced at the feet of the surprised party guests.

The baron burst through the window above. "Ubiytsa! Ubiytsa!"

Ahren didn't understand the words, but he understood the onlookers' gasps and horror-struck faces. He rolled to the ground as a man reached for him. Ahren shoved a screaming woman out of the way and snatched up the fallen brooch.

Men yelled and drew their swords as he sprinted across the courtyard. Stabbing pain shot through his ankle. The tight, fancy shoes bit into his feet. He pushed the hurt from his mind as he crashed through tables and leapt over rosebushes.

The gate guard unsheathed his rapier and charged. Ahren grabbed a plate and hurled it at the man. The flying porcelain exploded against his forehead. The guard fell to the ground holding his face, blood pouring between his gloved hands. Leaping over him, Ahren raced into the city street. A cacophony of screams and cries followed him into the night.

The streets of Ralkosty were mostly clear. Many of the shops and vendors had already closed for the evening. Ahren ducked into an alley just as a pair of riders raced past him in pursuit. Church bells rang an alarm, and it would only be a matter of time before the soldiers found him. He hurried to escape the noble district, keeping to the small avenues and alleyways.

Ahren slowed once he reached what appeared to be a merchant district. Peasants wandered the narrow streets, perusing the late-night stands as they moved between bars and brothels. Holding his arm over his stomach, he covered the dagger cut across his doublet. The red cloth easily masked the blood from his wound. It no longer bled, but he had yet to see its severity.

A trio of whores called to him from an open window. He knew his disheveled appearance and the torn, fancy clothes made him stand out. He thought about taking a room in a nearby inn. There might even be an innkeeper that spoke Mordakish. But this far inland in Rhomanny it wasn't likely. It didn't matter anyway; his only money was still wrapped inside his clothes at the baron's house.

An oncoming patrol of soldiers forced Ahren to hide in an alley. Holding his breath, he listened until their boot clomps faded away. He let out a sigh, then limped further into the alley. With a groan, he sat down on an empty barrel.

He pulled off the awkward shoes, and rubbed his swollen ankle. Now that the initial chase was over, its silent pain throbbed stronger. He'd be lucky if he was able to walk tomorrow. Not that it mattered. By now the entire city was looking for him. The city gates would already be closed and his hunters would be on the prowl. He had nowhere to go. The only man he knew had just thrown him out a window. He had no money, no way to speak to the locals, nothing but a stolen brooch with no fence to buy it.

Ahren hissed in pain as he shed the doublet and dropped it in a barrel beside him. It was a server's uniform and would only mark him. He ripped open the bloody tear across his shirt and examined his wound. Thick clumps of blood coated the hand-length gash. It wasn't deep, but with no barber to stitch it, it was only time before pus and fever set in.

He leaned back against the wall, remembering the fateful conversation that had led to this predicament.

"So where are you headed?" the baron had asked. He ran his hand along the twenty boxes freshly stacked in his warehouse. "Back to Frobinsky?"

"Yeah, I suppose," Ahren had said, wiping the sweat from his brow. "The *Seefalk* should be ready to sail by the time I return."

The baron nodded. "Did you ever wonder why the captain sent you to guard the shipment? I'm sure many of the other crew speak Rhomanic."

"I figured it was because he trusts me most."

The baron dabbed a handkerchief across his face. "The answer is because I had sent for a thief. The best thief the captain could think of. So he sent me you."

Ahren looked around. No one was in the warehouse with them. He studied the baron's fine clothing and neatly trimmed moustache. He eyed the silver rapier hilt at the man's waist.

"The captain made a mistake," Ahren said. "I am not a thief."

The baron's blue eyes sparkled. "Ah, I see. Then I suppose you wouldn't be interested in a small proposition. Seems unfortunate. I liked doing business with your captain. But if he can't tell a thief from an honest man, I have no use for him."

Ahren sighed. He didn't trust this baron. Something about him felt off. But Captain Hinstein had saved his life during a storm. He owed the man everything, and he couldn't allow himself to lose one of the captain's best clients.

"No one is *entirely* honest," he said carefully.

The baron grinned. "That's what I thought."

The cold edge of a blade against his throat jolted Ahren to the present.

"Vashi den'gii ili vasha zhizn," hissed a blond man holding the knife. He gave a wicked smile of rotted teeth.

Ahren looked at him with a blank stare. He didn't move. The words were lost on him, but the thief's intent wasn't. A second man with a scruffy black beard patted Ahren down. He easily found the bulge of the brooch hidden at Ahren's waist.

The dark-haired thief's eyes lit up as he removed the treasure and showed it to his accomplice. He shoved it into a pouch and continued his search of Ahren's body.

The blond man chuckled, his breath reeking like rancid meat, and held the blade more firmly. Ahren pulled his head back harder against the wooden wall.

His searcher pulled the bronze medallion out from under Ahren's shirt. With a hard jerk he broke the leather cord. Ahren braced himself. He had no more valuables. The two thieves would likely kill him now. The knife edge pressed against his throat, lightly breaking the skin. He felt the quiver in the blade as the man's arm tensed, readying to make the kill.

The bearded man slapped his companion in the shoulder and showed him the medallion. Relaxing the blade, the blond man took the bauble. His eyes widened as he flipped it over and examined it. They conversed back and forth in Rhomanic, seeming to question the trinket.

The blond thief returned the blade to Ahren's neck. "Otkuda vy eto vzyali?"

Ahren shook his head.

"Otkuda vy eto vzyali?" came again in the vulgar tongue.

"I … I don't speak Rhomanic," Ahren stammered, hoping the cutthroats understood him.

The toothless brigand nodded. He chuckled something to his companion who also nodded in agreement. They exchanged a few words, determining Ahren's fate.

Finally the knife withdrew from Ahren's neck, and he gave soft sigh of relief. The blond man pulled Ahren to his feet and motioned to the shoes lying on the ground.

Ahren bent over and pulled the tight shoes onto his feet. He groaned in pain when he tried to pull one over his swollen ankle. It had almost doubled in size within the past few minutes.

"Sleduyte za name," the man with the dagger said, motioning down the alley. Ahren nodded and hobbled in the direction he was pointed.

The two thieves led him through the dark back streets of the city, completely unsympathetic of Ahren's painful limp. Normally he would have looked for an opening, a moment he could escape. Now his mind focused solely on the pain of each step. He gritted his teeth and held his sliced stomach, fresh blood oozing between his fingers.

They led him to the back of a two-story building. The knife tip pressed firm into Ahren's back as the bearded man knocked on the door.

"Da?" came a voice from within.

The bearded man said something. The voice from inside replied.

The door opened and they led him into a small room. Dozens of shoes in every variety and state of wear lined shelves along the walls. An older man sat at a scarred table at the back of the room. He pushed aside a boot he appeared to have been sewing. His dress was simple, yet fancy enough to show he was not poor.

He spoke with the two men, his fatherly tone tinged with a sharp edge of impatience. The bearded man handed him the brooch and the medallion. Ignoring the gold, the old man grabbed the medallion. His eyes sparkled as he held it, and then returned to their previous composure. He gestured to the wooden chair across from him and the two brutes pushed Ahren into the hard seat.

The man ran his hand across his slender beard as he looked coldly at Ahren. "Ivan says you speak Mordakish."

Ahren nodded. "Yes."

He pursed his thin lips. "What is your name?"

"Ahren."

"What brings you so far from home? Ralkosty is far from Mordakland."

Ahren twisted in his seat. "I'm a sailor. My ship landed in Frobinsky three weeks ago. The captain sent me inland with the cargo to deliver it to the owner."

"You're a thief," the old man said idly. "And a murderer."

Ahren heart pounded. "No, I am a sailor. I don't—"

"Don't lie to me," the old man spat. "Word has already spread through the streets. A thief slipped into the house of Baron Krevnyet during a party, dressed as a servant, and stole a sapphire brooch from Countess Nyschev. The baron's young bride, Aglaya, found the thief hiding in a bedroom and he killed her. The baron caught the killer in the act, and tried to thwart him. In the scuffle, the rogue fell from a window, and fled into the night."

Ahren found it hard to breathe as he heard the story.

"The killer spoke to the baron in Mordakish. You look to have been in a scuffle, and even injured as the story describes. And you wear the poorly made shoes of a house servant at a formal affair." The old man leaned across the worktable. "There is a reward of a thousand gold bishkas for the killer. Dead or alive. For such a fortune, any man would bring you in."

Ahren didn't speak. He knew his face showed his admission to guilt. There was no use lying. "I didn't kill her," he muttered finally.

The old man's brow rose, but he said nothing.

"The baron paid me to steal the brooch. He gave me one of the servants' uniforms and told me to meet him in an empty room once I had gotten it. He would keep the gem and the rest was mine. But when I showed up, she was already dead. He took the gem and tried to kill me. I barely survived, I swear it."

The old man looked down at the gold brooch, missing its central stone. He leaned back in his chair. "Where did you get this?" he asked, holding up the medallion.

"In Lichthafen, when I was young. An old gypsy woman was selling trinkets and jewelry in the square."

The old man's eyes squinted with suspicion. "You bought it off a gypsy?"

Ahren swallowed. "She was blind in one eye, so I palmed the medallion from her blanket on her blind side. Somehow she saw me, and grabbed my hand before I could get away. She was fast, and her grip strong. I was terrified. But she didn't call the guards. She turned, opened my hand and put hers inside it. Then she just let go and told me to keep it. She said the medallion would save my life next time I was caught. I've worn it ever since."

The old man's lips turned into a slight grin. "Have you been caught since, before tonight?"

"No."

"Well, the witch was right. If it weren't for this trinket, you'd be a dead man right now." The old man smiled. "I am Kazimir. Tell me,

Ahren, do you know what this medallion is?"

For years, Ahren had studied and run his fingers over the jagged image of a mountain made of upturned dagger blades stamped onto the bronze disk. It symbolized power, of that he was sure. But its exact meaning was lost to him.

He shook his head.

"This is the mark of the Tyenee. A secret cabal of thieves and smugglers. Unlike any guild or local gang, the Tyenee influence stretches across the nations. Their existence is almost unknown, but their power knows no limitation." Kazimir looked back at the bronze medallion. "This was the badge of one of their leaders. A lieutenant wore this." He flipped it over and pointed to a small glyph scratched on its back. "This was the badge of Grigori. He ran a district of docks and warehouses in Lichthafen. He disappeared almost fifteen years ago."

Ahren leaned forward and looked at the medallion as if it were for the first time. "How do you know this?"

Kazimir pulled a gold chain from under his shirt, revealing a silver pendant. Ahren recognized the symbol instantly. It was almost identical to his own medallion; however, the delicate lines of Kazimir's looked to have been cast rather than stamped.

"He was my cousin," Kazimir said, returning the pendant beneath his silk shirt. "We joined the Tyenee when we were young men. We moved quickly through the ranks, and within a few years he was sent to Mordakland to maintain our interests. Five years later, he vanished."

"And you were sent to Ralkosty?"

The old man nodded. "I have been in this city for twenty years. Nothing happens here without my knowledge or consent."

Ahren couldn't help but let his eyes wander. Scraps of boot leather and metal tools littered the table. Shoes of every size and style covered the unsanded shelves. The pungent smell of leather and stale dust permeated the small room.

"I am a cobbler," Kazimir said calmly. "Every man, no matter how rich, needs shoes. And mine are some of the finest in Rhomanny. Would you prefer I sit in one of the giant houses like the baron, inside my city yet high above it, away from the day to day life?" He shook his head. "Too visible. Too disassociated from my streets. Too much opportunity for some young upstart to try to take over. No, I rule the city the way I want it, and will live in it to keep it that way."

"Why are you telling me all this?" Ahren asked. "You don't even know me."

Kazimir smiled. He poured two glasses of vodka from a bottle near the edge of the table. "Because you can't tell anyone. Ivan and Motya cannot understand us. They only know the symbol is important. With no one to go to, and no ability to communicate, you will be killed on sight if you leave this house, and the only reason I do not have Ivan cut your throat right now is because I believe your story and I believe I may have use for you." He set one of the glasses in front of Ahren, and then downed his own.

Tingles of fear danced up the back of Ahren's neck. For a moment, he had forgotten how precarious his situation was. "I … I only want out of the city. Nothing more."

"I understand that. But taking you outside the walls will require payment, and I think you have the skills to pay that debt. Besides, by the way you limped in here, I imagine it will be several days before you can walk. I will have someone come and look at your injuries. In the meantime, I will find a suitable job for you to repay your debt, and make you more appropriate shoes." He motioned to the glass Ahren hadn't even touched. "Now drink."

The foul smells and dingy streets were a quenching relief to Ahren. The woos of prostitutes and wailing songs of drunks had never been so welcome. Not even the long journeys aboard ship had been confining like the past four weeks trapped in a small room above the shop.

He had spent his days listening to customers chattering away in their unknown language. Nights were most often the same. However, visitors instead came in through the back door to the workroom, their hushed voices sometimes escalating into arguments. By listening to their tone and applying his minimal vocabulary, he learned more Rhomanic over the first week than he had after years of sailing into foreign ports.

Impressed with the speed Ahren adapted, Kazimir cut a small hole in the floor for him to watch and study the customers' mannerisms. After his ankle and cut healed enough for him to come downstairs, he spent a few quiet nights with his host. Often the conversations were short, interrupted by an errant visitor, forcing him back upstairs into hiding to watch through the tiny spy hole.

Ahren adjusted his wide-brimmed hat as he approached a pair of soldiers. They seemed more interested in beating a beggar child than they were in him. But there was no need for risk. His hair short and his newly grown beard trimmed, Ahren doubted anyone but the baron would recognize him.

The cobblestone streets widened as Ahren entered the noble district. The painted homes and shops grew larger, and further apart. No loud taverns cluttered the lanes. No beggars lurked in the alleyways.

He stopped in an alley a block from the baron's house. From there he surveyed the high stone wall surrounding the property, its only entrance being the black iron gate. He noted the thick vines intertwined over the rough stone as his mind wandered back to two nights before in the workroom.

"I have something for you," Kazimir had said. The old man put down his thick needle and handed him a roll of paper. Ahren opened it to see a poster of a man, similar to himself. The words above and below the picture were unknown to him.

Kazimir poured some drinks. "They call you Chernyy Voron. The Black Raven."

Ahren's brow rose.

The old man grinned. "A bit theatrical, I agree. It conveys the image of the dark thief flying from the window, escaping into the night. It's a good name. Trust me, there's much worse."

Ahren merely shrugged.

"That's a small fortune on your head. The baron will spend almost as much as he made on that sapphire to have you killed." He set a glass in front of Ahren and handed another to Ivan.

"Even more reason for me to leave the city as soon as possible," Ahren said, setting aside the poster.

"Ah." The old man smiled. "That is exactly what this meeting is about. Before you leave, I will require you to do a simple job. Something well suited for the Black Raven."

Ahren scratched his scruffy beard. "What is it?"

Kazimir's dark eyes twinkled. "I need you to break into Baron

Krevnyet's house."

Ahren snorted. He couldn't believe the perversity in making him return to the house of his enemy. The one place he would most likely be caught. "Why?"

"Don't look so grim," the old man chided. "Vengeance."

The guard inside the gate was bored or distracted, not noticing Ahren study the front lawn through the thick bars as he passed slowly along the street. The windows of the house looked dark, except for the lower east side where the servants lived. The west side of the grounds appeared the least guarded.

Ahren circled the property, keeping to the shadows of the alleys, and made his way to the western side. Patiently, he waited for a group of loud, young noblemen to pass before he crept to the wall and quickly pulled himself up the latticework of vines and jutting rocks.

He took a brief moment to peer over its edge.

"Do you enjoy cards?" Kazimir asked.

Ahren nodded, finishing his drink. "Yeah, a little."

The old man poured more of the clear liquor into Ahren's glass. "Are you any good?"

"A little," he replied, wondering where this was leading.

Kazimir chuckled. "Your friend the baron isn't. In fact, he's terrible at cards, but loves them nonetheless."

Ahren studied the cobbler's face. It told him nothing. "So?"

"A colleague of mine, a man by the name of Paook, owns a gambling house in Kossintry, many miles from here. The baron, it seems, has run up quite the debt. Over five thousand bishkas."

Ahren momentarily lost his breath. He couldn't imagine such a fortune. Losing it was beyond comprehension.

"Even a man such as the baron can't pay that lightly. The law looks down on gambling halls, but detests debtors even more. So he came up with the best solution to solve his problem."

"Theft?" Ahren asked, thinking of the sapphire he had stolen.

Kazimir shook his head. "Marriage."

The grounds looked clear. With one fluid motion, Ahren swung himself over the wall and dropped onto a soft flowerbed.

Staying low, he kept to the rows of rosebushes, following them to the edge of the house. The muted gray of his cloak blended with the stone and he skirted the wall to the rear of the house. During his short stay as a guest, he had noticed the doors to the lounge were held only with a small latch and usually unlocked. Unless the baron's paranoia of him returning was as great as he had made it appear, the rear doors would be Ahren's best way inside.

Ducking behind a stone vase near the door, he surveyed the scene. No guards patrolled the rear property. No lights shone in the lounge. The glow of candlelight peeked through the shutters of the third window to the left, and in the room above him.

Ahren scooted up to the doors. The baron had not installed a new lock. With a grin, he removed a flat roll of leather from his pouch; another gift from Kazimir. Ahren lifted the soft doeskin flap of the roll to see his picks and tools. Selecting a parchment-thin blade, he inserted it between the doors. Careful, so as not to make any noise, he slipped it upward. He felt it catch the door latch and lifted it harmlessly away.

He returned the blade to the toolkit and softly cracked open the door. Its fine, oiled hinges didn't betray his silent entrance. He slipped inside, closing the door behind him, and froze.

An older man, likely a servant, lay on a couch with a young maid, their half-naked bodies glistening with sweat. He snored softly beneath her as she snuggled against his bare chest.

Holding his breath, Ahren crept across the polished wood floors, swinging a wide circle around the lovers, to the door across the room.

The girl moaned.

Flinching, Ahren turned his head to see her brush a lock of blonde hair from her cheek and roll her head to face the other way. Ahren eased out a sigh and darted through the door before the couple could notice him.

Quickly, he made his way through the halls, his glove-leather shoes muffling every step. He dashed up the marble staircase to the second floor, stopping only to make sure the upstairs hall was empty. His palms began to sweat as he retraced his steps down the hall. Had he only known the baron's intent, he could have left through the front door that night a free man, instead of walking into that dark room.

He hesitated as he came to the fourth door on his left: the baron's room. He fought the yearning to sneak inside and kill the cad in his bed. Kazimir didn't want that; what the cobbler had in mind was worse than anything Ahren could do.

He continued down the hall to the fifth and last door on the left. Gently, he twisted the handle. Locked. He mouthed a curse and removed the tools from his side. Under the dim moonlight cast through the hall's window, Ahren chose his tools and slipped them into the keyhole. Chewing his lip, he blindly fumbled inside the lock. Each scrape and clink of the wire picks boomed in his ears. Even knowing only a mouse could hear him at work, the fear of the baron bursting through his door, sword in hand, danced in the back of his mind.

Ahren drew a sharp breath as felt the lock gave way. Carefully, he twisted the picks around and the click of the bolt thundered softly down the empty hall. He didn't hesitate. He returned his tools to their pouch and slipped through the door.

A sliver of moonlight cut its way through a gap in the velvet curtains, giving only a hint to the dark room's layout. He pulled them aside and opened the shutters, bathing the study in pale, blue luminescence.

Ahren opened the desk, sifting through piles of paper and empty ink bottles. He checked the drawers for false bottoms, and even felt along the underside and back of the desk. Nothing.

Opening a cabinet, he scoured through cups and trophies to no avail. He looked inside the ottoman, the drawers along a small table, and even behind the tapestries. Still nothing.

Undaunted, Ahren searched a bookshelf, opening, and looking behind every dusty tome. Finally, on the bottom shelf, he discovered the row of books was a façade. He pulled away the board covered in book spines, and found a heavy wooden box.

Nerves tingling, he placed the casket on the desk. A silver keyhole stared back at him. He removed his tools and picked the simple lock with ease. Ahren held his breath and opened the case.

He remembered Kazimir's smile as he had poured Ahren another drink. "At Paook's suggestion, Baron Krevnyet wed Aglaya

Vischkol, and then used her very wealthy dowry to pay Paook's debt. He actually had no interest in the girl aside from financial gain. In fact, he despised her. He maintained the image of a pair of newlyweds in love, while simultaneously plotting her murder. That's where you fell in."

Ahren had tongued his cheek, pondering Kazimir's story. "How do you know this?" he finally asked.

The old man had chuckled. "By his own hand." He pulled a folded letter out from under the table and dropped it before Ahren. The broken wax seal still held the mark of Baron Krevnyet.

Ahren glanced at the foreign words fluidly written across the page.

"That's just one of over a half-dozen letters the baron wrote to Paook, detailing their plot." He folded the letter and returned it to the drawer. "The Vischkol family has much influence here and in Kossintry. The news that their daughter's murderer was the very man they paid to wed her would eliminate the baron, allowing me to acquire his warehouses. Also, if Paook were to be the one to bring forth the incriminating evidence, he would be guaranteed their noble favor."

"Then why not bring the letters forward?" Ahren asked. "What do you need me for?"

"Paook has enough letters incriminating the baron, but not himself. However, the baron was smart enough to know that. So to protect himself, he holds the letters Paook wrote to him, proposing the union and the plot. Therefore, they are both locked together in blackmail."

Ahren shot the vodka back. "I believe I know what you want me to get."

Ahren pulled the folded letters out from the case and opened them. The words were unintelligible, but he had been taught Paook's signature. He thumbed through the papers. All four letters were there. He took them and dropped them inside his pouch.

A broad smile crept across his lips as he pulled out another piece of paper from the leather pouch: his reward poster. He dropped it inside the box and shut the lid. Carefully, he picked the lock closed, and returned the chest to its hidden shelf.

Ahren closed the window shutters and the curtains then quietly returned to the hall. He drew his tools to lock the door behind him, but voices from the stairway pulled his attention.

Light approached along the corridor. Ahren slipped behind a small table holding a vase just as a man and woman turned down the hall toward him. He pressed himself against the wall as tightly as he could, and pulled the excess fabric of his cloak from sight.

He held his breath. The couple drew closer. The man laughed something to his companion and instantly Ahren knew the voice. The baron.

Braving a peek, Ahren slowly lifted his head behind the vase. The smug baron staggered slightly, beneath the weight of a candelabrum in one hand and a woman on his other arm. Her rich red dress and powdered cheeks revealed her as a courtesan. The baron opened the door to his chamber and led her inside.

Ahren heard the door lock before he exhaled. He decided not to lock the office door, and quickly slipped down the hallway and down the stairs. Before heading back to the lounge, he detoured into the dining room.

Servants' voices came from the neighboring kitchen. Ahren crept across the room alongside the ornate table. Against the far wall a gold and crystal statue rested on a pedestal beneath a leaded glass dome. The letters paid Kazimir for four weeks of protection, but this would pay his safe passage out of the city. Ahren opened a nearby cabinet and removed a handful of yellow napkins, shoving them inside an empty cloth satchel he wore over his shoulder. He grabbed another handful and hurried across the room. He lifted the dome and set it carefully on the marble floor. He rubbed his sweaty fingers together and removed the statue from its pedestal. Wrapping it in the cloth napkins, he slipped it into the now cushioned satchel.

As he turned to leave, the kitchen door swung silently open, releasing a beam of orange firelight. An older housemaid stood silhouetted in the door frame, holding a tray of gilded glasses. She froze, seeing Ahren standing in the room. A sharp gasp escaped her lips. The silver tray tumbled from her hands.

Heart pounding, Ahren bolted from the room and into the hall as the crash of metal and exploding porcelain erupted behind him. The servant's screams filled the house before the shards finished tinkling across the stone.

Ahren slipped into the lounge and smiled in relief to find the room empty. He darted through the door, leaving it open behind him, and raced across the lawn. He glanced at the front gate to see the guard still standing oblivious to the commotion from inside.

With the grace of a frightened cat, Ahren clamored over the wall. He held the satchel close against his body and dropped to the alley on the other side. The shock of the hard ground stung his feet through the soft-soled shoes, but he didn't fall. He pulled the cloak around him, hiding the bulging satchel, and hurried down the street.

"Very good," Kazimir said, flipping through the letters. "They're all here. Paook will be very pleased." He looked at Ahren. "And your passage?"

Ahren removed the bundle of napkins from his satchel and unwrapped the crystal statue.

The old man smiled as he took the treasure. "Good. You have done well, Chernyy Voron." He placed the statue in a velvet-lined box and shut the lid. "There is an ale wagon out front, waiting to take you from the city." He nodded to an empty barrel in the corner. "There is your seat. Get in."

Ahren stepped into the barrel and crammed himself inside.

"Motya will let you out once you are far from the city. There is a ship leaving for Mordakland in two weeks, bound for Lunnisburg. I have already booked you passage."

"Thank you, Kazimir," Ahren said. "I cannot thank you enough."

Motya picked up the round lid, but Kazimir stopped him before he sealed the barrel.

"Here," he said, dropping a heavy wad of paper onto Ahren's lap. "This is yours."

Ahren unfolded the paper to see the gold brooch wrapped inside. He chuckled as he realized the wrapping was one of his reward posters.

The old man handed him a shiny copper medallion stamped with the glyph of the Tyenee. Ahren flipped it over to find the image of a raven crudely scratched on the back.

"Show that to a man in Lunnisburg named Fritz, he owns a tavern called The Mermaid's Tail. He'll find you work."

Ahren looked back at the old man with a puzzled stare. Before he could speak, Motya placed the lid onto the barrel. As it closed, he heard Kazimir's voice.

"Welcome to the Tyenee."

The Porvov Switch

"Come on, Whazzik. Who took it?" Volker strummed the taut rope stretching from Whazzik's tied wrists. The other end ran over a ceiling rafter to a large hanging bucket filled with bricks. A second rope connected the three-foot shopkeeper's ankles to the base of a wooden support beam, leaving the quellen suspended between them.

"I … I don't know," Whazzik screamed through gritted teeth. "It was … just gone."

Volker sighed. "Two more."

Ahren nodded, grabbed two more brown bricks from a pile in the corner, and dropped them into the pendulous bucket. The rope creaked tighter.

"I said I don't know!" Whazzik yelled. Beads of sweat ran off his forehead and into his hand-sized quellish ears.

Nonchalantly, Volker scratched his chin. "That's a real shame, Whazzik. I thought you knew every cutpurse and smuggler in the city. I'm sure you can think of it. Otherwise you're going to be a lot taller."

"I told you," the quellen moaned, his pained face reddened almost purple. "I got to the drop off … and it was just gone. Dolfus was already dead. I never … saw anyone."

Volker removed his cloth cap, scratched his bald head, and gestured to Ahren. Ahren dropped another heavy brick into the bucket. A sickly pop echoed from the shopkeeper's shoulders.

"Have mercy!" he squealed.

"Mercy?" Volker smiled. "I am. You're lucky I'm the one asking the questions instead of my friend here. They call him the Black Raven. His methods of persuasion make mine look like fun."

"Black Raven? Never … heard of him." The little quellen slumped his head back in an attempt to see behind him, but Ahren side-stepped behind the support pillar.

"He's new to the city. Big-time killer down in Rhomanny. He wanted to ask you the questions, but since you're my friend and all, I managed to convince him otherwise." Volker leaned close to Whazzik's large ear and whispered, "But I'm afraid that if you won't tell me what I need, he'll have to ask you. And neither of us wants that, do we?"

Ahren rolled his eyes at the big man's fantastic claims. He had never asked to do the interrogation. Torture made him queasy. He set another brick onto the already overloaded bucket and the shopkeeper cried out again.

"You can scream all you like," Volker said. "No one can hear us down here." He nodded up to the basement door. "Shop's closed, and these walls are mighty thick. Even if someone came inside, they wouldn't find this door. I remember you hiding me down here when the guards were after me. Searched your place for half an hour before giving up, remember?"

Ahren watched the hulking thug taunt his prisoner the way a wolf might circle a deer caught in a steel trap. Volker was brilliant. He spoke several languages, could read maps, and knew more obscure history and trivia than anyone Ahren had ever met. Had he chosen another profession, he might have been a scholar or a priest, but neither could satisfy Volker's true appetite for crime.

"I remember," Whazzik said with a forced laugh. "We've had a lot of good times."

"You're a good man, Whazzik. I'm really going to hate losing you. Unless of course, you can think of who stole my merchandise. Only someone who knew what it was would have taken it, and everyone knows not to cross you. So who was it?"

Ahren dropped another block into the bucket, now threatening to overflow.

"The Gravins," the shopkeeper screamed. "It had to ... have been the Gravins."

Volker shot a quick glace to Ahren as his brow rose. "Who?"

"Some new ... group," Whazzik groaned. "Just heard of them myself. Got ... some hideout in the Harbor District."

"Progress," Volker said. "Tell me about them."

"Don't know much about them." The quellen winced, futilely struggling with his bonds. "Just small-time heists … and stuff. But word is … their leader, Dolch, has got the power of a demon. It had to be them, I swear it."

"Demon, eh?" Volker sucked something out of his teeth. "Makes sense why they'd want the egg. A drake would make a good sacrifice … or pet." He leaned back down and growled. "You better not be lying to me."

Whazzik fervently shook his head. "No, no. All the … other gangs know me as a fence … and know Dolfus worked for me. They … wouldn't risk it." Tears streamed down his cheeks. "It had to be them."

"I believe you. But if you're lying …" Volker slid a thick-bladed knife from his belt and ran the tip along the quellen's shivering throat. "Good. Now I want you to find out as much about these Gravins as you can. I need to know where to find them and everything known about this Dolch. I'll be back in three days, and if you don't have anything, I'll let Black Raven do the asking."

"I'll find out everything," Whazzik said quickly.

"I knew I could trust you." Volker sliced the rope binding the shopkeeper's hands, sending him and the heavy bucket crashing to the dirt floor. "You're a good friend, Whazzik." He sheathed his knife and motioned to Ahren to leave.

They ascended the rickety stairs and crouched through the short, concealed door leading to the back of the shop. Passing the furniture and art cluttering the small store, they unlocked the door and stepped out onto the streets of Lunnisburg. A thin blanket of dark smog hung over the city despite the cool, sea breeze. Fresh smoke billowed from the Old Kaisers, the twenty-five statues forming the towers of the city's outer wall. The twelve patron Saints of Lunnisburg formed the tower walls of the Kaiser's citadel in the city's heart. Each figure held a constantly burning basin in their right hand. The fires served as navigation points for nighttime sailors, lit the streets in a constant glow, and consumed any trash normally found in a port city. They also covered the city in a gritty haze.

"Seemed a little extreme," Ahren said, closing the door behind them.

Volker snorted as he headed down the narrow street. "That little rat was screaming for mercy before we even added the first weight. Quellens do that because they're small. Truth is they can handle much more pain than you or I."

"Then why play along with it?"

"Because he's my friend. He just needed some encouragement in order to speak. Quellens rarely share anything unless it's to their advantage. So in lieu of gold, the best payment was his life."

Ahren shook his head trying to grasp the unnecessary complexity of quellens. "So what are we going to do about this gang?"

The big man shrugged. "We'll ask around about them, but probably won't know much until Whazzik gets back with us. He has a nose for gossip and such. By this time tomorrow, half the thieves of the city will know the Black Raven's name."

"And that's a good thing? There's probably still a price on my head down in Rhomanny."

"So? Rhomanny is far away, and Whazzik didn't get a good look at you even if he was stupid enough to tell anyone what you look like. The important point is people know the name, and learn to fear it."

"That doesn't help with the Gravins," Ahren insisted.

"We'll report to Fritz what we know. He'll tell us what he wants us to do about them. No gang of thieves can ever beat the Tyenee. Just because they might not know we are their masters does not excuse their sin. No matter what Fritz decides, these Gravins will learn who they really answer to."

"So we're to kill them?"

"With just you and me?" Volker asked with a smile. "I'm sure it would be a good fight, but a demon cult of thieves is probably best left for someone with more men, men we can afford to lose. No, I think Fritz will call for a Porvov Switch."

"What's that?"

"Saint Vishtin!" Volker exclaimed as he stopped and faced Ahren. "When Fritz told me we were getting a new member, I was excited. Even more so, when I heard you were a sailor and had traveled the world. I figured you'd be able to tell me all sorts of stories about places you'd been and things you've seen. And here you are, the Black Raven. You dazzled Kazimir into making you a member of the greatest cabal of smugglers and assassins in the world, and you don't even know the roots of the Tyenee. We came from Rhomanny and you can't even speak Rhomanic!" Volker's disappointment in Ahren had been a regular conversation since Ahren's arrival three weeks ago.

"That's why you're teaching me," Ahren reminded. "And the longer you delay in telling me what the Porvov Switch is, the longer you'll be forced to associate with an ignorant."

The bald man's stern grimace softened into a smile. "Good point." He turned and continued along the cobble street toward The Mermaid's Tail. "Come along. The sooner we report, the sooner you'll learn."

Shadows slithered along the streets and looming shop fronts under the red glow from the colossal statues surrounding the city. Most reputable businesses had already closed for the evening, but customers still filled the lanes, their faces hidden beneath hooded cloaks and wide-brimmed hats. They clustered around dark stands and alleys in search of the taboo pleasures and artifacts only available in the nighttime markets of Lunnisburg.

Ahren kept his head low as he made his way through the city. The folds of his gray cloak hid the heavy rope slung over his shoulder. Ignoring the calls from whores and vendors, he followed Volker through a crowded bazaar and into a dark street away from the Old Kaisers' watchful lights.

The steep engraved walls of Heiligstein Basilica loomed over Saint Faiga's Square and towered over the surrounding buildings. A pair of guards in breast plates and armed with long halberds patrolled the front of the building. Their capes were white instead of rich blue, meaning they belonged to the church and not the city.

Ahren's soft glove-leather shoes made no sound as he hugged the shadows along the neighboring buildings and passed the basilica. Two blocks further he stopped behind a smaller, and much less elaborate, domed church, and crouched between a short tree and the low wall surrounding a cemetery behind it.

A group of drunken sailors sauntered past, arguing about where they were. Ahren kept still, watching them from his hiding place. The men stopped beside a stone well and bickered for several long minutes before taking the road toward Kaiser Adelino II. A figure moved from the alley after they left, and raced toward Ahren. The clomping of its feet across the cobblestone echoed off the buildings.

"You're loud," Ahren whispered as Volker scurried into the bushes beside him.

"I never claimed to be the quiet one," the bald man hissed. "Just get me up to the top of that dome and I'll show you what I can do."

Ahren held back his response. He leaned out, braving a peek around the bushes. The streets were empty on either side. A lighted house window looked down on the cemetery, but appeared vacant. He drew a breath, grabbed the edge of the stone wall, swung his legs onto the other side, and dropped to the ground. Keeping low, he hurried past gravestones and urns to the rear wall of the chapel and hid behind a pillar. He watched the lit window as Volker hopped the wall and crawled over to him. Ahren pointed at his own eyes and then to the window. Volker nodded and slipped behind the neighboring pillar to avoid being seen.

Briskly rubbing his hands together, Ahren let out a deep breath and jumped, grabbing the carved awning lip above him. The heavy rope pulled him slightly to the side, but he managed to scramble up onto the narrow, slate-shingled ledge above the rear door. The smooth tiles creaked underfoot as he slipped behind a statue in a dark alcove. He scanned the streets from the shadows, and watched a lone soldier in a blue tabard walk down the quiet lane talking to himself, apparently oblivious of his surroundings. Ahren waited for several heartbeats after the guard walked out of sight before emerging from his hiding place.

He climbed up and over the heavy statue, then pulled himself up onto a narrow ledge running the perimeter of the church. The cool sea breeze from the harbor pulled at his cloak, ruffling it to the side. With his face against the rough-hewn stone wall, Ahren sidestepped along the six-inch ledge to a round window. Thick stained glass filled the opening. Breaking it silently would be impossible. He glanced over his shoulder to the empty streets. A figure moved inside the open window across the street and Ahren froze. A young woman sat at a table beside the window, deeply engrossed in her needlepoint. Ahren sighed in relief, then grasped the ornate window frame and pulled himself up. He dug the toes of his soft shoes as far as he could onto the one-inch rim of molding and reached up to the ledge marking the next level of the building.

His outstretched fingers wrapped around the rough edge of the shelf and dug in. He gave a quick jump, allowing his fingers to grip a good hold before gravity caught him. Quickly he pulled himself up and then over a low wall onto the domed roof. Sweat beaded his brow, and he caught his breath for a few moments before peering back over the wall to make sure no one had witnessed him. The streets were still empty.

Ahren wrenched the coil off his shoulder and tied it at the base of a stone globe adorning the wall. After pulling the line taut, he dropped it down to where Volker waited forty feet below. The rope straightened and shuddered as the large man pulled himself up. Ahren stood watch, waiting for his companion to join him.

"That'll wake you up," Volker gasped after pulling himself onto the roof.

Ahren nodded, surveying the great triple-sided dome beside them. Three small statues stood along the lip tracing the opening at the dome's summit. Hopefully they'd be strong enough to hold them.

Volker pulled up the dangling line so no passersby would notice it. Once finished he began untying the knot holding it in place.

"What are you doing?" Ahren hissed through gritted teeth. "We'll need that to get down."

"We'll need it first to get inside the chapel."

"That's what your rope is for."

The large man shook his head. "Mine's for the escape." He gave a sly smile. "Trust me."

Ahren shrugged, not having a choice in the matter. Until he had proven himself, Volker was in charge. Fritz had made that unquestionably clear.

Volker handed the coiled rope to Ahren and nodded to the top of the dome. Ahren pulled it over his shoulder, checked again to see if anyone was looking, and climbed up the rough dome to the top.

Pigeons cooed and fluttered from just inside the dome, giving him a momentary panic as he reached the lip. He lay on his stomach and looked down through the three-foot opening. The dark chapel appeared empty. A shallow pool surrounded by inlaid stonework rested directly below.

Ahren gripped one of the carved figures standing watch over the entrance and tried to jostle it. It felt secure. Quickly, he tied the line around the statue's base, and dropped the end into the cavernous church. Volker crawled up beside him and began fastening his own line as Ahren grabbed his rope and carefully lowered his legs through the yawning hole.

Plump gray pigeons fluttered from the rafters away from their invader. Ahren descended the line quickly, hand over hand; careful not to shake the rope too hard in case the granite anchor might not be as sturdy as he had thought. Volker's black, slender rope dropped down beside him, and the birds once again stirred as the large man crawled down from the roof.

Upon reaching the bottom, Ahren stretched his foot out and stepped onto the outer lip of the hallowed pool that the priests used to catch rain, the holy water of Arieth, The True God. A white, lumpy skin of pigeon droppings and feathers covered the "purest of waters."

Ahren dropped to the inlaid floor, careful not to disturb the priest sleeping in the room behind the eastern door. He hurried to an arched alcove. There, inside a box of beveled glass and under a massive copper lid, a withered green thumb rested on a gold- and jewel-encrusted plaque: the sacred thumb of Saint Theobold.

Volker crept up beside him and, without saying a word, grabbed the edges of the thick graven lid. Ahren took the other side and together they lifted the heavy covering. His trembling hands strained under the weight, forcing him to lean his back into it to keep from dropping it. Slowly, they lowered the cover, careful not to make any noise. The low scrape as it touched the floor echoed through the chamber, yet didn't even disturb the cooing birds. Ahren let out a sigh, shaking the feeling back into his curled fingers.

The bald man smiled and winked at him before slipping out of the alcove toward the altar. Ahren took another breath, reached inside the box and removed the plaque from the dusty velvet pillow. The thick gold and large jewels gave the eight-inch-wide tablet considerable heft. He opened the satchel at his waist and set it inside between two layers of folded cloth. Before refastening the flap, he removed a long black raven's feather and placed it on the empty green pillow. He smiled, imagining the priest's face tomorrow morning. The soft rattling of a chain pulled Ahren's attention back to the present. Volker stood before a great marble statue of Arieth, removing a golden, triangle-shaped pendulum from his hands. The holy icon was worth a fortune, but the relic inside Ahren's pouch was priceless. The church would do anything to retrieve it, likely forgetting about the triangle.

Volker tucked the treasure inside his satchel and gave the signal he was ready. Ahren tightened the ties to his pouch, adjusted the strap digging into his shoulder, and hurried to the dangling ropes.

Despite his size, Volker hurried up the line with a spider's grace. He had already untied and coiled his rope by the time Ahren reached the top. Ahren pulled his rope up and slung it back over his shoulder.

They scooted down the side of the high dome to the outer wall. Ahren made sure no one was watching as Volker tied his line to one of the spheres. A horse-drawn carriage rolled down the street toward them, forcing the thieves to hide in the shadows until it had passed. After the sound of hooves faded away, Volker motioned for Ahren to climb down.

Ahren took the round silk line and noticed Volker's irregular-shaped knot holding it in place. The gnarled series of figure eights didn't resemble any knot Ahren had ever seen. Making a note to show his mentor proper rope skills, he dropped the line down the other side and lowered himself to the cemetery below then hid behind one of the columns.

Volker zipped down the smooth rope and crouched beside the wall. Taking the end of the rope he tied a reverse version of the knot above. Once done, he pulled the rope taut and the coiled mass slid up the line to the top. He jerked the rope once more and it fell free of the wall. Ahren stared in bewildered shock.

"I spent two years with a traveling circus," the bald man said, re-coiling the silk line. "One of their acrobats taught me this trick, but you have to use a special rope for it. Maybe one day I'll teach it to you." He threw the coil over his shoulder and pulled his wide cloak around to hide it. "Let's go."

They slipped out of the graveyard, and followed the alleys back to Fritz's tavern.

Alarm bells rang early the next morning. Church and city guards raided every known fence and burglar in the city. Some even ventured into the dark undercity, hassling and evicting many of the vagrants in their desperate search. Whispers of the stolen artifact quickly spread, as rumors do. A trio of armored soldiers burst into Whazzik's shop and interrogated him for an hour after rifling through his merchandise. The six gold dreins Volker had given him ensured that they learned nothing but a mention that the Gravins might be involved.

Hammering echoed down the cobbled streets as reward posters were nailed to every post and chapel door: *Eternal Salvation for the return of Saint Theobold's remains, and one thousand dreins for the culprits.* Greed fueled suspicion, and rampant accusations filled the city.

Patrols doubled that night, especially near churches and government offices. Spies infiltrated the nighttime markets trying to uncover any mention of the stolen artifact.

Near midnight, Ahren and Volker left the security of the inn and headed into the city. Ahren's hand kept finding its way to the heavy bag hung over his shoulder. Every glance from other nighttime travelers felt like an accusation. He couldn't wait to be rid of the relic.

Volker leisurely led them down common streets, strolling the city as if nothing troubled him. Finally, they entered the harbor district, passing long piers heavy with moored ships. Gulls squawked and circled overhead, their white bodies cast red under the Old Kaisers' torches. The steady breeze off the sea carried low murmurs of dice games and fights. Tired whores, their tight bodices laced over crumpled dresses, stood prattling in a pack; one occasionally sauntering into an unlit alley with a customer.

The two men passed rows of blocky warehouses, each painted differently to signify its owner. Soldiers and private mercenaries patrolled the cluster of buildings like packs of stray cats in the shadows hunting for food.

A pair of burnt-out warehouses sat in the back away from the rest. Fire had all but consumed one, leaving but a skeleton of charred timbers, while its blackened neighbor still held its shape. The men slipped between a stack of empty crates, and watched the buildings. Whazzik had told them the Gravins' lair was there. Hopefully, the drake egg was inside, and still intact.

Volker tapped Ahren's hand and motioned to a lanky figure hovering near the rear wall. The man's gray and brown striped cloak blended well with his surroundings. The Gravin guard circled the abandoned warehouse once, before taking a seat on an overturned barrel.

Volker picked up a pair of rusty nails lying beside the boxes, then pointed to a pile of rubble between the ruined buildings, gesturing Ahren to go. Keeping low, Ahren followed the line of crates past the sentry's line of sight, and then darted across toward the heap of charred debris. Broken bottles and loose stones encircled the buildings, forcing him to move carefully to avoid making any noise. He reached the spot and crouched behind the mound of blackened brick and timber.

A sharp thud echoed in the silence followed by the cling of metal skittering off cobblestones. Ahren held his breath, listening for the man's footsteps. Another *thwack* sounded against the warehouse wall and the metallic ring of Volker's second nail.

Ahren waited.

Soft footsteps came close. Ahren slid his dagger from its leather sheath. A shadow passed over him as the oblivious guard circled past, investigating the sounds of Volker's nails. Once the man's back was to him, Ahren sprang from his position, clapped his hand over the sentry's mouth and brought the dagger pommel down hard against his head. The body fell limp to the ground. He untied the man's tattered cloak, revealing a short, thick-bladed sword at his waist, then winced, hearing Volker's heavy bootsteps racing toward him. "You're still too loud," he hissed as the man crouched beside him.

"Why didn't you kill him?" Volker asked.

"I have an idea." Ahren pulled off his own cloak and hat and put the man's striped cloak on. It stank of smoke and fish.

"Ah." The brute nodded. "Good idea. Take his sword, too."

"It'll get in the way when I'm climbing."

"Manage," Volker growled. "First, it helps the disguise. Second, you might need it."

Grumbling, Ahren untied the leather cords securing the blade to the man's leg and slid the sheath off his belt. The unconscious brigand stirred. Volker whipped out his own knife from his boot and sliced the man's throat. Blood, black under the faint light, gurgled from the wound and pooled beneath the guard, running down through a grid of slender valleys between cobblestones. Ahren glanced away. Death wasn't uncommon among his profession, but he preferred not to be a witness.

After hiding the body behind the debris pile, the two men circled to the main warehouse entrance. The heavy door was barred. Ahren squinted through a knothole in one of the planks, but a heavy cloth had been hung on the inside, covering the hole. A dim light flickered through the coarse fabric. He put his ear to the hole and held his breath. Vague murmurs came from within.

"Are they in there?" Volker whispered.

Ahren nodded. "I can't make out what they're saying or how many there are."

"Let's assume it's all of them, and be careful."

They hurried around to the rear of the building where the guard had sat, and there they found a smaller door. A pair of rough-cut boards straddled the entrance, discouraging beggars or vagrants from entering. Ahren studied the timbers, finding that they were only nailed to the frame. The door itself could still be opened. Footprints in the ashen dust outside the entrance verified its frequent use. He scanned the eaves above him. The flat roof angled slightly down the building from front to back and he couldn't see how much of it was still intact.

"Give me a boost," he whispered, motioning to the roof. "I'll try to get inside and get the egg."

Volker dropped to one knee and laced his fingers together. Ahren put his foot in the big man's hands and Volker hoisted him up with a grunt. Ahren grabbed the edge of the roof and pulled himself forward, cursing the uncomfortable position of the sword that restricted his leg's mobility.

The dreary roof sagged under its own weight. Faint light glimmered up from an ominous fissure on the opposite side. Twin valleys of drooping shingles showed a support beam running between them all the way to the dark hole. Hopefully the timber could hold his weight.

"What do you see?" Volker hissed.

"There's an opening. I can probably get inside there and get the egg," Ahren replied softly. "Stay out here just in case." To his relief, the bald man nodded and took position behind one of the broken barrels beside the door. The roof wouldn't hold Volker's clumsy weight, and besides, Ahren preferred the thought of stealth. He crouched to his hands and knees to spread his weight and followed the straight beam to the fissure. The spongy wood creaked and bowed slightly under him. He crawled faster before it had time to give way. Stopping where the roof curled down along the edge of the opening, he leaned his head inside. A low voice crept up to meet him.

"'Are you afraid, Dolch?' it asked me."

A charred, narrow loft littered with debris and fallen timbers lay only a few feet below him. Ahren slithered down through the opening and dropped gently onto it. The sword brushed a loose shingle, sending it clattering down onto the ledge. He froze. Sweat beaded his brow during the heavy silence.

"But I was too afraid to answer," the voice continued. "The little light from the basement window behind me had been eaten up by the surrounding darkness. I heard its voice again from all sides. 'Are you frightened because you cannot see, my child?'"

Ahren wormed his way over burnt boxes, careful not to touch any loose floorboards, until he came to the loft's edge. Several milky tallow candles and smoking oil lamps flickered near the back of the warehouse. Half a dozen men sat on slapdash benches of boards and chipped bricks. A man in a black hooded cloak stood before them. The yellow candle light seemed to dim around him.

"'I can save you, my son. I can cure the wound slowly killing you. I can show you the darkness as no mortal has ever seen it. But for a price ...'"

The men hung on the speaker's every word. Ahren pulled his attention away from the hypnotic sermon and scanned the rest of the room. Several boxes and bolts of fabric stood along one wall. Nine moldy cots clustered in the far corner near an unsanded table. Crumbs and cards littered the tabletop amidst globs of melted wax. He peered through the slats to find a crude altar directly beneath him. Gold jewelry glinted from the ebony velvet that covered the wide pedestal. A pitted, oblong rock lay in the middle of the altar before a mirror of polished obsidian. The drake egg! Ahren's eyes widened. The ugly stone was no larger than a child's head, yet in another year it would be the size of a man's and then the creature inside would break free, fully grown.

"So I pledged myself to the darkness and took it into me," the leader hailed. "And my wounds healed and my eyes could clearly see everything in the darkness around me. In that moment, it told me its secret. A secret I can spend a lifetime sharing with you." He held out his hand and black flame erupted in his palm. The rayless fire danced in his grasp, consuming more of the room's already faint light. Inky drops ran between his curled fingers and fell sizzling to the floor.

Ahren stared at the accursed flame, then scooted back over the cluttered shelf and moved to an unlit corner away from the cult. The narrow ladder-like steps that had once led up from the floor had long since collapsed, but a thick wooden pillar supported the loft and the ceiling above. He wrapped his arms around the sooty column, and slid silently down to the floor.

"But the darkness demands sacrifice."

A sense of foreboding surrounded the squat altar. Ahren knelt before it, and opened his satchel. Careful to not make any noise, he removed the golden placard and slipped it beneath the shimmering velvet blanketing the shrine, where he hoped no one would find it by accident.

Volker had told him that in the early years of the Tyenee, when they first infiltrated the great Rhomanic city of Porvov, a powerful gang already ruled the streets. The Tyenee, aware they couldn't beat them in an all-out war, staged a heist, broke into the royal palace, and stole the czar's coronation scepter. The search to reclaim it had been fierce and dozens of men suspected of the crime died upon the rack. Finally, an anonymous note found its way into the czar's hand, revealing that the scepter was stolen by the other gang, and told where to find it in their hideout. After the execution of every member of their rival, the Tyenee rose and took hold of the city's underworld.

"Who among you is ready to make the eternal pledge?" Dolch asked.

"I," the men intoned in unison.

Ahren caught his reflection in the black mirror as he reached for the egg. The sinister image stared back at him with a knowing look—and smiled. Terrified, Ahren snatched the heavy stone egg from the table and crawled quickly away; his fiendish doppelganger watching with amused glee from inside the obsidian mirror.

"Who among you would die for it?" Dolch's voice filled the room.

"I," the thieves replied.

The egg was too wide for his satchel, forcing Ahren to hold it tightly under one arm as he shimmied back up the support pillar. Sweat ran down his face, and coated his palms. His slick hand slipped on the soot-coated beam, but he squeezed tighter with his knees in order not to fall. The sword handle at his waist dug painfully into his thigh, and his heart labored with fear and exertion. He struggled over the loft's edge and crawled up onto it.

Dolch's sermon grew to a crescendo. "Then I ask you, my children—"

A weak board cracked under Ahren's knee. Its loud pop silenced the room.

Dolch's eyes narrowed. "Intruder," he screamed, hurling the ebony fire in Ahren's direction.

Ahren ducked. The fire struck the roof behind him. Penetrating cold erupted around him, engulfing the area in shadow. He fled toward the exit in the roof, frost coating his clothes and the creaking floor.

"Stop him," Dolch shrieked.

His fingers numb, Ahren reached the hole and jumped through it as another explosion of stygian fire narrowly missed him. The light from the Old Kaisers had never felt so inviting. He scrambled up onto the roof, the egg still tucked under his arm, and rushed to the nearest edge. His foot plunged through the weak roof and he fell, face first. The egg flew from his arms, bounced off the shingles, and vanished over the edge. He ripped his foot free and jumped to his feet as Dolch leapt from the large hole.

Dolch gave him a wicked smile. The inky flames ignited in his hand again.

Ahren jerked a dagger from its sheath and hurled it. Dolch tossed the ball of black fire. The spell collided with Ahren's blade in the air between the men and exploded in an icy blast that hurled Ahren from the rooftop. He fell to the street and hit the hard cobbles with a thud. Groaning, he looked up as Dolch leapt off the roof with a tiger's grace. The demon-man laughed, and lifted another handful of his cursed fire. A blurred figure rose up behind him, knocking him to the ground. Volker, clutching the drake egg, kicked the fallen gang leader, and drew his knife. Dolch swept Volker's legs, sending the brute to the ground and the knife skittering away. He flew up to his feet like a marionette being pulled by invisible strings and jet flames erupted from his fist as he turned to face Volker.

Forcing himself to his feet, Ahren pulled the small sword from his hip, and lunged with a scream of rage.

Dolch turned in surprise as the thick blade lashed down. The iron tip sliced through his face, ripping one of his eyes and sending a fan of blood across the alley. He staggered back, clutching his bleeding face.

The cries of the thieves bursting from the warehouse warned Ahren he was out of time. He hurled the sword at his wounded enemy. The ill-weighted weapon missed the man's chest, but skewered his arm and knocked him back to the ground. Ahren reached for Volker, grabbed his friend's hand, and pulled him up. Volker, still clutching the egg, raced with him through the streets away from the gang's howls and curses.

They hurried through a maze-work of cluttered alleyways until they reached a populated square, then slowed to a casual stroll, huffing and coated in sweat, past the scant crowd and wary guards. They meandered along a wide street to the other side of the market, then ducked into the alleys and doubled back toward the safety of The Mermaid's Tail.

Later that night, a street urchin dropped a letter in the slot outside the palace gate. The "Rat Hole," as it was called, allowed any and all citizens to report injustices, or denounce criminals without fear. Before sunrise, a unit of soldiers stormed a burnt-out warehouse in the Harbor District. The thumb of Saint Theobold, as well as other stolen goods, was recovered and six thieves were arrested. The body of a seventh brigand was found outside with a cut throat, but their leader was nowhere to be found. Rumors spread that an unholy altar had been discovered inside their den.

Before dying on the gallows, some days later, one of the thieves declared, "Dolch will have his revenge." How the convict had been able to speak so clearly, without a tongue and while swinging from the noose, would be debated and argued in taverns and barracks for years.

Meanwhile, Ahren and Volker enjoyed lounging in the comforts of Fritz's inn, and the frequent comments that Ahren needed to prove himself became nothing more than a memory. He continued his tutelage, receiving less supervision from his seniors and assuming more responsibilities, yet every night he kept a burning lamp beside his bed to chase away the darkness.

The Reluctant Assassin

A loud *thunk* startled Ahren from his sleep. The walls hummed with echoes of shouts and laughter from the three-story bar room below. Even up in his fourth-floor refuge, they invaded his domicile with the incessant sounds of drunken shouts and music. He had grown accustomed to noise, almost never noticing it, but the sound that woke him came from inside his room.

Drawing a short dagger hidden between his bed and the wall, he scanned the room for an intruder, but found no one. The lamp on the bedside table filled the humble flat with dim yellow light. Barefoot, he crossed the cold wood floor and pressed his ear to the door.

"Who's there?" he asked loudly.

Nothing.

He unlocked the door, slid the bar from across it, opened it cautiously, and peered down the hall. It was empty, except for a man and one of the resident whores kissing and fondling each other in the far corner, oblivious to him. Ahren shrugged. He closed the door and slid the bar back in place.

Rubbing gritty sleep from his eyes, he turned to go back to bed, and stopped. A metal spike tip protruded from the shutter of his window. Sharp splinters of wood peeled back from the point that had struck it from the outside. The dark shutter slats were too tightly fitted to let him peek through. He blew out the lamp, immersing the room in darkness, and blindly unfastened the shutter latch.

With his back to the wall to prevent any more archers a clear shot, he pushed open the right shutter. The red glow cast from the burning basins atop the thirty-seven graven towers in and around the city of Lunnisburg spilled through the window, illuminating the room. Ahren waited several seconds, then quickly peered outside.

The adjacent rooftops and streets below were empty. He braved sticking his head out to see a thick metal crossbow bolt jutting from the closed left shutter. Its steep angle indicated the shooter had been street-level, and a small cork capped the back end. Puzzled, Ahren wrestled the bolt free, removed the cork, and shook a tightly rolled parchment from the tube. It unfurled to become a small note.

Black Raven,

Ahren's heart froze. Only a select few knew him by that name. His alias in the criminal world was his most guarded secret. He took a deep sigh to calm his trembling hands, then continued reading the letter.

Your reputation as a thief and an assassin are legendary. I have undertaken the difficulty to find you and have a job that requires your particular finesse and skill. In return you will be handsomely rewarded.
If you wish to accept, hang a red scarf outside your window tomorrow night. If not, hang a blue one, and I shall take my business elsewhere.

A Friend

Ahren read the letter several times. The flattery left out one small detail. Aside from the mounting bounty he had earned in Lunnisburg, the Vischkol family in Rhomanny still offered one thousand gold pieces to avenge the murder of their daughter, even after it had been revealed that he had been framed and the real killer, her husband, was captured. Anyone who had gone through enough trouble to discover his name and track him down would also have learned of the bounty.

Until he learned his blackmailer's identity, he had no choice but to play along.

Ahren's filthy dun cloak stank of manure and the sour beer he had poured over himself. He huddled in an alleyway beside a chipped wooden bowl containing three brass coins, dressed in dingy rags, and clutching a half empty bottle. A pair of men sneered at him as they sauntered past. Ahren gazed up with pleading eyes. "Spare a coin, brother?" he begged in a dry voice.

One of them cursed at him as they walked away.

Ahren watched their retreating backs for a second, then glanced up at the shuttered fourth-story windows across the street. Even in the faint red light cast by the torches that the Old Kaisers held high above the city, he could clearly see the crimson sash dangling from his window, fluttering in the breeze.

Horse hooves clomped down the lane toward him. Moments later, a black carriage rolled into view. The driver pulled back on the reins, stopping a pair of brown horses just below the weathered sign of The Mermaid's Tail.

Ahren tried to look disinterested as he studied the simple ebony coach accented with glinting silver. A *thunk* echoed from the shuttered window above, the driver popped the reins and the carriage hurried away. Ahren leapt to his feet, knocking the bowl and coins aside, and raced after it down the narrow street. He sprinted to keep up, but the horses were too fast. The coach turned onto an adjoining lane and vanished from sight. Gasping, Ahren reached the intersection and looked down the empty street, but the carriage was nowhere to be seen. "Damn it."

The coins, as well as the bowl, were already gone by the time he returned. Frustrated, Ahren walked back inside the busy tavern, and ordered a drink before heading up to his room. As before, a sharp-pointed bolt jutted through the back of his shutter. He opened the window and ripped it free. Inside, he found another note.

There is a ship called The Pelikan docked in the harbor. The captain's name is Odell Tabstein. He wears a gold ring set with an emerald. Kill him, and take the ring. In his cabin you will find a letter addressed to a Mister Gren Schmied in Lichthafen. Wrap the ring and the unopened letter in a yellow cloth and drop them in a white empty barrel in Saint Faiga's Square at noon three days hence. Then leave.

You will be paid once I receive them. Don't disappoint me.

A cool salt breeze glided over the docks, flapping Ahren's muted gray cloak as he slipped in through the ship's aft window from a narrow ledge outside. The ship creaked against the heavy pier ropes as if the vessel were trying to escape, desperate to return to sea.

The stout odor of mildew and dirty clothes dominated the small cabin. Rolls of parchment cluttered a pair of shelves above a narrow desk along the side wall. An open bottle rested on a small table in the middle of the room and beyond it, a dun-colored hammock hung above a brass-bound sea chest.

Leaving the curtains open for light, Ahren crossed the dim, red-lit cabin and searched the shelves among the worn maps and charts. Nothing. He picked the simple desk lock, and lifted the lid to discover a clutter of paper and poorly carved baubles. He sifted carefully between trinkets and empty inkwells until his fingers located a neatly folded square parchment. Holding it up to the light, he read Gren Schmied's name in a smooth flowing script.

Hard boot steps approached from the deck outside. Quickly, Ahren closed the lid and crouched behind the door as it swung open.

A stocky man with thinning blond hair staggered inside, accompanied by a pungent waft of cheap wine. He paused to stare at the open window, shook his head, then peeled off his shirt and stumbled toward his hammock.

Wood grated as Ahren dropped the bar across the closed door.

"Who the—" The captain whirled around.

The rasp of Ahren's drawn dagger cut him off. "My name is unimportant. But my business is." He gestured to an empty stool. "Sit."

The captain kept his eyes affixed on Ahren's blade as he slid onto the hard wooden seat.

"Captain Odell Tabstein," Ahren said, "someone has gone through a lot of effort to have you killed."

"So you're here to kill me?" the captain growled.

Ahren shook his head. "I've come for information."

"About what?"

"Do you have any enemies, Captain?"

Odell squinted at the blade in Ahren's hand. "None that I know."

Ahren held up the square of folded parchment. "Someone wants your ring and this letter. Who is Gren Schmied?"

"So that's what this is about," Odel bellowed, his lips curling in anger.

"Who is he?"

"It's time for you to leave." Odel yanked a knife from his boot and stood. "Get out!" He squeezed the bone handle so tightly his knuckles turned white.

"Whatever your business, I don't care, I just—"

Knocking the small table away, Odel lunged.

His blade sliced Ahren's cloak as he sidestepped the attack. "Halt!"

The captain swiped the knife again, but Ahren ducked the swing and caught his arm. A huge fist smashed into Ahren's face, knocking him back, and the combatants crashed to the floor. Wrestling over the captain's blade, they rolled across the cabin, crashed into the wall, and Odel scrambled on top of Ahren. Odel lay across him and pushed his weight down onto the handle, inching it toward Ahren's chest.

Ahren drove his knee hard into the man's side. Odel gritted his teeth in pain but continued to press the blade closer. With another hard kick, Ahren knocked the captain off, sending him sprawling. Ahren got up and readied for another attack.

"Captain?" a voice shouted from outside.

"In here," Odel called, rolling to his feet. Clutching his knife, he rushed Ahren again.

Ahren grabbed the captain's wrist and pushed the knife aside as their bodies collided, knocking them against the wall. A gasp squelched from the captain's open mouth and he staggered back then stared down at Ahren's dagger protruding from under his own ribs.

Crimson blood burst from the wound and gushed down his body as he pulled the blade free.

With a crash, the door jolted against the locked bar.

"Captain!" someone shouted

The dagger fell from Odel's limp fingers and he collapsed to the wooden floor, a trickle of blood dribbling from his lips.

"Idiot," Ahren hissed, dropping to the man's side.

Odel rolled his head and grinned as if seeing Ahren for the first time. Wood cracked as the door shook under its onslaught. Biting his lip in anger, Ahren pulled the golden ring from the captain's bloody finger and crawled quickly out the open window. He grabbed the aft mooring line and pulled himself rapidly across the rope as the door inside burst open. Curses and furious screams echoed behind him as he reached the pier and fled.

Accordion and violin music filled Saint Faiga's Square from a trio of street performers playing beside a stone well. Ahren studied the crowd hoping to see if anyone paid him any interest, maybe even his anonymous blackmailer. But he noticed nothing unusual. He wandered past a pack of urchins kicking a tired leather ball back and forth, and meandered through the square until he found a white barrel near the alley beside a butcher's shop. He stopped at the barrel, gave a last furtive glance around, then dropped a yellow cloth inside as he bent over to adjust his boot.

The deed accomplished, Ahren straightened up and nonchalantly left the square. Killing Captain Tabstein had been an accident. But the man's blood wasn't on his hands; it was on the hands of whoever had sent him. The letter was sealed, and there was no way to open it without breaking the wax. Ahren had put it in the bundle with the ring, and a note telling his employer to keep his money and leave him alone.

Once he was no longer in sight of the barrel, Ahren circled back to an alley across the square, hid between a pair of crates, and watched.

One of the dirty boys left his game and ran over to the barrel. He leaned inside, pulled out the yellow bundle, then dashed off.

Leaping from the alley, Ahren raced across the square. The urchin darted down a side street. Squeezing past booths and carts Ahren hurried after him and turned onto a crowded street. Quickly, he scanned the area and spotted another young waif clutching the bundle running away. The boy turned down another street, and Ahren slipped through an alley to cut him off. He sprinted through the narrow passage, leaping over stacked baskets, and reached the street just ahead of the urchin.

The dirty child's eyes widened as Ahren leapt in front of him. The waif stumbled back and hurled the yellow bundle into the street. An older boy ran out from the opposite side of the street, grabbed it, and dashed down the road. Ahren pushed his way through the crowd, trying to keep sight of the bright yellow. A lumbering wagon nearly ran Ahren down, momentarily blocking the lane, and forcing him to stop for it to pass. Once clear, he ran down the road to where he had last seen the boy. Cursing, he searched the streets. Nothing.

The package was gone.

Two nights later, another hard *thunk* woke Ahren from an already restless sleep. An annoyingly familiar metal quarrel jutted through his shutter. He pulled it open just as the fading sound of horse hooves clomped away.

The bolt was heavier than the others. He opened it and poured five round sapphires into his hand. Shaking his head in frustration, he peered inside the tube, pulled out another bit of parchment, and unrolled it.

You have done well, Black Raven. There is another job I wish you to do for me. the Goldener Aal will make port in one week's time. The captain carries a letter to a Miss Viveka Khamleir. Kill him, wrap the unopened letter in a yellow cloth as before, and put it in a white barrel beside the tower of Kaiser Imre III. Then leave.

You will be paid upon my receipt of the letter.

A cool smile crept along Ahren's lips. His extortionist had made one deadly mistake: a name. The first letter was going to someone outside the city. But if the ship was arriving with the letter, the recipient could be a resident. He closed his window and returned to bed as a plan began to formulate.

A ship's bell rang across the harbor district as a vessel readied for launch. Sailors and docksmen scuttled around. Clucking hens fluttered uncomfortably inside their small stacked cages, oblivious to their inevitable fate at sea.

Confidently, Ahren strolled down the street, his brass-tipped cane tapping against the cobbles with every stride. His face felt naked without his goatee and moustache, and the fine velvet doublet hugged him tighter than he was accustomed. He suppressed his amusement at how the crowd seemed to part before him at the sight of his rich clothes.

A two-story building came into view and Ahren headed for

it, stopping at its entrance to gaze up at the wide sign stretching below the eaves. *Khamleir's* it read in deep letters. He adjusted his collar and strode through the door.

A thin-faced clerk looked up from his desk. "May I help you?" The room smelled of cedar and old smoke.

"Yes," Ahren said in a pretentious tone. "I wish to speak with Miss Khamleir."

The clerk closed his ink pot. "Is she expecting you?"

Ahren shook his head. "Tell her the Count of Eichefurt is here to see her."

"Wait here." The clerk stood and headed through a door near the back of the room.

Ahren tapped his cane on the tile floor as his eyes surveyed the room. The quellen shopkeep Whazzik had told him that Khamleir's had been operating in the city for over thirty years. The rich furniture and sturdy building only verified that business had been profitable.

The door opened and the clerk reentered, followed by a beautiful young woman. Golden ringlets of hair cascaded down her shoulders toward her ample breasts, held firmly behind an emerald bodice.

"I am Viveka. How may I help you, Count Eichefurt?" she asked in a delicate, yet strong voice.

Ahren blinked, momentarily taken aback by her youth. "Miss Khamleir? I have a matter of business I wish to discuss. A … friend recommended you, and I feel that we could come to a … mutually advantageous arrangement."

She smiled. "I see. Are you looking to ship goods? Or produce?"

"It is a bit more complicated than that, and I would prefer to discuss such business in private, if you don't mind."

She nodded and motioned to the door behind her. "Then let us go up to my office, Count."

Ahren followed her billowing silk skirt up the stairs to a richly decorated room. A thick burgundy and azure rug covered the oaken floor before a dark polished desk. Behind it, through an open window, the harbor glistened in the sunlight.

"Would you care for a drink?" She motioned a delicate hand

toward a padded chair across from her desk.

"Most certainly." Ahren sat and watched the young woman pour two goblets of wine from a gilded bottle.

She handed him his drink, then lowered herself onto the high-backed seat across from him. "So tell me, Count Eichefurt. What is the nature of your business?"

Ahren sipped the smooth wine. "Very good. I do admit, you are much younger than I would have thought. And far lovelier."

"Thank you." She smiled warmly, yet her blue eyes studied him. "This was my father's business. I inherited it after his death two months ago."

"My condolences. It must be hard to be a woman such as yourself and in charge of such a complex operation."

"I grew up here." She took a sip of wine, then regarded Ahren over the rim of her glass. "I took over when my father first became ill. My captains all know and trust me." The tone of her voice took on a slight chill. "My only challenge is clients who deem me unfit to handle their interests. That, and potential suitors who only want my business."

Ahren grinned. "Any man who only sees you for your money is a blind fool. Fortunately, I am neither."

Her hard gaze softened momentarily. "I'm sure the count has not come all this way to flatter me."

"True." Ahren set the goblet on the desk and leaned back against the leather cushions. "It has come to my attention that you may have an enemy. Someone who could profit by eliminating the captains of your ships."

Anger flashed across Viveka's face. "What do you want?" she asked coldly, her eyes narrowing.

Ahren held his hand up to calm her. "To help you. Several nights ago, someone murdered the captain of one of your vessels in exchange for a small fortune. The killer stole the captain's ring, as well as a letter sent to a Mister Gren Schmied."

Viveka's thin hands balled into tight fists and her penetrating glare could have stopped a charging horse.

"The same individual is also planning to murder the captain of the *Goldener Aal* when it makes berth tomorrow. I believe there is a second letter involved."

"What are you after?" Viveka growled. Her flushing cheeks made her even more beautiful.

"To find out who wishes to do you harm. Tell me, who is Mister Schmied? A lover?"

"My uncle. I ask his advice on certain matters."

"Ah. Is there anyone who would be willing to kill in order to keep you from receiving his advice?"

The young woman's creamy breasts rose against her bodice as she drew a deep breath and sighed. "How do you know this? What's in it for you?"

Ahren's lips pulled into a half-smile. "Let's just say that I have many connections with … less than reputable people. People who wish to know the identity of our … mutual enemy."

She traced her finger along the goblet rim until it rang with a crystal tone. "And what will happen when you find this conspirator?" She gazed at him under a veil of thick lashes as she took another sip of her wine.

"Such a fate a young lady shouldn't wish to know." Ahren's tone was flat, but his eyes glittered with anger.

Viveka's eyes sparkled with the sinister mischief of a cat spying an unwary meal. "I'm no lady." She set her glass down firmly on the table. "And you, whoever you are, are not a nobleman." She ran a long finger over her chin, sizing him up in a way that made the hairs arch along the back of his neck. "I'll pay your assassin's fee if the problem is taken care of permanently."

Aroused by the young woman's ruthlessness, Ahren adjusted his position in his seat to relieve his tightening pants. "You're right, on both accounts. Keep your pay. Consider it an apology for the accidental death of one of your captains."

A devious smile answered him.

"Now." He slid his hand slowly up his cane. "Who would wish ill to a woman as beautiful as yourself?"

Konrad Amkire leaned over his desk, reading the manifest for the next shipment, when his office door cracked open. Bayard leaned his head inside. "There is someone here to see you, sir."

"Who is it?" Konrad didn't look up, busy as he was filling in the spaces for his latest customer's inventory. A week ago the ship had been empty. Now, finding enough room for the cargo was the problem.

The old clerk shifted uneasily. "A Count Eichefurt, sir. He says he has important business to discuss."

Konrad paused his scribbling and stared vacantly at the open book as he tried to recall the name Eichefurt. His business demanded he be aware of any potential clients, and an unknown name troubled him. He closed the manifest. "Send him in."

Bayard gave a short nod and vanished behind the door. Konrad rose from his leather chair and approached the small table near the back wall. He brushed his fingers along the sparse hairs covering his head and buttoned his doublet. Footsteps echoed up the stairs and he hurried back to his seat just as the door opened.

"The Count of Eichefurt," Bayard announced, stepping away from the door and revealing a young man dressed in rich velvet the color of parchment.

Konrad stood and extended his hand. "Welcome, Count. I am Konrad Amkire, owner of Sudwinde Shipping."

"Good day."

The count grasped the offered hand and shook it firmly. "Your company comes highly recommended."

"Please." Konrad gestured toward a chair on the other side of his desk. "Have a seat." He seated himself, propped his elbows on his desk, and laced his fingers into a single, loose fist. "How can I help you today?"

The count sat and fidgeted with his brass-knobbed cane. "I am in need of a vessel to carry a shipment of wool and other goods from here to Rhomanny. Frobinsky, in fact. Depending on how my business fares, I will be in need of more vessels and would want a long-term relationship with my shippers."

"I understand. When would this cargo be ready?" Unable to hold back his excitement at a permanent client, Konrad stood. "Would you like a drink, Count?"

The count stiffened and a frown tugged at the corners of his mouth. "I need to ship as soon as possible. I was ready last week, but one of the captains of the shipping company was murdered aboard his ship. A second captain almost met the same fate, though I am informed that the killer was apprehended." He dismissed the situation with an impatient wave of his hand. "Regardless, I can't afford to do business with a company so prone to losing ship's executive personnel and thus losing my shipment." He grasped the cane firmly, walking his hand idly up it as he made a visible effort to calm down. "I apologize, I get carried away." He inhaled deeply, released it and gave Konrad a thin smile. "I would love a drink."

Konrad stared at the young noble in shock. "They caught …"

The count nodded with a half-shrug. "Late last night. Miss Khamleir assured me the threat was over, but I cannot afford to take any chances."

Konrad dabbed his forehead with a small cloth and stood. "Let me fetch your drink." He crossed the room to the small table. His hands shook slightly as he unstopped the bottle and filled two glasses with amber rum. "I'm sure Miss Khamleir was devastated by the loss of one of her captains," he said, watching the count's reflection in the mirror. "Rumor is that many of his crew left after the murder. I'm afraid many more will leave now."

"Perhaps." The count's hands twisted his cane knob. "But hopefully that will cease to be a problem once they've finished questioning the assassin."

"He was captured alive?"

"He was. Or so I'm told." The count turned a probing gaze on Konrad.

"Good." Konrad set a glass down in front of the count. "Miss Khamleir and I may be competitors, but she is a good woman from a good family. And sailors gossip. If this continued, her men and mine may all decide to find a different line of work." He settled back against his chair and placed his glass before him on the desk.

The count nodded, sipping his drink. "That makes sense. But back to my offer …"

Konrad chewed his lip. "I'm sure we can do business. However." He knocked his drink back. "I need to see about fitting your cargo onto the next voyage. If you can give me size and number, I can have a date and price ready for you by the morning."

The count finished his drink, his pale eyes sparkling. "I understand." He flashed Konrad a smile as he removed a folded parchment from his doublet. "The warehouse cost in this city is damn near criminal. I need these shipped before I have to pay another week's fee."

Konrad glanced over the paper and scribbled down the information in his ledger. "I have several warehouses that you can use any time you need." He handed the parchment back to the count.

"I would be very grateful for that."

"I'll have everything ready for you by tomorrow morning." Konrad stood. "Let me escort you to the door."

Konrad stood in the doorway until the nobleman was out of sight before sending Bayard home and locking the door. The shipper paused for a moment staring at the inside of the door, his heart thudding painfully, then set his jaw and left his office on an errand of utmost importance.

The evening breeze chilled as sunlight waned. By the Old Kaisers' light, Konrad briskly walked down the Lunnisburg streets past vendors closing for the night. A creeping tingle slithered up the back of his neck. He looked sharply over his shoulder, scanning the streets behind him, but no one paid him any attention. A nervous chuckle escaped his lips and his pace quickened until he reached The Tiger's Coat, one of the city's finer inns.

The smell of warm food greeted him as he stepped inside, and the talk of men enjoying a drink after a hard day's work filled the air, but Konrad barely noticed. He crossed the bar, dashed up to the third floor and hurried down a narrow hall to a white door. "Helmuth," he called, pounding his fist into the door.

It creaked open and one of Helmuth's green eyes peered out. "What are you doing here?" His sour breath reeked of wine.

"We need to talk." Konrad glanced over his shoulder. "Let me in."

The door squeaked open. Helmuth towered before him, his blond hair tangled and silk clothes disheveled. He held a thin-bladed sword at his side. "Out," he snapped at a young, red-haired wench clutching the bed sheets over her ample bosom.

The girl scrambled out of bed, snatched her garments from the floor and wriggled into a short chemise. Her eyes flashed angrily at Konrad as she scurried out into the hall, a crumpled bodice clenched tightly in one hand.

"What is it?" Helmuth growled. He waited until Konrad stepped inside then closed the door. "You ruin my sport."

Konrad balled his hand into a fist but didn't raise it. "Your assassin was caught! I paid *you* to kill the captains, not hire a killer."

An amused grin grew across the bounty hunter's face. "So? He doesn't know who we are." He tossed the silver-hilted sword onto the unmade bed and pulled his hair back. "I admit I'm disappointed." He twisted the hair into a tangled ponytail. "I didn't spend months tracking him all the way from Ralkosty just to lose out on the bounty. You're fortunate you approached me right before I found him."

"But he didn't get the letter!" Konrad objected furiously. "Now she's—"

"So we change plans," Helmuth interrupted with a shrug. "A small setback, nothing more." He removed a small crossbow from a table and set it on a brass-bound trunk beside the bed. "You look terrible. Go downstairs and get some food, bring back a bottle of wine, and we'll decide our next move."

Konrad took a deep breath and ran his hand over his face. He opened his mouth to speak, then shut it, turned and left the room.

Several minutes later, his hands full with a plate of food and two bottles of wine, he pushed the bedroom door open with his shoulder. "I was thinking," he said, closing the door with his foot. "We could use some of the docksmen …"

Helmuth sat motionless in his chair, his mouth hung open in an expressionless stare.

"You all right?"

The bounty hunter made no reply.

Konrad set the plate down and touched the man on the shoulder. "Helmuth?"

The blond man fell limply to the floor, a metal quarrel jutting from his back. Konrad dropped the bottles, sending a plume of wine and broken glass gushing across the polished wood. A black raven feather protruded from the hollow metal tube.

Terrified, Konrad looked around. The room was empty, and the shutters closed. Turning to run, he slipped on the blood- and wine-soaked floor. He slid and nearly fell, but regained his footing, dashed across the room and burst into the hall, knocking over a patron, as he raced down the stairs. Shouted curses followed him as he shoved his way through the bar and fled out into the chilly night.

He bolted down the narrow streets, dodging traffic and ignoring the shouts of guards. His legs faltered. His breath came in raging gasps and a burning pain shot through his side. He stopped and slouched against a shop front and sucked air in heavy gulps. As the red haze faded from his vision, he forced himself to look around.

A wooden sign creaked in the wind on rusted rings. "Spielder's Mercantile." Konrad smiled; he was almost home. He dabbed the sweat now coating his face and bald head and began walking toward his house.

He made it a block before a familiar tingle danced up his neck. He jerked his head around and glanced over his shoulder to see a lone, cloaked figure walking down the street behind him. Red shadows hid the figure's face, but the determination in his pace rejuvenated Konrad's fear. He cut through an alley and hurried across a small square, then risked another glance behind. He was still being followed. Konrad's heart pounded faster and he dodged into the maze work of alleyways.

After some minutes, Konrad skidded around a corner and came face-to-face with a dead end. He spun around to double back, but stopped. The steady sound of bootsteps echoed from the alley walls.

Trapped.

He swallowed and looked frantically around, then ducked into a door niche. Pressing against the door, he struggled not to pound on it and draw his pursuer's attention. He held his breath and prayed not to be seen, listening as the footsteps came closer. And closer. And closer. Then stopped. Konrad gulped, straining to hear anything in the sudden silence.

"Mister Amkire."

Konrad nearly screamed. He slowly turned his head and forced himself to look. A dark-haired gentleman stood in the alleyway, his rich parchment clothes now hidden under a dark cloak. "Count Eichefurt." He forced a slight chuckle. "You surprised me."

The count nodded, but said nothing.

"Count," Konrad's voice shook. "I think someone's following me. A ... a ... cutpurse or some brigand. Can you look back to make sure no one's there?"

The count didn't move. "There's no one back there. We're alone."

"But I heard him!"

The count nodded. "You did. The fact remains, we're alone." He let fall a long black feather. It drifted down and settled at Konrad's feet.

Konrad's gaze lifted from the feather to the count's face. The count narrowed his eyes. Konrad bolted. The Black Raven's cane cracked against Konrad's knees as he fled past. He stumbled and fell, sprawling onto the filthy cobblestones.

The cold brass tip of his attacker's cane pressed into the side of his throat.

"Did you really think I wouldn't find you?"

"It was Helmuth," Konrad sputtered. "He tracked you down. It was his idea. I had nothing to do with it." Tears streamed down his face. "Have mercy. Please."

"You went along with it," Ahren said, his voice cold.

"I'll pay you," Konrad blubbered. "Whatever you want! Please don't kill me! I'll do anything!"

Ahren shook his head. "Miss Khamleir and I have an arrangement, and I am a man of my word."

"Please, I—"

The Black Raven twisted the round knob of his cane and a slender stiletto point sprang from the tip. The pick-like blade jabbed into Konrad's neck.

Blood gurgled into his throat and out his mouth. He clutched the wound, trying to staunch the pulsing flow of silky blood pouring between his fingers. Gulping like a fish, he tried to scream, but only gurgled. His killer stood above him, watching with apathetic eyes. Coldness crept in, the world dimmed and faded to nothing.

Ahren let out a sigh as Konrad's twitching body fell still. He pulled back on the knob, retracting the blade into the shaft, then locked the mechanism before pushing the handle back to its normal position.

Stepping around the pool of dark blood now filling the narrow lane, he picked up the black feather, and tucked it in the dead man's doublet. A satisfied smile grew along his lips as he turned to leave the alley, slowly strolling like a gentleman should.

Tomorrow, he would tell Viveka that it was done. She had told him to report back immediately. And as much as he would love to pay a late-night visit, he had more pressing business. Tonight, he would sleep well for the first time in days. Tomorrow, he would collect his reward.

Race for the Night Ruby

"You have the hands of a sailor," the whore whispered as Ahren took the glass from her. She ran her long fingers along his. "Yet delicate." She released his hand and gazed up at him with vivid green eyes, the only part of her face not hidden by a red silk veil.

Ahren couldn't help but smile at the whore's advances. Fortunately, she couldn't see her small victory through the gray veil concealing his nose and mouth. The Nadjancian fashion did more than just protect the wearer from the stench of the watery streets, it gave anonymity. Something a wanted man, like Ahren, could always use.

She dropped a nugget of incense into the brazier, adding to the thin sweet haze filling the room. "We could be good together." She leaned closer with the catlike grace of a courtesan, pressing her bare breasts against him. "Magical."

A short weasel of a man stepped through the curtains, followed by a pair of whores. The youth of their eyes, and small pomegranate breasts, suggested they were no more than fifteen. Tiny golden bells jingled from their thin veils.

"Ah, Black Raven," Mashkov said, flopping onto a cushioned chair. "I am glad to meet you."

"That name, as is our business, is private," Ahren said.

Mashkov scanned the small chamber. "We are alone."

Ahren nodded to the girls doting over their master.

"Ah." His eyes gleamed with amused understanding. "Leave us!" Silently, the women stood and slipped through the heavy velvet drapes to the hall.

Ahren surveyed his surroundings. The carved walls, adorned in thick red curtains, left dozens of crevices for a spy hole. He didn't like it.

Mashkov poured himself a glass of vodka. "I see you have met Karolina." He motioned to the doorway. "You like her? You can have her every night during your stay." He knocked back the glass and set it on the small table between them.

He was stalling. Ahren could smell it. In his two years since joining the Tyenee he had met many of its reputable members; killers, extortionists, smugglers. Yet Mashkov, the ruler of Nadjancia's brothels, was one of the most famous. So far, Ahren had yet to be impressed.

"And how long is my stay?" he asked, removing his gray veil and sipping his drink.

"Straight to the point. They warned me about that," Mashkov chuckled. "Not long. Have you ever heard of a dubrald?"

Ahren nodded. "A night ruby. A magic gem that makes the user invisible. The dream of every thief. I can't think of anyone I've ever heard of actually possessing, or even seeing, one."

"Baron Rusukny." He refilled his and Ahren's glasses. "Rumor has spread that the baron, through luck and fortune, has somehow acquired a night ruby." He unrolled a map on the table between them. The artist's crude drawings didn't take away from the floor plan's massive size. "He keeps it here, in his house." Mashkov pointed a ringed finger to a small room on the fourth floor. "It's well protected. The baron's longtime feud with the Grevenik Family has made his home a veritable fortress, complete with armed guards."

Ahren leaned closer, running his finger across the inked parchment hallways. A circled X marked where guards were often posted. The city's canal streets bordered two sides of the house, meeting at the northwest corner. The same corner which held the room he needed to enter. "It'll take me three weeks."

"You have *one* week."

Ahren's brow rose.

"Word of an artifact such as this has drawn a lot of attention." He leaned back in his chair stroking his thin moustache. "My sources say that a local group called the Children of the Rat has already begun plotting for it."

"The Tyenee usually doesn't concern itself with local gangs," Ahren said, returning to the map.

"True." Mashkov nodded. "But their leader, a man named

Krisah, has aspirations higher than just a neighborhood, or even a city. He's a growing irritation that will soon be dealt with."

"Irritations like that are best handled before they become annoyances." Ahren didn't hide his contempt. A general of the Tyenee shouldn't be so careless. His finger tapped an inked window on the fourth floor. "Who drew this map?"

"One of my agents."

"I'd like to talk to this man."

"I'm afraid that isn't possible."

"Why?"

"Because he was found in an alley with this in his back." Mashkov held up a broken black and green glass knife. The swirled glass was beautifully crafted into an ideal grip. Its jagged, broken end showed to have once been a tri-bladed stiletto. "The blade shattered inside him."

Ahren's heart grew heavy as he eyed the handle. "Polnoch."

"We've been trying to recruit the bastard for years, but all we've got from him are more of these," Mashkov said, handing it over.

Tingles of discomfort slithered up Ahren's spine. Polnoch's reputation as a thief and assassin was near mythical. In fact, aside from his signature weapon, nothing else was known about him. Ahren set the handle on the table, happy to be rid of it. "Well, at least we can tell he's human."

"How?"

"The handle is too long to be quellish."

"Maybe he's just a smart quellen trying to throw us off track," Mashkov snorted. "Regardless, with Polnoch on the hunt, we can't afford to wait."

"How long can you give me?"

"The new moon is in nine days. On a dark night like that, you can be guaranteed one of our adversaries will try for it then. You have to get to it first."

Ahren flexed his muscles as best he could, trying to combat their urge to cramp inside the small, uncomfortable box. Slowly, he rolled onto his left side to find a short moment of comfort before new joints and muscles joined the protest. With a deep sigh, he listened to the ferryman's oar paddling through the city. He felt the boat slow.

"What do you want?" a man asked, his voice muffled by the wooden lid.

"Good evening," the ferryman called. "I am here to fetch your master. He wishes to go gambling tonight."

"He said to be here at nine. You're half an hour early."

"My apologies. I did not wish to be late. May I moor my boat and wait for him?"

Ahren held his breath. The guard's reply could be the difference between failure and success. With only nine days to plan the heist, there had been no time for a contingency.

The guard finally broke the silence. "Fine. Pull inside and wait."

Ahren let out a sigh as he heard the clanking chains and a soft cascade of water pouring from the moss-covered portcullis. The boat edged forward and turned before coming to a stop.

"Wait here," said the guard. A heavy door slammed shut, quickly followed by the sound of a bar sliding into place.

"Okay, we're alone," the ferryman hissed. "Get out."

Ahren crawled out from the hollow seat-box and put the cushioned lid back in place. The lantern dangling from the narrow boat's bow cast a flickering light across the stone room. Water still trickled from the raised iron portcullis behind them and a narrow stone dock ran along the walls over a foot above the watery floor. A single iron-bound door sat in the stone wall to his right. "Well done," he said, handing the ferryman a bag of gold.

The ferryman slipped the purse under his vest. "Go now. If anyone catches you …"

"You don't know me. I don't know you."

The veiled ferryman nodded.

Ahren stepped from the boat onto the low steps leading from the brackish water, careful not to slip on the thin skin of slime left from high tides. His soft leather shoes made no noise as he hurried past the door to the back of the chamber where a barrel of rubbish rested against the wall below a square hole no more than a foot and a half across. He pulled his veil tighter to block out the refuse's stink, and stuck his head through the opening.

Bits of debris and mold clung to the chute's rough stone walls. High above, Ahren could see evenly spaced slivers of light from the trash chute doors on each floor. The third and last one, fifty feet above, was his target: the fourth floor. Ahren slid on a pair of gloves, then pulled himself over the angled bottom and crawled inside the shaft.

The uneven stones gave Ahren's fingers more than enough purchase to climb. However, the tiny ledges held their own surprises: splinters of broken glass, rusted shards, or slick bits of rotted food lay inside each of the narrow crevices. The soft rain of debris from his questing fingers forced him to keep his head low, preventing him from seeing where he put his hands. He pushed his toes into the crags as he climbed, driving his back against the jagged wall behind him.

The baron's affinity for gambling was well known throughout the city. Arranging for Yevin, the owner of Nadjancia's most notorious gambling halls, to send the baron a personal invitation to sit at his table this night had been a simple task for Mashkov. The brothel owner's rise to power in the Tyenee was now apparent. It seemed everyone owed him a favor, or would do one for cheap. Ahren couldn't help but be impressed. However, the diversion wasn't without its drawbacks. With the baron gone on this moonless night, Ahren's competitors would inevitably take advantage of it themselves. He just had to get to the night ruby first.

He had made it to the opening on the second floor when he heard the iron door in the dock room below grate open.

"Come, Konstantin, we haven't got all night." Boot steps on stone echoed up the shaft.

Ahren braced himself against the wall and remained still.

"Take my hand, Baron," the ferryman said.

"You're early," Baron Rusukny replied. "I wish more of your kind were as prompt."

"It is my duty to serve you, my lord." The ferryman's overly sweet tone bordered on mockery.

A sharp stone digging in Ahren's back forced him to shift his weight, knocking down a small shower of dust and filth. He clenched his teeth as the miniature avalanche poured down the shaft into the room below.

"Konstantin," the baron yelled. "I'm waiting."

"I'm here, father," called another voice. Ahren had never met the baron's eldest son, but his reputation as a duelist was legendary throughout the city. Despite his foppish appearance, few men would dare cross swords with him. Water splashed as Ahren heard the second man step into the boat.

"To The Golden Wheel," the baron ordered. The paddle swished, taking them away. The heavy door boomed shut, and Ahren was once again alone. He let out a long breath, and continued his climb.

After several long and tiresome minutes, Ahren reached the fourth floor. He pressed his ear to the wooden door.

Silence.

Carefully, he cracked it open and peered inside. The empty halls were a welcome sight. He pushed the door open, crawled through the small opening, and lowered himself to the floor. An uncurtained window at the end of the hall offered little light. Only the glow from lights across the canal illuminated the moonless scene outside. Ahren unclasped his filthy cloak, wiped the clinging refuse from his gloves and shoes, then wedged it back inside the chute. Its stink would only give him away.

He shut the small door and crept silently down the hallway. Dark silhouettes of statues and suits of armor, like silent sentries along the walls, added to his paranoia.

Light suddenly spilled into the hallway ahead as a door squeaked open. Ahren dove behind a copper statue as a man in green and gold stepped into the hall. His hand resting on his sheathed rapier hilt, the guard turned in Ahren's direction.

Pressing himself into the shadows, Ahren remained still as the sentry strolled past.

Ahren waited several seconds after the guard had left before releasing his breath. At no time during his surveillance had he spotted patrols on this floor. He scanned the hall again, before slipping from his hiding place.

He turned at the hall's end and made his way down another long passage lined with paintings and unlit sconces. His eyes locked onto a heavy door at the end, the last obstacle before the prize.

A brass keyhole perched above the thick door handle stared back at him. Removing his gloves, Ahren knelt before it and drew a roll of doeskin from his pouch. He unrolled the soft leather, exposing a large collection of picks, shims, and various delicate tools. Gently, he slipped a pair of slender picks into the opening and stopped.

Something wasn't right.

Ahren withdrew the picks and examined the keyhole again. From the outside, the lock appeared simple, yet well made. The vertical slot, capped with a round hole, was perfectly cut into the decorative pattern swirling across the brass plate. He saw nothing unusual, but something made the small hairs along the back of his neck tingle.

He ran his finger along the hole and realized what troubled him. No one used it. The edges of the polished plate, where brass met wood, were dull, and the subtle tarnish where servants' rags could not clean it suggested the lock had been there for a while. However, the keyhole's edges were sharp and unblemished. No brass lock, no matter how well maintained, could escape the tiny scratches and dulled corners from a key sliding in and out. It was a trap.

Ahren conducted another search of the door for other keyholes, then ran his hands along the carved doorframe. Within one of the crags of the ornate wood he found a hidden hole nestled in the molding. He eased his picks into the new lock and worked the mechanism. The bolt's hard click echoed down the hall. Ahren slid his tools back into his pouch and opened the door.

He slipped inside, quietly closing the door behind him, and looked around at the small room. Faint light from a barred window glinted off the wood-paneled walls adorned with paintings and rich drapes. Several small chests rested in a far corner, a pair of bronze statues stood on either side of a second door, and in the center of the chamber, a silver and bronze box rested atop a short, marble pedestal.

Silver dragon heads, their mouths open in fearsome growls, adorned each side of the metal chest. Ahren ran his fingers across their ruby eyes and sharp, arrow-like tongues. The face looking upward from the top of the flat lid moved under his touch. He slid it aside on an unseen hinge to reveal a narrow keyhole lined with gold.

Ahren had just removed the tools from his pouch when he heard soft footsteps coming closer. The lock to the room's second door rattled. He slid the dragonhead cover back and ducked into a dark corner behind a curtain as the door creaked open. He held his breath, pressing himself against the wall.

The door closed and someone crossed the room to the metal box. Ahren braved a peek from behind the heavy velvet folds to see a man dressed in simple clothes of brown and gray carrying a slender hooded lantern. Setting it on the box, the stranger raised the hood and candlelight filled the room. He examined the box, quickly discovering the concealed hole, and carefully worked a pair of picks into the lock.

Ahren slid his hand to his dagger, grasping the leather-wrapped handle.

The lock's soft click filled the silent room. The thief put his tools away, placed his lantern on the floor, and slowly lifted the lid. Drawing his blade, Ahren slid out from behind the curtain.

A quick series of pops rang from the box, followed by thuds from the chamber walls. Ahren looked down to see a narrow dart imbedded in the dark panel beside him.

The thief staggered back and pulled a similar dart from his stomach. A tremor ran through his body and with a hollow gasp, he collapsed into a fit of jerky convulsions. Ahren froze. Looking back at the small arrow, he saw thick fluid spattered around where it had hit.

The thief rolled on the floor, his arms and legs lashing out as if he were a tangled marionette, unable to control his own body. Only a hissing groan escaped his lips as a bloodstain spread across his veil, wetly clinging over his mouth and nose.

Ahren crossed the room. The thief's eyes, red with hemorrhaged veins, looked on him with fear and pain. Ahren knelt down and thrust his dagger between the man's ribs into his heart. Fear faded from his eyes, and his body grew limp.

Ahren wiped the blade and returned it to its sheath. The ornate lid of the metal chest still sat open. Cautiously, he peered inside and saw four small crossbows aimed out of the mouths of the silver dragonheads. A bowl lined in black velvet sat nestled between the weapons and a dark gem lay inside. He removed the stone and examined it. The round ruby was no bigger than a man's eye. A black cloud swirled inside the stone like smoke. Ahren had never even imagined seeing a dubrald. Now, as he held it between his fingers, he felt entranced by its dark beauty. The inky wisps danced seductively within their crimson walls.

Mashkov had been right in denying Ahren the knowledge to unlock the gem's power. Had he known the secret, Ahren questioned if he'd be able to give the treasure to someone else. Begrudgingly, he pried his eyes from the stone and slipped it securely in his pouch. Before closing the deadly chest, he removed a long black feather and placed it in the velvet bowl.

He stepped back to the door he had entered and put his ear to the narrow gap between it and the doorframe. Nothing. Quickly, he slipped from the room and crept down the hall, past the busts and statues, and stopped beside a large window.

He peered through the wavy glass and thick iron bars and saw the top of the outer wall running thirty feet along the courtyard's edge, ending just below the eaves of the neighboring roof. The house guards paid little attention to the yard, making the wall an almost perfect roadway into the house. However, once making it to the house the locked bars made it an impregnable entrance. Ahren clicked the inside latch, and swung the window open.

As he suspected, no guards patrolled the courtyard. With a fluid motion, Ahren hopped over the windowsill and lowered himself onto the flat-topped wall. He hurried down the thick stones toward the adjoining rooftop when a shadow ahead caught his eye. Ahren slowed, momentarily searching for what had moved. A soft clatter from another rooftop drew his attention. A figure, clad in gray and brown, crouched low against the roof, his dark clothing perfectly matching the tile and stone. The dead thief hadn't come alone, and the Children of the Rat were now lying in ambush.

Ahren crouched, grabbed the outside edge of the wall, and jumped down. His fingers held his weight. The distance to the streets below now halved, he let go, dropped onto the hard cobblestone, and ran.

Most of Nadjancia's twisted, narrow streets were no more than alleys. At many places, Ahren could simultaneously press the flats of his hands against shop fronts on opposite sides. The tall buildings leaned over the streets, blocking out almost all light from above. Only sparse lamps, along the black stone buildings, cast dim illumination within the labyrinth's walls.

Soft clacks of someone tapping roof tiles echoed down from above. More tapping on clay and wood shingles replied from up ahead. His rooftop pursuers knew where he was. Shadows flew across the tops of the narrow streets as men leapt from roof to roof. Ahren turned abruptly down the streets, hoping to confuse and lose his hunters. The alley stopped at a canal and he raced along the street beside it, hoping to find a bridge. The canals were too wide for the thieves to jump.

He just needed to get off this block.

A wall blocked the street ahead, forcing Ahren to abandon the canal and plunge deeper into the dark winding streets. Tapping came from ahead and to the left. He turned right and ran until he heard it ahead of him again. They were trying to herd him. Ignoring their warnings, Ahren kept straight.

The narrow canyon opened up into a small square. An ornate stone well rested in its center. A dingy canal bordered the far side. Relief swept through Ahren's tired muscles upon spotting a narrow bridge arching over the canal. Feet on shingles clamored up behind him as he raced to the bridge.

A caped figure stepped onto the bridge, his rapier aimed at Ahren. Stabbing eyes peered from the shadows beneath a leather-brimmed hat. The light gray veil, pulled tautly across his face, had been painted, giving him the appearance of a skull. It was Krisah, the ambitious gang leader. He moved back and forth across the bridge as a serpent, seeming to pivot off the unmoving needle-tip of his sword.

Ahren felt his pursuers' eyes along his back. His gaze darted away from the swordsman long enough to see a dozen figures crouched along the roofs overlooking the square.

Krisah advanced slowly, his steps delicate as if it were a dance. Ahren's obvious lack of a sword gleamed like a victory in the man's dark eyes.

Ahren took a step back, holding his left hand up between him and his adversary. As Krisah neared the bridge's edge, Ahren swung his hand far to the left, drawing his opponent's eyes, as his right hand drew and hurled his dagger. The blade whipped through the quiet air and sank into the man's stomach.

Krisah's sword clattered to the ground. Staggering back, he fell into the dark canal. The audience of thieves pounded their fists in silent fury. Ripping up the flat, square roof-tiles, they hurled them down at Ahren. The clay shingles exploded on the stones around him as he raced across the bridge and vanished into the streets beyond.

The shadowy streets, encased with black, stone buildings, turned and wove into a maddening maze. Ahren struggled to keep his bearings, but the steep walls of building fronts blocked any view of the city's taller landmarks, and fast-moving clouds blew across the heavens, shielding the stars.

The distant thuds of many feet racing on cobblestone echoed from behind. Ahren hurried faster, but kept on his toes, hoping the softer steps would not betray his location.

Many small alleys joined, forming a wide lane feeding into another square. He saw the Central Canal ahead. Forty yards across the canal's slow waters, sat the Pleasure District and the safety of Mashkov's brothel.

A row of boats, tied for the night, bobbed against the canal's banks. Ahren raced to the pier's end and leapt into one of the slender ferries. He yanked and unhitched the mooring line, then pushed the vessel free of the dock. With a sigh of relief, he slipped the oars into their locks and began rowing to the other side.

His reprieve was short-lived. As he reached halfway across the canal, three men in gray and brown climbed into one of the boats and continued after him. He rowed faster, but with two men manning the oars, his pursuers quickly shortened the gap between them.

Reaching the other side, Ahren steered the boat down one of the smaller canal streets. The men behind him drew closer. One of them stood on the bow and hurled a lasso. The rope splashed in the water beside him. The man coiled the line, readying for another throw. If he caught the docking cleat or lantern hook, Ahren knew he'd have to escape into the water. He wouldn't be able to cut free. His only blade had been lost in the belly of their leader. Frantically, his eyes searched for the best place to climb ashore if he had to swim. Sheer building walls lined the banks. The stone statues above watched with emotionless eyes.

The other boat was within fifteen feet when the man readied for another throw. Ahren unlocked the boat oar, ready to defend himself. Just as the man reared back to throw, a soft shower of dust fell from above. He looked up and cried out, as a falling statue smashed into the men's boat, ripping it in half. Water exploded in a column of splintered wood and flailing arms. The thieves screamed and howled as waves from the statue's wake pulled them under.

Ahren looked up to where the statue had come, but saw no one along the dark rooftops. He was close to the brothel, and Mashkov must have had runners out looking for him. It was the only explanation.

He guided the boat to the brothel steps and leapt out. He hurried past the doorman and through the lounges of veiled whores and clouds of incense. His heart still pounded in his ears as he ascended the stairs and stepped through the curtain to Mashkov's chamber.

"I got it," he announced.

Mashkov sat, leaning back on one of the cushioned chairs.

"I couldn't have done it if you hadn't had someone up on the roof …" Ahren froze. The glass handle of a stiletto jutted from the thin man's throat. Wet blood coated his red clothes and dripped into pools on the floor.

A sharp sting stabbed into Ahren's side, and his hands grabbed at a slender dart imbedded above his hip. He spun to see a figure in a wide hat step out from behind one of the heavy drapes. *Polnoch!* His vision blurred and his body became heavy. He reached in vain for a nearby table but collapsed to the floor.

Footsteps came from behind him, and Ahren felt his attacker rifle through his pouches and remove the night ruby. Polnoch rolled him onto his back, and slipped one of the signature glass stilettos into Ahren's limp hand.

"You have the hands of a sailor," said a familiar voice.

Ahren's heart lurched. He looked into the fierce green eyes peering from behind Polnoch's veil.

"Something for you to remember me by, lover." She pulled her veil away, unmasking the delicate face he had known over the past nine nights. Long curls of auburn hair spilled down her shoulders as she removed her hat and leaned closer; her soft lips trembling against his. "I let you live knowing my face, Black Raven, because you will be the last to ever see it." Her bittersweet perfume flooded his mind with fond memories, soothing his pounding heart. She kissed him, softly tugging his lip as she sat up.

She smiled seductively. "You're welcome for my help in the canal." She slipped the smoky gem into her mouth and vanished.

The Ferrymaster's Toll

Ahren stepped through the golden velvet curtain into a small room. He no longer noticed the heavy clouds of incense since taking the brothel over a month before. Anna, a bare-breasted whore in a green veil, filled a glass chalice with vodka and handed it to the man sitting in one of the large padded chairs. A black-hilted sword leaned an arm's reach beside him and a poorly concealed dagger bulged beneath his loosened doublet. Ahren nodded and the pale-skinned girl bowed then left the two men alone.

"I was to meet with Mashkov," the man said, removing his brown veil. Deep scars pitted his narrow face.

Ahren took the chair opposite him. A long wooden case rested on the low table between them. Ever since Mashkov's assassination weeks before, Ahren had assumed responsibility until the Tyenee could send a suitable replacement. "You must be Kirril." He unclasped the veil from over his nose and mouth. "My name is Ahren. Mashkov had urgent business outside the city, and left me in charge of his affairs until his return."

Kirril's eyes narrowed. His fingers inched toward the hidden weapon. "Mashkov never said anything about leaving. My business is with him alone."

"I understand." Ahren sipped his drink. "I can assure you, however, that I am quite capable of handling *all* of his business while he is away."

Kirril said nothing.

"If you'd prefer to wait until Mashkov returns, I understand. However, I couldn't even tell you how long that will be."

The thin man chewed his lip for several long seconds before speaking. "I cannot wait. Tell me, Ahren, Mashkov promised me the Black Raven for the job that I have. Do you know him?"

Ahren winced at the name. Mashkov's penchant for saying things he shouldn't had been his downfall. "I know him."

Kirril's shifting seemed to ease. His hand relaxed and slid away from the concealed blade. "Wonderful. Is it true he stole a dubrald from Baron Rusukny's home?"

Ahren smiled, but said nothing.

Kirril chuckled. "I thought so. If he was able to do that, then Mashkov was right in saying he would be perfect for this."

"And what exactly is your job, Kirril?"

Kirril downed his chalice in one gulp. "What do you know about the ferrymen's guild?"

Ahren shrugged. "It's the only guild not controlled by one of the Nadjancian noble houses. Anyone who has tried to work outside the guild or to control it has met with disastrous results."

"Very good." He poured himself another drink. "But how? How does the most powerful guild survive its independence when the houses command every other major guild in the city?"

Since coming to the Veiled City, Ahren had seen many of its customs and myths. But in a place where mystery and decadence reigned as virtues, only one name symbolized its horrors. "The Ferrymaster."

A faint smile twisted on Kirril's thin lips. "That's right. Have you seen him?"

Ahren shook his head.

"Live here long enough, and you'll see the King of the Canals," Kirril said. "Upset his ferrymen, and you'll meet the drowned."

Ahren swirled the clear liquor in the bottom of his glass. He'd heard of the ghostly guild master his first day in the city. The ferrymen who navigated their slender boats up and down the watery streets all owed him their allegiance. Ten percent of all they made, they dropped into the canal as their tithe. Anyone crossing the ferrymen, or their master, wouldn't be able to ride the canals again. Otherwise, the bloated corpses of all who had drowned in the canals would exact the Ferrymaster's revenge. If a customer was upset at his ferryman, the custom was to toss his pay into the water, to pay the master but not the servant. "Who was he?" Ahren asked.

"His name was Vooshkae. When Nadjancia was young, and the ferrymen disjoined, it was known that whoever controlled the canals controlled the city. Before the Grevenik and Rusukny's war ran blood into the canals, two other houses feuded for control. The Deshirit and Glothrev Families vied for domination. Docks were burned, brawls erupted across the canals, and the city suffered. Any ferryman not under the protection from one of the houses was often found floating down the street. Vooshkae was a young man then, and when a member of the Glothrev Family asked whom he paid tribute, Vooshkae beat him with his oar. The Deshirits assumed that meant he swore allegiance to them, and when they sent a man to collect their cut, Vooshkae sent him back with a knife in his neck."

"That must have upset them," Ahren said.

Kirril gave a nervous laugh. "Vooshkae rallied the ferrymen together, saying that the power of the waterways belonged to those who worked them. He set a standard of pay for the workers and anyone who refused to pay it, found that no one would give them a ride. Eventually, the Glothrev and Deshirit Families sent assassins in order to regain control. But they all went missing. After that, no ferryman would take anyone associated with either house onto the canals. When they tried again, Vooshkae's fury was merciless; any member of either family who entered the canals was drowned by the ferrymen. Men, women, young and old, he killed them all.

"To appease the Ferrymaster, the Deshirits and Glothrevs united and presented him with a jeweled oar cap, declaring him 'King of the Canals.' With his guard down, they sent one last assassin." Kirril leaned forward, his voice low. "The story goes that when the would-be killer tried, the bodies of his drowned predecessors rose from the water and dragged him screaming under the surface. After that, no one threatened Vooshkae's authority."

"It's an interesting story, Kirril," Ahren said, trying to hide the chill creeping up his spine. "But what does the Ferrymaster's tale have to do with the Black Raven?"

The scarred man straightened and sipped his drink. "It was said that the jeweled oar cap was what made him king over the canals, even those who died in them. When Vooshkae died, the new guild master erected a tower on the Isle of Muritzka for him. He was buried with the oar cap. And every guild master since is entombed there as well. Whoever owns that cap controls the canals and the city. But only the reigning guild master has the key to Vooshkae's tower."

"And the Black Raven is to steal this key?"

Kirril's eyes sparkled. "No." He patted the long box. "My job was to get the key. But the Ferrymaster's tower is filled with deadly traps. Black Raven's is to steal the oar cap."

Ahren's eyes narrowed. He opened the wooden box to find a golden rapier inside. His mouth opened, trying to form the question on his lips, but Kirril answered it first.

"The guild master's sword is the key."

"How did you get it?"

"The Ferrymaster knows all that happens on his canals, but his domain doesn't reach onto the land." He gave a killer's smile. "It'll be a few days before the ferrymen realize their master is missing, but waiting for Mashkov to return isn't an option. I promised Mashkov the key. He promised me a cut of his fortune. Ten percent, of ten percent of what every ferryman is paid, is enough for me." He sipped his drink. "But if you don't wish to honor Mashkov's deal, I'm sure I can find another buyer. However, time is short. If word of the guild master's death—"

Ahren snapped the wooden lid shut. Whether he liked the idea or not, control over the canals was something the Tyenee would want, and there was no time to hesitate. Until an agent was sent to take permanent control of the brothels and the city, Ahren had to make the decisions. "No. I am willing to honor his agreement."

"So the Black Raven will fetch the oar cap?"

Ahren nodded. "I will pass the key to him, and he will bring us the Ferrymaster's oar cap."

"Wonderful," Kirril beamed. He raised his glass. "To the new Kings of the Canal," he toasted. "May fortune smile on us both."

Ahren knocked back his drink. "Return in one week."

Kirril refastened the veil across his face and stood. "I will see you then, Ahren. I wish luck to the Black Raven." He bowed his head, slid his sword into its sheath, and left.

Ahren sat quiet for several seconds before pouring another drink.

"I don't trust him," Klanya said, stepping out from the curtain behind Kirril's empty chair. The brown-haired whore sheathed her curved dagger. "He means to kill you, Black Raven. I'm sure of it."

Ahren handed her the glass. "Thank you, Klanya. I'll be careful."

A cool breeze coursed narrow valleys between buildings, sweeping away the canals' putrid stink. Ahren guided his craft down the dark watery streets. Narrow boats lined the canals, moored for the night. Their wooden hulls softly banged against the stone walls like floating wind chimes. The yellow lantern hanging from his prow cast long shadows across an empty market as he floated past. Gray rats scurried across the flagstones as they raided the lingering scraps from the butchers' tables.

Crossing the Central Canal, Ahren passed fat nobles and jeweled courtesans in silken veils enjoying the private gambling house courtyards overlooking the water. He steered through the Warehouse District near the Grevenik Docks as drunken sailors brawled over dice and threw away their coin on soured drinks and weary whores.

He paddled his small boat out from the floating city and into the calm harbor water. Once there he lowered the metal hood over the lantern and guided himself by the pale light cast from the half-moon above. Ahead, Muritzka's sheer walls loomed out over the water. Dark silhouettes of towers and steep tomb roofs rose behind the imposing parapets. A pair of iron torches burned on either side of the portcullised entrance. Beneath them, two guards in blackened chain and dark veils stood silently, watching Ahren approach.

Ahren slowed his craft to a stop before the iron gate. Reaching inside a velvet bag, he lifted out a fistful of golden coins. Letting them fall from his fingers they clinked back into the pouch with musical rhythm. "I've come to pay my respects," he said, cinching the bag closed and tossing it to the sentry's feet.

The guards said nothing. With both hands, one turned the winch wheel beside him. Chains rattled and grated and the rusty gate rose. Water cascaded from the dark moss wrapped around the portcullis bars.

With a nod, Ahren guided his boat under the dripping gate and into an ornately engraved canal. Statues and obelisks lined the sides like silent guardians. Behind them, thousands of lavish mausoleums spread out across the manicured island like a miniature city.

The wide canal led straight to the island's center, where it opened into a rectangular lagoon hidden beneath a latticed canopy of leafy vines. Far to the side, near the twenty-foot wall surrounding the island, an onion-domed tower loomed over the necropolis. Ahren moored his boat beside an empty funeral barge, grabbed his lantern, and stepped out into Nadjancia's great cemetery.

Dark tiles paved the pathways between the stone monuments. Graven saints and gargoyles stared down at him with lifeless eyes as he passed. Ahren couldn't shake the discomforting feeling from the many lifelike marble and bronze figures standing above the graves. With his lantern high, he wove through the maze of tombs until finally reaching the Ferrymaster's tower.

Blue veins coursed through the gray marble covering the building. An intricate relief of ferrymen navigating the city's bustling canals encircled the tower's wide lower portion. A pointed archway in the monument's side broke the artistic scene. The shallow alcove, adorned with mermaids and gold leaf, went in only four feet and ended at a green copper wall.

Running his fingers across the cold metal, Ahren searched for an opening. Unsuccessful in finding a hinge or keyhole, he spread out his examination to the alcove walls. The elaborate carvings created a seemingly endless number of places to conceal the keyhole. Raising his lantern, Ahren scanned the graven façade.

A carving of a large fish caught his attention. Its scaly body waved back and forth, as if frozen in a moment of swimming, and its round face swept upward, into the alcove. Its thick lips formed a dark hole.

Kneeling, Ahren peered into the fish's mouth. The smooth opening was wide enough to slide a finger into. Two slender grooves ran down the left side. Ahren set his lantern down and drew the gold-hilted sword from his waist. A swirling design interlaced with tiny gemstones ran up the middle of the blade. An open flower, with three pearls, capped the pommel.

Ahren had spent hours studying the ornate weapon, trying to understand its secret. While the keen blade was well crafted, its adornments and misbalanced weight made it a poor weapon. Kirril had called it a key, but nothing about it appeared useful as one.

Holding the handle tight, Ahren unscrewed the pommel. He pulled out a slender tube running up the handle length. The brass cylinder ended in a jagged ring of squared teeth. Two flat-topped bumps rose from one side of the otherwise smooth tube.

Lining the notches with the grooves, Ahren carefully inserted the key into the fish's mouth. It slid in perfectly. In his many years of burgling, he had never seen a key or lock as this. He leaned in closer, trying to study how it worked. It appeared ready, but something about it still made him feel uneasy. Remembering Kirril's warning of traps, Ahren leaned away.

Holding it with only his thumb and forefinger, he twisted the key to the right. The lock clicked and a nine-inch spike shot from the hollow key in the fish's mouth. Ahren froze, staring at the needle-like blade. Had he not moved, it would have stabbed him.

Pulling himself to his feet, he checked the copper door. It was unlocked.

Cautiously, he pushed it, but it didn't move. He tried again, driving his weight into the door. Slowly, it swung open. The spike jutting from the fish's mouth retracted as the opening widened. With a soft click, the trap re-armed.

A sigh of stale air wafted out the dark doorway. Pulling his veil tighter across his nose to block the foul odor, Ahren raised his lantern and peered inside. Bright mosaics sparkled in the dim light. Ragged tapestries of dusty cobwebs hung from the ceiling. A honeycomb of niches, each containing a moldy skeleton in a rotted shroud, covered the back wall. Marble busts, accented with gold and tarnished silver, lined the walkway past engraved vault doors covering the walls and floor.

Careful not to set off another trap, Ahren removed the cylindrical key from the wall and returned it to the sword handle. He glanced over his shoulder one last time and then stepped through the tower door.

Ahren followed the narrow path between the sculpted busts of the former guild masters. Jeweled masks, silver ferry figureheads and other bizarre treasures leaned in the corners and decorated the walls. To the left, between a pair of gold oars, an arched doorway led to a spiral staircase.

A faint breeze trickled down the stairway as Ahren followed the tight spirals upward. The passage opened up onto the second floor, to a vaulted chamber decorated in amber. A ring of stone sarcophagi encircled a white statue of a veiled woman playing a violin. Ahren only glanced inside before continuing up the steep stairs.

He passed two more floors before reaching the highest level in the tower. Pale moonlight shone through the narrow, barred windows lining the room. Blood-red tiles decorated the inlaid floor. A full-size stone statue of a canal ferry dominated the center of the chamber. Its veiled pilot stared out ahead, holding his bronze oar with both hands. An ivory coffin, decorated with black pearls, rested inside the narrow craft. Its lid was carved into the form of a man lying on a draped cloth.

Amazed by its haunting beauty, Ahren circled the dark statue before finally approaching. He ran his fingers across the smooth ivory, wiping away a thin layer of dust. Placing his hands firmly against the lid near the top, he pushed. The heavy stone didn't budge.

Taking a deep breath, he braced his feet against the floor, and pressed against the sarcophagus cover with all his weight. Stone ground on stone as the thick lid inched aside. A sliver of blackness widened as the casket slid open. Suddenly, a small pop came from the lid, followed by a loud clank.

With a screech, the ferryman statue whirled around. Ahren ducked just as its bronze paddle whooshed past, knocking the hat from his head. Chains rattled as an iron portcullis slammed down over the stairwell entrance with a thunderous crash, sealing him in.

Catching his breath, Ahren slowly rose to his feet. A thumb-sized metal pin protruded up from the casket's inner walls where Ahren had slid away the lid. Hesitant to move the lid any further, he raised his lantern and peered through the narrow crevice into the sarcophagus.

A dried skeleton lay inside. It held a black, tarnished oar cap against its chest. Gold and jeweled rings covered white boney fingers. Carefully, Ahren slipped his hand through the narrow opening and removed the artifact from the corpse's grasp.

Glistening square diamonds rimmed the oar cap's hollow end. The round knob at the other end was formed like a ruby-eyed skull, accented with gold.

Removing a wide strip of cloth from his satchel, Ahren wrapped the cap tightly before tucking it into his bag. He drew a thick raven's quill from his pouch and slipped it into the Ferrymaster's dead hands with a smile.

Now that the prize was his, Ahren surveyed his situation. Rusted iron bars covered the windows. One by one, he pulled and pushed, hoping one might be loose, but the thick rivets holding them in place were too strong.

Outside, over the island walls, he could see the swinging lanterns aboard the boats and ferries in the harbor. Shouts and ship's bells echoed across the nighttime water. Behind them, the quiet cityscape stood like a jagged silhouette, broken only by yellow-lit windows.

Sweat trickled down his face and into his eyes as he wrestled with the last set of bars before finally surrendering. It didn't matter. Even if he managed to pry one free, the tower was sixty feet of smooth marble before the ground, and he didn't have a rope.

Wiping his brow, he turned his attention to the wide portcullis blocking the stairs. Chips of stone tile lay scattered around where the gate's spear-like points had shattered them when it dropped. He could tell by looking that it was too heavy to lift.

Creeping panic began to take hold. He was trapped.

Given enough time, Ahren could escape unscathed. But he didn't have time. Someone outside must have heard the thunderous noise the falling portcullis had made. He had bribed the guards outside the cemetery, but the burglary of one of the city's most prominent tombs wouldn't be ignored. Even if no one had heard him, the guards would want him gone before their shift ended. His boat was still moored at the docks. The tower door was still open. Someone would notice.

He spied an alabaster figure of a mermaid in the corner near the door. The statue itself was useless, but its stout, waist-high pedestal was perfect. If he could lift the portcullis enough to lay the pedestal under it, he could squeeze out. He just needed a lever or something to pry up the gate.

Ahren's eyes fell onto the bronze oar that had nearly taken his head off only a few minutes before. The nine-foot pole would be enough for him to lever the gate. If he couldn't pull it out of the ferryman's stone hands, he'd break the statue at the wrists.

Grasping the oar at the paddle head, Ahren pulled with his entire body. It didn't move. He pushed and jerked harder, trying to wiggle it in any way. The statue moved at the waist-seam which had spun before. Ahren heard chains rattle as he jostled the mechanical sculpture.

Pushing against the side of the oar, Ahren moved the statue again. The hollow rattle of chains echoed from somewhere in the walls. The same chains had rattled when the portcullis had dropped. Ahren pushed harder, straining against the metal oar. Across the room, the iron gate groaned and lifted less than an inch.

Excitement swept through Ahren's veins, as he watched the portcullis lift. He relaxed his pressure on the oar, and the bronze pole nearly swung into him as the gate dropped back to the floor with a clang.

Lifting the gate was no longer a problem, but keeping it up long enough for him to get out was.

The portcullis was too far away to slip a brace under, so he'd have to keep the winch arm from spinning when he let go. He looked at the mermaid statue's pedestal, but it was too short to block the bronze oar. Scanning the chamber again, he spied the sarcophagus lid still resting on the box. He could have used that, if he hadn't been worried there might be more traps hidden beneath, but then he remembered the pin.

Returning to the ivory casket, Ahren depressed the small metal pin hidden along its inside wall. Holding it down with a dagger blade, he dug his fingers into a narrow crevice on the carved lid and pulled the heavy stone back. His fingers strained as he slid the stone lid back enough to cover the pin and keep it in place.

Shaking his hand to restore the feeling to his numb fingertips, he grabbed the bronze oar and pushed. Chains rattled and the iron gate inched higher. The portcullis had risen about a hand's breadth above the floor when something inside the rotating statue clicked. And Ahren relaxed his hold long enough to see the door didn't fall.

Ahren drove his weight against the oar again, lifting the door another few inches.

Click.

The gap was almost enough to squeeze through. He drove himself against the oar again and again, each time lifting the gate a little higher as clicks locked his progress in place. Sweat poured down his forehead and into his eyes as he propped himself against the lever one last time. The gate's bent spear points hovered almost two feet above the floor; there was more than enough space to slide under.

Nodding his farewell to the Ferrymaster's grave, Ahren slipped under the black portcullis and retreated down the tower stairs. He reached the bottom and crossed the tomb room without even a glance at the riches displayed along the walls. He had entertained the notion of keeping a few of the jeweled treasures buried in the tower, but after the commotion and near catastrophe of being trapped inside, it was better to leave with the Ferrymaster's treasure than risk another mishap.

A fresh breeze blew from outside as Ahren reached the doorway. He was about to step through when a shadow moved in the cemetery ahead.

A figure stepped out from behind one of the mausoleums, a crossbow tucked against his shoulder. Ahren jumped behind the door just as the bolt whizzed past, sparking off the stone and skittering into the darkness.

"He's here!" someone yelled.

Boot steps raced toward the tower.

Ahren drove his shoulder into the copper door and pushed it closed just as the pounding footsteps reached the alcove. The door lock snapped into place with a metallic thump.

"Damn it," someone shouted, the voice muffled behind the door. Something slammed into the thick copper. "You missed him."

Ahren backed away, nearly stumbling into one of the marble busts. His mind tumbled over possibilities, trying to figure out who the men were. They weren't dressed in uniforms. They hadn't tried to capture him. They had been waiting for him.

The door rang as someone pounded a fist against the other side. It would take hours before anyone could batter it down. Ahren had until then to figure a way out. There were no windows except for in the Ferrymaster's room, and Ahren hurried back up the stairs to identify his assailants.

He slipped back under the gate, and peered down from the barred window onto the area in front of the tower's door. Four plainly dressed men in veils stood outside talking amongst themselves. One carried a burning torch, while two others held stout crossbows. The fourth man clutched a rapier. He carried himself with authority, and the others appeared to look to him for instruction.

Ahren squinted to see if he could recognize the leader's hidden face. The man looked up as if he'd felt Ahren's eyes. He unclasped his brown veil and smiled.

"Ahren," Kirril called. "I thought it was you."

"I was about to say the same thing," Ahren replied.

Kirril chuckled. "So you're the Black Raven. I must congratulate you on your accomplishments. First you plundered Baron Rusukny's house and now you survived the Ferrymaster's tower."

"So you meant to double-cross me?"

"Nothing personal, Black Raven. But I had an offer from another buyer who promised a larger cut than Mashkov."

Ahren's gaze ran across the cemetery to the open canal gate leading outside.

"Oh, don't worry about the guards," Kirril said casually. "We took care of them. We wouldn't want anyone disturbing us."

One of Kirril's henchmen began lifting his crossbow while Kirril spoke.

Ahren backed away from the window.

"Put that away you idiot," Kirril snapped. "The door's locked. We can't get inside."

"That puts us in a delicate situation," Ahren called.

"I wouldn't say that." Kirril smiled. "You're in a cage, Black Raven. You might have the key, but you can't get out. You have no food. No water. Nothing."

"Someone's going to notice the missing guards," Ahren said. "I don't think you'll want to be here when they come looking."

Kirril laughed. "Nice try. But I don't see you calling down from that tower for them to rescue you. You've broken into the Ferrymaster's tomb. It won't be hard to believe you killed the guards."

Ahren chewed his lip. His eyes returned to the bronze oar in the ferryman statue's grip. "Then what do you propose, Kirril? If I die in here, you don't get the oar cap and your buyer won't be happy."

"Easy. Just drop the cap out the window, and we'll leave. I'm sure the Black Raven can figure a way out of there."

"No deal," Ahren called. "If you want the cap, you'll have to come get it."

Kirril's blue eyes chilled. "I'd love to."

Ahren smiled. He unscrewed the sword pommel at his waist and removed the cylindrical key from the handle. "Here," he said, holding it out through the bars. "Here's your key. It fits in the fish's mouth. Come up here if you're man enough." He let it fall from his grasp.

Kirril snatched the key before it hit the ground. "You're a fool, Black Raven." Holding the key, he marched into the door alcove and out of sight.

Ahren didn't have much time. He leapt toward the bronze oar and drove it back. It clicked as the gate crept higher. Grinding his teeth, Ahren pushed with all his strength. The ferryman statue twisted around.

Click. Click.

Outside, from below, someone screamed. A wide smile curled along Ahren's strained face. Kirril had found the door trap. They'd be coming up the tower any second. Bracing his feet against the floor, Ahren pushed the winch harder.

Click. Click. Click.

The portcullis was high enough to walk under, but he needed it higher. Driving himself harder against the lever, he spun the winch a full revolution, hoisting the gate higher.

Click. Click. Click.

Torchlight grew in the stairwell as the men drew closer. Backing away from the statue, Ahren removed the jeweled cap from his satchel.

"There you are!" Kirril barked and he came up the steps. Blood dripped from the brown veil wound tightly around his hand.

Ahren just smiled.

A towering brute in a dark-blue veil followed Kirril into the room. A sword-like knife gleamed from his clubbish hand. Two more henchmen, each armed with crossbows followed him up.

"Give me the cap." Kirril growled, squeezing his rapier handle with his good hand. He circled around the room on Ahren's right. The hulking thug moved to the left, blocking Ahren behind the sarcophagus. One of the crossbowmen stood in the doorway, aiming his weapon at Ahren's chest.

"Right here." Ahren held up the silver and jeweled cap.

The men moved closer.

They were almost on him when Ahren flicked the oar cap across the room. Its red gemstones sparkled as it flew in a high arc, end over end toward the doorway.

"Get it," Kirril shouted, lunging his blade at Ahren.

The crossbowman in the doorway dropped his aim to catch the treasure flying toward him.

In one motion, Ahren brought up his foot, kicked the pearl-studded coffin lid and leapt over it. Screeching, the ferryman statue spun around. Its bronze oar whipped through the air. Ahren curled his legs, allowing the oar to fly beneath him and strike the massive brute in the mouth. With a hard crack, blood and broken teeth exploded from under his veil as the whirling oar knocked him back across the room.

With a shriek of grinding iron, the portcullis dropped from the ceiling, smashing into the crossbowman in the door, impaling him on its spikes. The oar cap hit the tiles with a *ting* and skittered down the stairs beyond

Tumbling to the ground, Ahren slid across the floor and under the falling portcullis briefly suspended by the henchman's crumpling body. The gate slammed shut behind him with a meaty squish.

The other crossbowman stood dumfounded in the stairwell. Leaping to his feet, Ahren tackled the man against the wall. He smashed the man's face with his elbow and knocked him to the floor.

Kirril screamed in fury.

Ahren snagged the oar cap off the floor and raced down the stairs. He flew blindly through the dark stairwell, leaping steps two to three at a time. After passing the other two floors, the stairwell opened up onto the ground floor.

A wedge of pale moonlight shined through the open copper door. Clutching the silver oar cap tighter, Ahren ran into the cemetery.

Cool air hit his face as he burst outside. For a short moment, Ahren felt the exhilarating rush of victory, moments before a blur flew out from the shadows.

Something hard slammed into Ahren's stomach, knocking away his breath. He doubled over in pain as his attacker stepped into the alcove wielding a scarred and scratched belaying pin. Rearing it back, the man swung it like a club. Ahren tried dodging, but the cudgel cracked against his head and spots swam before his eyes. The silver cap fell from his grasp as he staggered back. His vision cleared long enough to see the club smash into his cheek.

Blood's tang filled his mouth.

The man swung again, but Ahren ducked. The club smacked against the tower's marble carvings, chipping off a siren's nose. Ahren ripped the jeweled rapier from its sheath and brought it up just in time to block another swing. The cudgel's blow knocked the poorly-weighted sword from Ahren's grasp.

Jumping back to avoid another attack, Ahren tripped over an uneven flagstone. Ahren kicked his attacker in the knee and scrambled to get away.

"Get him, Yurlik," Kirril shouted from a window above. "Kill him!"

Ahren stumbled to his feet, his vision still lurching in and out of focus. Yurlik charged again, raising the short club high. Ahren side-stepped the attack and punched him in the kidneys.

The man's body went rigid and then he fell to his knees. Ahren raised his fist to finish him off when the crossbowman from within the tower burst through the door.

Ahren leapt to the side behind a tomb before the crossbowman could take aim. His weapon tucked into his shoulder, the man hurried to his fallen companion and helped him to his feet.

Kirril pointed out from the tower window. "He's over there!"

Keeping low, Ahren hurried away. The two henchmen followed him through the narrow labyrinth of tombs and monuments. Ahren slipped into a dark niche behind a statue and hid.

"Right there," Kirril shouted.

A bolt whizzed through the air, shattering the statue's hand beside Ahren's head. Ahren scrambled away before the man had time to reload. He wove his way quickly through the narrow streets, trying to keep out of Kirril's searching sight. His pursuers circled like sharks, herding him deeper into the city of tombs.

He came to a small garden and ducked beside a hedge. The henchmen's shadows moved between the buildings as they drew closer. Ahren picked up a fist-sized rock and hurled it far to the side. The stone clattered off roof tiles and the men hurried toward it.

As fast and quietly as he could, Ahren crept the other direction. Following a row of short, bushy trees, he came to the island's vault-lined outer wall. He headed right, back toward the tower. He hadn't seen the men pick up the oar cap after he dropped it. With luck, he could sneak in and steal it out from under Kirril's nose.

The wall turned, and Ahren found himself boxed in a tight canyon of unmarked mausoleums. He doubled back but stopped. Yurlik turned down the narrow footpath coming toward him.

"Over here!" he shouted.

With nowhere to go, Ahren grabbed onto the vault doors beside him and clamored up the wall.

Yurlik charged, swinging his club, but Ahren climbed faster. "He's getting away!"

Ahren pulled himself onto the top and ran down the wide wall. A crossbow twanged and a bolt flew past. Racing away, he left his pursuers in the necropolis maze, and followed the perimeter walls back to the unguarded tower.

He circled almost half the island before nearing the Ferrymaster's tower. Ragged clouds swept across the sky, obscuring the moonlight. A soft breeze blew in from the sea, washing away the harbor's stench. Ahren slowed to a jog, searching for a good place to drop off the wall.

The clouds opened up and pale moonlight bathed the cemetery grounds. Ahren froze.

Kirril stood in front of the tower door, aiming a crossbow. The iron trigger clicked and the bolt shot through the air.

Ahren sprung away but the bolt stabbed into his side. The sharp point bit into his hip, wheeling him around. He tumbled over the low parapet and fell. City lights and the crescent moon spun past in a blur before he slammed into the cold water and everything went black.

Ahren awoke with a gasp. Putrid water rushed over his head as his sudden movement shattered his body's natural buoyancy. Stabbing pain shot through his body as Ahren kicked his legs. Reaching down, he felt the jagged tear the bolt had left in his side. The deep cut ran a finger-width above the hip bone.

He pulled his way back to the surface and spat out the foul, salty water. Ahead, the yellow city lights shimmered off the calm harbor surface. He floated no more than fifteen feet from the wall he had fallen from. A dark shape bobbed aimlessly along the stone block walls. Squinting he could make out a piece of driftwood.

Clutching his hip with one hand, Ahren paddled over to the floating chunk of wood. A thin film of grime coated the stout timber. Barnacles encrusted one end. The faded paint spiraling up the broken pole indicated it had been a mooring post. Pulling it under his arms, the floating wood held his head above the water.

Ahren sighed, trying to plot his next move, when the echoing rattle of chains broke the silence. Rolling his head around, he saw the fore and aft lamps of Kirril's boat as it glided out of the cemetery gate.

He was getting away.

Fury surged through Ahren's veins, numbing the pain from his wounds. Kirril had betrayed him and left him for dead. He couldn't let him escape.

Aiming himself and his broken post in the direction of Kirril's boat, he kicked off the wall and began his pursuit.

He expected Kirril to head back into the city, but the small skiff followed the shoreline instead. Struggling to keep up, Ahren paddled harder. The small craft glided past the sailing vessels berthed at the Western Docks and then deeper out into the harbor.

A faint bell rang from a wide sailing barge floating ahead. Kirril's boat steered toward the larger vessel and slowed.

Ahren watched as a veiled sailor aboard the barge tied a rope around the skiff's prow. Kirril and his two remaining henchmen climbed up onto the low ship, and were escorted into the stern-side cabin, leaving two men alone on deck.

Glass lamps hung from the vessel's masts, their flickering lights sparkling off the ship's gilded woodwork and polished accents. As Ahren neared, he could make out the crewmen's rich dress of green and gold. The signature colors only verified his suspicions as to who owned the luxurious vessel: the Rusukny Family.

Not only did Baron Rusukny have the gold to buy the oar cap, his bounty on the Black Raven was well known throughout the city. Now, Kirril would be collecting them both.

Injured, and outnumbered, surprise was Ahren's greatest asset.

His enemies thought he was dead and that they were alone. No matter what was going to happen, he swore Kirril would die before sunrise.

Ahren slid off the driftwood pole and lowered himself behind it. Quietly, he paddled closer, trying not to disturb the water's surface any more than he had to.

One of the sailors on deck stood at the bow, staring out over the city, the other atop the rear cabin, holding the tiller. Neither seemed to notice as Ahren grabbed the lip of the low-lying hull.

He pulled himself along the side of the barge to where Kirril's tied skiff banged rhythmically with the waves. Muted voices came from inside the cabin. Reaching down to his belt, he slid the dagger from its swollen leather sheath.

A light breeze from the rear-facing window circled the room, and fluttered the lamplight. Outside, the soft sound of water sloshed against the rocking ship. Kirril sat silently, watching the young noble across from him inspect the jeweled oar cap.

"That's a substantial price you're asking," Konstantin Rusukny said, setting it back onto the table between them. "How do I know you're not trying to swindle my father?"

Kirril grinned. "Only a fool would try to swindle Nadjancia's greatest swordsman. I assure you, this is Vooshkae's oar cap, and the price is very reasonable."

The young noble casually swished the clear vodka in the bottom of his glass. Javor, the bearded bodyguard beside him, sat with crossed arms, staring coldly at Kirril and his men. The ruffian of course was unnecessary. If there was any truth to the duelist's near mythical reputation, Konstantin could kill all three of them before anyone could even draw.

"Agreed," Konstantin finally said. "The price you ask is acceptable." He raised his bowl-shaped glass and knocked it back.

Kirril's heart pounded. Fifty thousand gold bishkas was more than he'd ever seen. That, and fifteen percent of whatever profits the Rusuknys made from the ferrymen, would make him one of the most powerful men in the city. Hiding his excitement, he downed his drink as well, sealing the deal.

"Now." Konstantin set the glass on the table and leaned forward.

"Are you sure the Black Raven is dead?"

"I shot him myself," Kirril said, his lips tightening into a wide smile. "Right now, he's feeding the crabs."

The duelist's gray eyes narrowed. "How can I be sure he is dead?"

Kirril displayed the bloody veil wrapped tightly around his right hand. "Because there is no way I could allow the man responsible for this to survive."

Konstantin refilled the glasses from a crystal decanter. "Then let us toast to the death of the Black Raven."

A hard thump trembled the ceiling. Kirril gave it a momentary glance before raising his glass. A sailor above the cabin must have slipped.

"My father will of course wish to discuss the details of his death with you," Konstantin said after the toast. "Once he is satisfied, the reward will be yours."

A crash sounded from outside on the deck. Turning around, Kirril gasped. Flickering orange light flooded the triangular window inset in the door.

"Fire!" Javor yelled. Jumping from his chair, he crossed the cabin in two strides and wrenched the door open. Bright flames blanketed the raised fore-deck.

"Quick," Konstantin shouted. "Put it out."

Kirril's men rushed outside after the bodyguard. Konstantin stepped out onto the deck behind them, shouting orders. A crossbow twanged from atop the stern cabin. The green globe lantern suspended above the three men exploded, showering them in oil. An orange ball of fire erupted as the oil touched the blaze, engulfing the men in flame. Screaming, the burning men staggered back and tumbled off the deck into the water.

Shielding his face from the smoke and heat, Kirril turned away. His eyes widened in horror as a man swung down and through the rear cabin window. Blood stained his wet, grimy clothes. His fierce eyes stared out from behind tangles of dripping hair. A slender dagger gleamed in one hand as he snatched the oar cap off the table with the other.

"Help," he screamed. "The Black Raven is here."

Over Kirril's shoulder, Ahren saw Konstantin Rusukny wheel around, his gold-hilted rapier in his grasp. Ahren flipped over the oak table, knocking half-full glasses across the room. With a hard kick, he drove the table into the door, slamming it shut.

"This is between us," he growled, tightening his grip on the horn-handled dagger.

Kirril clumsily drew his rapier with his wrapped, injured hand and thrust at Ahren's chest. Ahren side-stepped the blade and slashed upward. With a wild swing, Kirril dodged it. His sword nicked the small candle chandelier hanging from the ceiling. Shadows danced and spun along the walls as the fixture swung back and forth.

Ahren feinted to the right, then circled the blade around, slicing Kirril across the wrist. Crimson blood burst from the gash and poured down the man's arm.

The door shuddered violently as it was struck again and again. The table shifted, allowing the opening gap to grow with each blow.

Kirril swung his sword, slinging blood across the room. Ahren ducked and stabbed at his enemy's open belly. Kirril jumped back, but not before the dagger tip nicked his stomach.

Kirril's face contorted with fury. Screaming, he brandished his sword high and charged.

Stepping into the attack, Ahren caught Kirril's sword arm. He thrust his dagger, but Kirril managed to grab his wrist. Their arms locked. Straining, they wrestled over the sharp blade between them.

Kirril hissed through gritted teeth as he drove his weight through his arm, pressing the dagger tip against Ahren's breast. Ahren's tense muscles burned as he struggled to move the blade away. His wounded hip spasmed in pain, threatening to buckle under him. His slashed flesh tore wider and fresh blood spread across his already stained clothes.

With a crash of battered wood, the door flew open. Konstantin stood panting in the doorway, silhouetted against the raging fire engulfing the fore deck behind him. The shimmering light gleamed off the gold rapier in his hand.

Wrenching his body around, Ahren knocked Kirril off and kicked him hard in the stomach. Kirril flew back and screamed. A slender blade erupted from his chest as his body slammed into

Konstantin, knocking him down and driving the duelist's sword through his body.

Jerking his blade from the dead man's corpse, Konstantin staggered to his feet. With nowhere else to go, Ahren sprung out the cabin window and grabbed the upper deck. Climbing to the top, he pulled his legs up just as the duelist's blade swept past.

Quickly, he shoved the silver oar cap into his soaking satchel. He was about to jump the flaming barge when one of the yardarm ropes gave way. With a crash, the heavy pole slammed against the deck, knocking the ship askew.

Falling against the deck, Ahren slid along the smooth wood and into a post. The oar cap tumbled from his bag and skittered toward the edge. Lunging after it, Ahren managed to grab the treasure before it could fall into the black water.

A voice sneered from behind him. "There you are."

Ahren rolled to the side to see Konstantin maneuver up the slanting steps to the upper deck. He held his rapier in front; its needle-like point transfixed Ahren.

"I've been wanting to meet you for some time, Black Raven." He advanced down the sloping deck toward where Ahren lay. "I was disappointed when Kirril said he had killed you."

"It is not as easy as it appears," Ahren said, inching his fingers toward the dagger tucked into his belt.

"I doubt that. You seem to bleed like any other man." The young man stepped past the dead helmsman's body sliding toward the edge. The hull creaked and the ship leaned further to the side. Water crept up onto the lower deck, extinguishing flames with hissing plumes of steam.

Working the dagger out from under his belt, Ahren slid the handle up under his forearm and pinched the blade near the tip. "Then try it."

Grinning, Konstantin closed the distance between them. He reared his arm, readying for the fatal thrust.

Ahren flung the dagger at the duelist's face. It twirled toward its mark, but Konstantin deflected the blade with his sword. The dagger sailed out into the darkness and plunked into the harbor.

Before the swordsman could recover, Ahren scrambled away. He jumped down onto the lower deck where Kirril's body lay in the doorway, staring up at him with dead eyes. He still held his rapier in his bandaged hand.

Running footsteps pounded from above as Konstantin charged. Ahren grabbed the sword from the dead man's grasp and raised it, just in time to block the duelist's blade. Metal rang and Konstantin attacked again with a series of quick blows, driving Ahren back.

The slender blades whipped back and forth with blurring speed. Backing away, Ahren moved along the raised port side of the listing ship. Furniture and cargo crashed from inside the hull and cabins, unbalancing the barge even more. Water surged in through the open doors and the ship rolled further.

Parrying Konstantin's sword, Ahren hopped over the deck rail and onto the ship's side. As if immune to the rolling footing, the duelist stepped onto the narrow strip of hull still above water.

"Give it up," Konstantin shouted, driving Ahren back with a quick thrust.

Ahren swung his blade at his opponent's open side, but the swordsman caught the blow with his rapier. He hooked one of his quillons through the open bars of Ahren's hand guard and pulled. The sword flew from Ahren's hand and into the water.

Konstantin brought his sword tip to Ahren's throat. "Goodbye, Black Raven."

Trying to back away from the sharp point, Ahren slipped and fell on the wet hull. The swordsman chuckled and moved in for the kill.

Ahren shoved his hand into the satchel and pulled out the Ferrymaster's jeweled oar cap. "Back," he shouted, holding it out over the water.

The young Rusukny relaxed the blade, but held his ground. "If you drop that—"

"You'll have nothing," Ahren spat. "Now back away!"

"Your death will last six months if you drop it." Konstantin reared the sword back for a thrust and extended his other hand. "Give it here, and you'll die with honor."

Ahren met the swordsman's cold stare. "You'll never be the Canal King." He opened his hand and with a plunk, the oar cap was gone. "I pay the master, but not you."

Konstantin's eyes widened and his face twisted with rage. "You idiot," he screamed.

Smiling, Ahren braced himself for the strike.

Konstantin's muscles tensed. His eyes seethed with hatred. "Die!" He stepped into the lunge, but the ship jolted beneath his feet, knocking him off balance. The duelist staggered back but didn't fall. He raised the sword again.

A spongy, green hand exploded from the water and grabbed Konstantin's leather boot. He shrieked as a bloated head rose to the surface and stared up with bulging white eyes. Yanking his leg free, Konstantin stumbled away from his gruesome attacker.

Water poured from its mouth and nose as the corpse pulled itself up onto the sinking barge. Dark sludge and slime coated its skin and patches of thin, tangled hair. Torn and filthy rags mixed with seaweed hung from its dripping body. The overpowering stench of rot filled the air.

Another arm thrust up from the water, as another corpse crawled onto the ship behind him.

Konstantin stabbed with his rapier. The blade passed through its soft body almost effortlessly. Dingy brown water poured from the open wound. Flesh fell in chunks from the creature's boney fingers as it reached out.

Screaming, the swordsman slashed with his rapier, splitting a wide gash across the creature's belly. Water and worm-ridden intestines gushed out onto the wooden planks. The corpse continued forward, stepping on its own entrails. It seized Konstantin by the doublet.

"Help," the swordsman wailed, struggling to get away.

The putrid corpse grappled around Konstantin's torso as the other seized him by the hair.

Terrified, Ahren scrambled away off the boat and into the water.

Behind him, Konstantin's scream echoed across the harbor, followed by a violent splash. Wood creaked and groaned and the remains of the barge fell below the waves.

Swimming as fast as he could, Ahren struggled to get away. His muscles burned with exhaustion and his wounded hip stung with almost paralyzing pain. Fighting to keep his head above water, he gulped air in desperate breaths.

He felt himself sinking. His legs gave out and he slipped beneath the waves.

Hands grabbed him by the waist. Ahren screamed, releasing an eruption of bubbles.

More unseen hands seized his legs and shoulder. They lifted him to the surface. Disoriented and weak, Ahren gasped for air.

The city rushed toward him as the hands dragged him with incredible speed. He pulled against their grip, but they held fast. More hands slid under him, almost cradling his body still below the water.

They carried him to the stone edge of the city and released their grip. Ahren reached up for a mooring ring above his head, and he felt himself lifted up toward it. Grabbing the iron ring, he pulled himself out of the water and onto the land.

Shuddering, he felt up and down his legs, making sure nothing was still holding him. He rolled onto his side and looked out over the harbor. In the moonlight, a single black ferry drifted past. The smooth craft glided across the water without disturbing the surface.

A well-dressed ferryman in black and burgundy stood at the rear, his face hidden behind a long silken veil. With a sweep of his oar, the boat stopped. Glittering rubies sparkled off the silver knob capping his oar.

Frozen in terror, Ahren stared back at the Ferrymaster for several long seconds. The ferryman held up a long raven's feather, then let if fall into the water between them. The black quill floated toward him, as if carried by an unseen current.

Ahren reached down and removed the feather from the water. He looked back up, but the Ferrymaster had vanished.

Lovers' Quarrel

A faint breeze swept across the nighttime road and out over the sea cliffs. Ribbons of moonlight shimmered off the black water, waves crashing into the rocks below with steady cadence. Ahead, a walled, fortress-like manor overlooked the bay and the adjoining port.

Keeping to the shadows beneath the trees, Karolina followed the sinuous path toward the house. A sudden gust swept her blue cloak and pushed against the basket in her arms. She adjusted her grip until the wind subsided, all the while maintaining the appearance that the empty vessel was heavy.

Her skin tingled with anticipation. She slowed her breath to prevent it from steaming in the chilly air. Excitement coursed through her body, spiking her senses. She heard the scuttle of mice in the leaves. The sweet taste of salty air danced across her lips, and she smelled the flowered vines creeping through branches above.

Nearing the house, she turned and circled to a clump of large rocks bordering the property. She crouched behind them and watched. A pair of guards, armed with rapiers at their belts, stood at the wrought iron gate. Through the bars, she spied at least one more patrolling the grounds inside. Slivers of yellow light peeked through the manor's shuttered windows. Two on the third, and highest, floor hung open. A dark figure walked between them, silhouetted by lamplight. Guard or a servant, Karolina couldn't tell. Both would be plentiful within the house. Somewhere, hidden within the ivy-drenched walls, Mikhail Svelovich thought he was safe.

Karolina untied the bothersome cloak and shoved it into the basket. There was no more need for disguises.

Unclasping the slender leather box on her belt, she removed a round gem from its padded cradle. Even in the moonlight she could make out the wisps of inky smoke that swirled and danced within the inch-wide ruby.

She slipped the stone into her mouth and shuddered, a sudden jolt shooting through her flesh. To the world she was invisible, but when she looked at her own hands and body, she saw black curls of fog confined to her form. Pressing her tongue against the gem so it wouldn't roll back into her throat, she stood and walked across the clearing toward the manor. She moved softly to not make any noise or overly disturb the grass.

The gossiping voices of the two gate guards became clearer as she neared the ten-foot wall.

"I'm not lying, it's the size of my head," said one in a high-pitched voice.

"It can't be," the other replied.

"Tomorrow we'll go to town and I'll show you."

Their voices faded as another gust of wind swept them away. Karolina followed the stone wall to a narrow patch devoid of vines. She grabbed hold of one of the worn rocks and quickly scaled to the top.

Peering over the edge, she surveyed the property. A sentry stood alone at the front door, but the side servant's entrance appeared unguarded. A lone patrolman circled the grounds; his blank expression said his mind wandered on other things. Patiently, she waited for him to pass out of earshot before dropping quietly to the ground.

Steering clear of fallen leaves, she made her way around to the side of the manor. She maintained slow breathing so the plumes would not give her away in the unlikely case anyone looked her direction.

She reached the side door and listened. Nothing. The hinges faced inward, making it impossible for it to suddenly open and hit her. Carefully, she knelt, swung the metal cover away from the keyhole, and peered through.

A slender, mousey-haired maid worked quietly at a table rolling dough. Karolina watched for a few minutes, but the woman made no sign she intended to leave the kitchen for a while. She slid the keyhole cover back in place and continued her circle.

A white marble statue of a woman holding a lily stood in a hedge garden behind the house. Beyond it, a knee-high wall ran along the rear of the property where it fell away to the sheer sea cliffs. A double door set with large glass windows looked out from the manor. Inside, several chairs and sofas lined the walls leaving the inlaid floor open. On other nights the ballroom might comfortably hold forty people, but tonight it lay empty.

Karolina checked the door. Locked. She removed a small set of picks from her belt and unlocked it within seconds. Taking a quick moment to be sure the patrolling guard was not near, she softly cracked it open and slipped inside.

An impressive, life-size painting of Mikhail Svelovich hung on the side wall between two doors. Gray stripes accented his dark, curly beard. A fleet of merchant ships filled the ocean behind him as he stood poised in a regal stance.

His rival, Igor Vshlaci, had offered her five thousand gold bishkas to bring an end to the blood feud. It was just like a merchant to offer gold as payment. How would he expect her to move it out of the city, let alone carry it? Besides, five thousand bishkas was far below her price. She was Polnoch, and if her clients wanted the best, they had to pay for her reputation. Of course Igor tried to haggle at first, all good merchants do. But in the end he agreed to twenty Merciñan emeralds, each the size of a robin's egg, all in advance.

Tonight, the Merchant Kings War would end.

After checking the door, she crept out into a long hallway. According to the ex-servant she had coaxed, Mikhail spent most of his evenings either in the library on the second floor or his chambers on the third. The servant, like most young men, was eager to please, and drew a very detailed layout which she memorized.

Karolina turned up a tight staircase to the second floor. Lowering to her hands, she ascended like a cat to prevent the wooden steps from creaking loudly. As she reached the top, a thin-nosed guard walked past, his legs coming within inches of her face. She froze and watched him continue on, completely unaware she was there. He strolled down the passageway until it turned before she stepped out into the hall.

A long rug ran the length of the hall. Her map had said the library was located near the southeast corner of the house. Silently, she followed the corridor until it came to a dark oaken door.

Her tongue rolled along the magical gem in her mouth as she quietly crouched at the keyhole. The soft, red glow of a dying fire flickered across the room. Carved shelves packed with tomes rested along the walls between paintings and heavy curtains. A lone figure sat in a high-backed chair facing the fireplace.

Resting her ear to the keyhole, she heard nothing but the popping of embers.

Opening the door would give her away. Her prey might cry out in alarm and rouse any nearby guards and servants. Relying on her invisibility would be reckless and unlike many of the others who had owned the magical gemstone in its long and bloody history, she was a professional. Mikhail would have to leave eventually and all she needed was patience.

She retreated to a nook in the hallway, periodically checking to see if her target had moved, and waited.

The patrolling guard made his rounds one more time. After another twenty or so minutes, the kitchen servant came down the hall carrying a silver tray of food. She stopped at the library door and pushed it open with her hip, brass hinges groaning.

Quickly, Karolina made her move. She slipped through, behind the maid, and slid to the side of the door.

The thin woman kept her eyes low as she approached the leather chair. "I brought you your dinner, sir," she mumbled.

The seated figure gave no response.

She set the platter on a low table beside him. "I will leave it here for you." The woman shifted uncomfortably, bowed, and quickly left the room.

Karolina waited until the door closed. Luxurious paintings and elaborate vases decorated the spacious library. Curtains of lemon-yellow velvet draped across the ceiling and down the walls. A thick, fringed rug dominated the room, almost completely covering the wooden floor's intricately inlaid pattern. Warmth issued from a mahogany fireplace filled with flickering red coals.

Carefully, she approached the lone chair. Normally, the footprints she made in the soft rug would concern her. But with her prey's back to her, no one would see the telltale signs.

The man sat quietly with a thick tome lying open in his lap. His hanging head said he was asleep.

Reaching to her belt, she removed a glass stiletto from a padded leather sheath along her back. Squeezing its smooth, twisted handle she poised it inches from her victim's neck beneath his gray beard. With a sudden and hard thrust, she struck. A triangular hole opened in the man's throat as the invisible blade drove through his flesh. His body jerked. The stiletto scraped against his vertebrae and with a twist, she broke the glass blade inside him.

She withdrew her hand, releasing the weapon, and the blue-swirled handle appeared jutting from the wound. It fell to his lap leaving shards of glass as crimson blood burst from the hole and ran from his mouth.

His eyes sprung open in disbelief and she saw his face for the first time. Something about him looked familiar. She'd seen his pudgy cheeks and thick eyebrows before.

Wheezing and gurgling, he shuddered, knocking the book from his lap. Tight brown cord bound his hands, cutting his wrists. The thick beard slid unnaturally as he convulsed. Karolina ripped it off his face and gasped.

Igor Vshlaci, her employer, sat dying before her. With a final shiver, his body fell still. She removed a long black quill clutched in the dead man's hand.

Movement reflected in the azure vase in front of her. Spinning around, she saw a figure step from behind one of the curtains against the wall. She froze in shock.

His familiar blue eyes narrowed as he drew a black sash across his mouth with one hand and pulled a hanging silk rope with the other.

With a hard tug, Ahren yanked the smooth rope. A bell sounded as white flour spilled from the velvet slings along the ceiling, filling the room in clouds of fine powder. His eyes focused on an empty hole in the chalky fog. Metal rasped as he drew his rapier and stepped forward. He'd waited for this meeting for a long time. "Surrender."

One of Mikhail's guards burst through the door, holding his sword.

The invisible figure grabbed a nearby vase and hurled it at him. He ducked and the porcelain exploded behind him. The assassin leaped from the floor and across the room.

The guard hesitated, obviously confused by the scene before him. Polnoch lunged, her outstretched arm just a blur of emptiness silhouetted in white. The guard's neck caved inward and he fell to his knees, dropping his sword as he clutched his throat.

Cursing, Ahren chased after her. He leapt over the wheezing guard and into the hall. White footprints led to the left. He turned to see the streams of flour trailing from nothingness as she ran.

The hallway intersected ahead, and she took the right passage. A woman screamed.

Ahren raced around the corner to see a housemaid against the wall, pointing toward the stairwell. The flour on Polnoch's feet was thinning, but there was still enough to leave faint marks. Squeezing his rapier handle, he hurried down after the echoing footsteps.

He stopped and looked around as he reached the first floor. The elaborate, multicolored rugs hid any trace of white dust. Listening, he walked a few steps one way then the other. Guards were shouting the alarms above and outside. But he heard nothing from his quarry.

From the corner of his eyes he noticed a pale smudge in an alcove wall beside him. He feigned a glance the other way as his arm shot into the niche. His fingers caught fabric and he closed his fist. She fought, striking his arm and he wrenched her out. She twisted and the rapier dropped from his hand as they both crashed to the floor.

Struggling, Ahren managed to get his weight on top of her. A hand grabbed his throat, digging in its nails. He found her wrist and pulled it away, pinning it down. Through the flour he could smell her breath and skin. The familiar scent of her sweat trembled through his brain. She twisted like an insane cat wrestling to be free. A fist smashed into his cheek. Stunned, he nearly lost his grip. The unseen fist struck him again and he tasted blood. Dropping his weight, he slung his head forward. His forehead knocked against hers, banging it into the floor.

She yelped in pain.

In that quick instant as her lips parted, he saw her. Her fierce green eyes were just as he remembered. He found her other hand as she vanished again and grabbed it, slamming it into the floor above her head.

"Nice to see you again," he growled.

Bucking her body, Karolina wrapped her legs around Ahren and crushed his sides, driving the wind from him. She wrenched her weight to the right, throwing him off her. Ahren struggled to hold her unseen wrists, but her knee slammed into his groin. Gasping, his body seized in pain. With another hard kick, she tore from his grasp. The imprint in the carpet vanished and footsteps raced away.

The guard from the library burst down the stairs, clutching his rapier. Staggering to his feet, Ahren grabbed his sword and they hurried after her.

The kitchen door stood ajar. He looked in to see the handle of the outside exit rattling. Holding thier swords in front so she couldn't charge, the two men stepped inside.

The door handle stopped clattering. Ahren advanced slowly into the small kitchen. His gaze swept across the floor, but found no trace of flour. He cursed the cleanliness of Mikhail's staff. There wasn't even dust to help give her away.

The cellar door burst open and her soft shoes padded down the steps. Ahren crossed the room and followed down the dim-lit stairs.

Wooden shelves packed with dusty casks lined the cellar walls. Rows of narrow wine racks ran the length like dominos. Ahren stopped at the foot of the steps to get his bearings when a bottle flew at him from the darkness.

He side-stepped as it exploded beside him, showering him with glass and burgundy wine. "Shut the door!" he hollered to the guard silhouetted at the top of the stairs. He darted behind a row of cases as the door above closed, pinching off the only light and flooding the cellar in blackness. If he couldn't see her, it was time to even the field.

Hugging the wall of barrels, he crept further from where she had last seen him and listened. The room lay silent. "You can't escape this time," he said. "The exits are all blocked."

He slid further away and knelt beside one of the freestanding cases. His eyes strained to see anything from the dim light peeking under the door above. "Your employer is dead, Polnoch. You failed."

Wood creaked. Glass shattered as something slammed into the rack beside him. Ahren leapt out of the way as the case fell over then crashed into the adjoining one with a terrible clatter. He crouched beside a support pillar and listened, but heard nothing. Cold liquid ran between his fingers against the floor as decades worth of wine flowed over the stone.

"Are you all right," shouted a voice from behind the cellar door. "We're coming down."

"Keep that door shut," he hollered. "She'll escape if you open it."

Finally she spoke. "You're just wanting me alone in the dark again."

"Now we're even," he continued. "Or have you forgotten how you got that night ruby in Nadjancia?"

"That was different."

Ahren's eyes locked onto the direction her voice had come. If she was talking it meant the night ruby was out of her mouth. "Not really. You killed my boss, shot me with a drugged dart, and stole it."

Tinkling glass came from the broken bottles across the fallen racks.

"I let you live," she purred. "Your plan for revenge doesn't give me the same option."

"You left me to answer to my superiors. The Tyenee doesn't forgive easily." He slinked away from where he had last spoken and waited beside a stack of boxes.

"Poor Ahren," she condescended. "Does the mighty Black Raven have a master? I always wondered why you would subjugate yourself to the Tyenee. Maybe you aren't as brilliant as you think."

Anger flashed, and then a chuckle escaped his lips. She was toying with him. "I foiled you, didn't I?" He ran his fingers across the wet floor until he found one of the broken shards. Softly he crept further back behind the crates to where they opened up into the main storage area of the basement. Faint strips of light peeked in from the outside cellar door far in the back of the room. He only hoped she hadn't seen it.

"I'm not beaten yet." Her voice came from where he had hidden after the racks fell.

The guard behind the kitchen door called again. "Are you all right, down there?"

Ahren flicked the wedge of glass out several feet in front of him. It skittered across the floor stones. He held his breath and waited.

Unable to see, he heard nothing, yet the air in front of him moved slightly. He lunged forward, hoping she was there. His hands found her shoulder and he grabbed tight.

She thrashed, trying to get away, but he threw his arm around her neck and held on. Her elbow came back and jabbed into his stomach. Stumbling back, they crashed into a row of boxes, knocking them to the floor. Gasping for air, the night ruby fell from her mouth. She appeared suddenly in his arms as the round gem pinged on the ground and rolled away.

A small knife glinted in her hand. He released his sword just in time to catch it as she stabbed behind her. Pulling her hand away, he knocked it against the floor until the blade fell from her grasp.

She pressed back against his chest and purred, "I missed you too, lover."

"Give up, Karolina."

"You know that isn't an option." She twisted against him. "That's not what you really want."

He tightened his hold. "Surrender."

She turned her head so her smooth cheek brushed his chin. "I always said we'd be good together, Black Raven. Just you and me."

He pulled his face from hers, but not before he had caught her scent. Memories of Nadjancia flickered in his mind.

"Just you and me. And only one night ruby between us."

"Don't tell me it was that important to you. I hurt your pride. You wanted revenge." She slid her back up and down his chest. "And more. Don't tell me you haven't considered it. Or is vengeance your only dream about me when you go to bed at night?"

Her words stung. He struggled with himself to keep his tight hold of her. "You used me," he growled. "You stole from me."

"You used me too," she cooed. "I saved your life, remember? Then I spared it when I could have killed you. It was more than just business between us, you know that. Why else would I have let you live?"

Ahren pulled them up to their feet and moved toward the door. Yanking her hand free, she twisted around to face him. It was too dark to see her clearly, but he felt her soft lips tremble against his.

She whispered her words into his mouth. "We'd be magical together."

His grip loosened despite himself. Her leg slid up behind his as her hands glided up his chest.

The kitchen door burst open, spilling yellow light down into the wrecked wine cellar. He jerked in surprise and caught a glimpse of a guard boot starting down the steps.

Karolina's lips pressed Ahren's and kissed him. His flesh tingled as he returned the kiss, but suddenly her hand shoved away. Tripping over her leg, he crashed into a cluttered table and then onto the floor.

"There she is!" a guard cried, charging over the fallen wine racks.

Karolina hesitated, scanning the floor once. Then she raced to the outside cellar doors. Ahren rolled to his feet just as she unlatched the exit and threw it open.

One of the guard's feet broke through a fallen case as he climbed toward them. "She's getting away."

Something caught Ahren's attention just before he stood to start after her. The night ruby lay on the floor under the table. He scooped it up as the guards ran past.

Cries of pursuit came from the yard above. Ahren's lips still tingled from her kiss. He popped the night ruby into his mouth and bounded up the stairs. Cold night air hit his sweat-streaked face as he looked around. A black-clothed figure ran around to the front of the house.

The outside guards yelled and gave chase. She doubled back as she saw them and ran the other way. Ahren sprinted across the lawn past the gardens after her. He swiped with his hand but missed. He leapt, grabbing her waist and tackling her to the ground.

He scrambled up and held her down on the damp grass.

It was the first time he clearly saw her. Wisps of her auburn hair had pulled from her ponytail and hung across her face. Her emerald eyes darted to the closing guards.

"I wouldn't let you die this way." No lies, no seduction, just the truth.

"I can't *let* you escape," he said, the round gem clinking in his mouth as his body blinked into visibility.

"You didn't." She smiled then struck him aside the head. The stone fell from his mouth as he clutched his ear in pain. Snatching the night ruby from the grass, she pulled herself free and ran.

Two pairs of guards, their swords drawn, closed in from either side. Karolina hopped up onto the low wall overlooking the cliffs and turned back.

Ahren met her eyes and she gave a wink. Leaping over the wall, she slipped the gemstone in her mouth and vanished.

His heart pounding in fear, Ahren ran to where she had stood and looked over. White waves broke against the cliffs thirty feet below. The water looked black in the moonlight and he searched the surface for any sign of her. There was no body, no shape of her swimming away. Nothing.

She was gone.

Thieves' Duel

A warm, salty breeze blew across the harbor, carrying the sounds of ship bells and squawking gulls. Thousands of seamen chatted and shouted curses along the dock in half a dozen languages. Docksmen hurried along the piers lugging barrels and crates to and from the ships and cargo wagons along the wharf.

Adjusting the leather straps digging into his shoulders, Ahren sauntered down the pier. The fifteen silver the captain had paid him was more than they'd originally agreed. But the bribe to keep him aboard as a member of the crew wouldn't work. He slipped the jingling cloth bag into his vest and away from the greedy hands of beggars and thieves. The heavy chest on his back rattled as he followed the boardwalk to the cobblestone streets. His eyes wary, Ahren made his way to the nearest harbor gate. He melded into the bottlenecked crowd and passed under the high stone archway and into the busy city.

It had been a decade since Ahren had boarded his first vessel to escape Lichthafen. He'd sworn to never return. As Mordakland's largest port, Lichthafen was difficult to avoid. But he had. Until now.

Blue paint still flaked from the tailor's shop. Plump gray pigeons lined the shoulders and outstretched arms of the green copper statue in the square. Ahren wondered if anyone ever knew the monument's true identity. An ugly boot-shaped sign still hung above Kamler the Cobbler's. Nothing had changed.

Weaving through the winding, narrow streets, Ahren plunged deeper into the city. The tall buildings loomed high above, their peaked roofs leaning across toward one another. A pack of children played dice in the alley beside an unpainted tavern. An older boy with a filthy blue cap carved his name into the wall with a short knife, not ten inches from where Ahren had put his at that age. A small bell jingled as Ahren opened the tavern door and stepped inside.

Fresh stew bubbled in a cauldron hanging inside the fireplace. A square-jawed man with gray temples peeled potatoes on the bar. Ahren crossed the narrow room and put his back to the counter. He lowered himself until the chest *thunked* onto the bar top and then he slipped off the shoulder straps.

"What can I get for you, sailor?" the man asked while wiping his hands on a dingy apron.

Ahren said nothing.

The barkeep glanced to the hinged box on the counter. "Are you selling something? 'Cause unless you got a pair of goats in there, I ain't interested."

Ahren grinned. "That's a shame."

"That it is. So now that we've cleared up that I ain't interested in what you've got, why don't you tell me what you …" The man's eyes widened. "Saint Vishtin," he gasped. "Ahren?"

"Hello Griggs."

"I can't believe it!" He slipped around the counter and gave Ahren a strong hug. "How long's it been?"

Ahren smiled trying to hide his discomfort at speaking to the man he'd once considered a father. "Ten years."

"Katze," Griggs shouted. "Come down. Ahren's home!" He clapped Ahren on the shoulder. "This calls for a drink. I can't believe you're here."

A lean young woman with curly black hair glided down the barroom stairs. "What a surprise," she said, her dark eyes narrowing. "Where have you been?"

Ahren swallowed. He remembered Griggs' daughter as a scrawny little girl with frazzled hair who had always tried to tag along. Her annoying fascination with Ahren had been a source of constant ridicule from his peers. His eyes traced along her hips and firm breasts rising from her leather bodice. Things had changed. "Hello, Katze. I've been seeing the world."

Smiling, Griggs set a stein on the bar. "So what brings you back, my boy?"

Ahren knocked back a long swig and unlatched the box on the counter. "I brought these in for you." He unwrapped a thick clay tankard and set it on the bar. "Picked them up in Frobinsky."

Chuckling, the barkeep wet his lips. "That's very nice," he said picking it up and examining the swirling pattern along the rim. "But I don't really need them."

Ahren shrugged. "My mistake. Viston said you'd like them."

Griggs' smile vanished. "Viston?"

Ahren sipped his drink. "The diamonds are baked inside to pass them through customs."

"I see," he said, forcing a laugh. "Very clever." He reached into the box and removed two more tankards and a stack of thick plates. "So you work for Viston? I had thought someone else was bringing the shipment."

"The Black Raven?" Ahren asked.

Griggs froze. "So you know him?"

Ahren leaned across the bar and removed the copper pendant from under his shirt. "I always knew you were up to more than just organizing gangs of children. But I'd have never thought you were involved in anything like the Tyenee."

The man's smile faltered as he stared at the Tyenee's glyph stamped onto the medallion. He glanced at his daughter standing attentively beside him, and then back to Ahren. "You're … him?"

"I am." Ahren slipped the pendant back beneath his shirt. "However, my reputation demands that you not openly refer to me by that name."

Griggs nodded. "I understand. Let me show you to your room."

An eye-watering haze of candle and pipe smoke filled the tavern as patrons packed around the small tables, trading stories and playing games. Ahren sat in the back, watching from a small booth. He recognized only a handful of the men as boys he'd once run with. Most of the others were now rotting in prisons or graves. He had chatted with Clauser, an old cohort he remembered as a wiry stutterer. A deep knife scar now marred his once boyish face. He worked for Griggs as a fence in the Market District. Marten, a weasel-faced bully, worked as a hired thug, and Feschtek was a pimp. A new generation of Alley Cats now worked the streets, too young to remember their predecessors the way he and Clauser did. He wondered if Griggs even remembered all their names. Did he remember Tretan?

"So Ahren," Katze said as she slid into the seat beside him, "It seems you've done well for yourself. Father was right about you. You'd never leave the life."

"Seems so," he replied.

"Are they true?" she asked. "The stories we've heard?"

"Thieves gossip like whores. You shouldn't believe everything you've heard."

"I see." She took a swig from Ahren's tankard on the table. "So if you didn't quit the life, why did it take you so long to return?"

Ahren gnawed his lip. "I was busy."

"You were afraid." She leaned closer. Her skin smelled of rose oil and smoke. "Afraid we'd know what you'd become."

He snorted.

"I cried for a month after you'd left. We never heard anything. I never knew if you drowned at sea or got killed by pirates. First Tretan, and then you. That wasn't fair."

"It wasn't about you."

She shook her head. "Of course not. I was young and in love. Fortunately," she purred, "there were many others to teach me about love."

Her words stabbed and gnawed his gut. "You seem to have done well, Katze."

"And you as well." She ran her fingers along his shoulder. "A bounty hunter came by last month on a tip you'd be in the city. Father took care of him without even knowing who you were. It must be nice to live by a legend you did nothing to earn. Are *any* of the stories about you true?"

"More than enough of them," he said, pulling away.

Katze smirked. "Are they? There's probably a dozen thieves in Lichthafen more skilled than you, even me. That's why you stayed away. You didn't want anyone to outshine the Black Raven's legend."

Ahren's cheeks grew hot. "Not likely."

"That's just what I wanted to hear," she said with a triumphant smile. Katze slammed her fist into the table and leapt up onto her seat. "Attention!"

The bar fell silent and all eyes turned to Katze.

"Ahren, our wayward brother, has challenged me." Low chuckles echoed across the room. "As Master of Thieves, I am left with little choice but to accept."

Master of Thieves? Ahren groaned, realizing what had happened. The setup was obvious, and he'd fallen right into her hands.

Griggs' eyes narrowed from across the room at his flamboyant daughter. "Very well. If a challenge has been accepted then a Thieves Duel shall be set. Three nights from tonight. Wagers shall be settled here."

Commotion erupted through the tavern as jokes were passed and bets placed.

Katze stepped down beside Ahren and grinned. "Now we'll see how true the stories are."

"I didn't challenge you," he growled.

"Yes, you did." She leaned closer and whispered, "And if you try to back out, I'll tell the world the Black Raven cowered from a duel."

His eyes narrowed.

"You have three nights to re-learn the city. I suggest you get started."

Ahren's gray cloak fluttered in the nighttime breeze as he crossed Dishik Plaza past a stone statue to where two figures stood patiently at the mouth of an empty alley. Dark clouds sailed across the heavens, partially blocking the half-moon above. He ran a final mental inventory of his gear: picks, two daggers, two shoulder satchels, one vial of lopiune, ten gold coins tightly packed to not jingle, dark green cloak packed into a satchel, raven feathers, and a short knife hidden in his boot. All more cumbersome than he would normally carry. But the night's surprises might warrant each of them.

"Good evening," Griggs said as Ahren approached.

He nodded to Griggs and Katze beside him. A tight braid of black hair looped out from her burgundy cloak.

Griggs held up two folded and sealed parchment squares. "The rules are simple. You will both be given identical lists of items around the city. Each are worth points based off how difficult they are. Whoever returns to the bar before dawn with the most point's worth of items is the winner. Understand?"

Katze and Ahren both nodded.

"The only other rule is that neither of you can kill the other player." He shot a cold glare at his daughter. "Anything else goes. In the event of a tie, the first one back wins. Got it?"

"Understood," Ahren said. His skin began to tingle as he readied himself.

"I'll see you both by morning." Griggs handed them each their list.

As Ahren took the letter, Katze's boot smashed into his groin. Doubling over in pain, he fell to his knees.

"Good luck," she said, and raced away.

Tears welled in Ahren's eyes as he tried to shake the stabbing pang shooting through his body.

"I'll second that," Griggs said unsympathetically. "You're going to need it."

Leaning against a brick wall, Ahren pulled himself up and opened the list. His eyes scanned it over several times before locating his first mark. Catching his breath, he slipped the paper into his pouch and hobbled quickly from the plaza.

Nighttime dealers and merchants called out, hawking their goods as he passed their booths and carts. Whores and hustlers prowled the dark streets among the near endless supply of easy targets. Turning down a narrow lane, Ahren surveyed a wide indigo tavern dominating the corner intersection. Purple grapes spilled from an overflowing gold chalice on the hanging wooden sign. A burly man with a thick moustache stood at the door watching the passersby with contemptuous eyes.

He stepped before the doors as Ahren approached. "Where are you headed?"

"Inside."

Chuckling, the broad man shook his head. "The Golden Goblet is for gentlemen, not peasants."

Ahren threw his shoulders back and curled his lip. "I have spent the past three weeks aboard a ship with ale-swooning scum. Before I can bathe and dress in something more human, I wish to wash the taste from my mouth." He drew four gold dreins from his pouch and held them up. "A peasant wouldn't carry my purse and unless you want your master to horse-whip you for rejecting my patronage, I suggest you let me pass."

The man's eyes widened as he stared at the coins in Ahren's palm. "I … I …" he stammered.

Dropping the coins back in his purse, Ahren pushed the doorman aside and marched through the door without a word. Music from a minstrel trio filled the smoky air. Men in silk shirts and brocade doublets laughed and drank while richly dressed courtesans in gold and perfume doted over them. Ahren strode to one of the blue-vested employees standing beside a massive wine rack along the sidewall behind a marble-topped counter. A black bottle rested on a wooden stand beside him.

"How may I help you, sir?" the waiter asked.

Keeping his pretentious manner, Ahren cleared his throat. "Your doorman's incompetence is inexcusable."

"My apologies, sir."

"Are you the owner?"

The young waiter shook his head. "No, he is upstairs."

"Then it is his apology I want." Ahren glanced at the bottle displayed on the edge of the counter. The Golden Goblet's crest stamped the purple wax seal atop the cork. Many of the other bottles on the rack bore the same insignia. "It has been a long while since I tasted Falkeblut."

"We are the only hall that serves it, fine sir. May I pour you a glass?"

Ahren looked back at the open door behind him, and set a pair of gold dreins on the counter. "I would like a bottle," he said, holding the coins under his finger. "I would also enjoy words with your owner. Fetch him for me."

The waiter licked his lips nervously.

"Now," Ahren growled.

With a nod, the waiter hurried from behind the counter to a doorway. The instant he vanished from sight, Ahren scooped the coins back into his purse and quickly removed the unopened bottle from its display. Holding it under his cloak, he dropped one of the raven's quills onto the bar and then strode across the tavern and out through the door. He felt the doorman's eyes on his back as he followed the road away until turning down a side street.

Opening his satchel, he nestled the bottle inside. Falkeblut was only three points, but it was a start. He unfolded the list and found the next closest target: Vathristern Cathedral.

Several blocks later, the streets opened up and the imposing walls of the great cathedral rose before him. White-cloaked church knights in polished breastplates stood watch beside the entrance. Slowing his jog to a casual walk, Ahren crossed the square, passed the grand pouring fountain, and ascended the steps to Vathristern's great bronze doors.

A waft of incense smoke greeted him as he entered. Men and women knelt along the mostly empty pews, their muted whispered prayers softly echoing through the great chamber. Marble statues stared down from the walls above with pupiless eyes. Keeping his head low, Ahren entered a deep alcove to the right. Short, fat candles of every color flickered along a high, tiered stand coated in hardened wax, forming a wall of flame. Across from them, a gold and jeweled urn rested inside a wrought iron cage between a pair of golden candlesticks.

Ahren knelt before the stand and lowered his eyes. A pair of young women prayed beside him, asking for their brother's health to return. Ahren remained silent until they finally left. He glanced around making sure he was alone, then rose and faced the great urn behind him. Still feigning contemplation, he brought a hand to his lips while his other removed a black quill. He checked one more time to be certain no one was watching, then licked his fingertips and snuffed out the slender taper burning beside the metal cage. Pulling the candle free, he tucked the heavy gold candlestick under his cloak and dropped the raven feather in its place.

He turned and slowly walked from the alcove as a hooded figure stepped inside. As he neared the arched front doors, a woman's voice pierced the cathedral's silence.

"Thief!"

Ahren looked back to see Katze standing before the golden urn, her finger pointed at him. Both candlesticks were missing.

"Thief," she shrieked. "I saw him."

Two dozen eyes turned to Ahren still standing twenty feet from the door. A bearded priest nodded to one of the soldiers. Whirling back around, Ahren bolted toward the door. A church knight's gloved hand reached for him, but he ducked, and plowed straight into his hard breastplate. Screaming, the soldier fell back and tumbled down the wide steps to the street.

"Stop him!" someone shouted.

Hurtling down the steps, Ahren ran back across the square and down into a narrow alley. Shouts and bells sounded behind him. Unclasping his billowing gray cloak, he let it fall as he turned into another lane. He followed the tight alleyway to an intersection. Pulling the thin green cloak from his satchel, he threw it over his shoulders then casually stepped into the street.

The candlestick was five points, but if Katze had one as well, the points were in vain. He sighed deeply, trying to quell his hot anger. Mutilation was the price for stealing from the Church. The golden sticks would have cost him his eyes, maybe his hands. She would have been happy to let them do it. This was more than a simple challenge now. It was personal.

Sticking to the narrow valleys of lanes, he briskly entered the Merchant District. Pale light spilled from only a handful of stores. Closed wooden shutters sealed off most of the shops' windows. His eyes studied the painted signs, dimly lit by street lamps. As the street slightly curved, he spied a hanging sign cut into the shape of a key: Hetstier's Locksmith. A large silver inlaid padlock dangled from the painted door.

Stopping before it, Ahren looked around. A group of teenage boys lounged on the steps two shops away. Beyond them, several pedestrians roamed the streets and a clump of people gathered at a still open boutique.

"Nice night," Ahren said approaching the young men. "Any of you interested in making some easy coin?"

A pimple-faced boy with a faint moustache nodded. "Wherever we can." The others chuckled in agreement.

Ahren held up two of the dreins from his purse. "How about these?"

The boys' eyes widened as they eyed the gold. "Who you want dead?" one asked.

He shook his head. "Nothing so brutal." Ahren gestured to the open shop. "Does that store sell rings?"

"Yeah."

"I want you all to go in there, and grab everything you can." He tossed one of the coins into the boy's hand. "Meet me in Kammhar

Park in twenty minutes and I'll pay you the rest."

The grubby teens nodded eagerly.

"Don't get caught. Now go."

Laughing to themselves, the boys got up and hurried to the boutique. Ahren turned back to the locksmith's. A slender keyhole adorned the padlock's side face. He removed his leather roll of picks and selected a pair of slender wires when a commotion erupted from the store.

"Halt! Halt!" someone shouted. Glass broke followed by furious cries. The boys charged out into the street, their arms full. Knocking people aside, they raced the other direction toward the park.

"Stop them. Someone stop them!"

Quickly, Ahren slid the picks into the keyhole and worked them around. Picking a lock on the side of an open street was suicide. Hopefully the diversion would work.

"They're getting away!"

"They went that way," a woman cried.

Ahren stuck one of the picks between his lips and selected a different one. He worked it into the keyhole until he found the tumbler latch inside. With a twist of the wrist, he wound it around the central post until the lock's curved iron shackle popped out. Removing the shackle from the door, he dropped it and the lock body into his pouch. He slipped a black quill through the door latch and walked the other way down the street.

Hetstier's unmarred lock would fetch him ten points. Better still, they were points Katze wouldn't be able to duplicate. There was only one.

He checked the list again for his next job: the small azure vase from Widow Dinstet's window. Her late husband had been a well-known captain when Ahren had lived in the city before. It was an easy five points. Holding the heavy satchels against him so they wouldn't bounce, Ahren hurried across the city.

A pair of Church Knights in white tabards marched down the lane toward him. The bells of Vathristern Cathedral still tolled not six blocks away. Fighting the urge to run, he remained calm, and casually strolled past them. He let out a sigh as they continued on, not giving him a moment's glance. Shops and taverns gave way to packed narrow homes.

Ahren followed for several blocks before stopping in front of a white and brown house. The simple dwelling was no more than fifteen feet wide, but rose four stories high. A tiny blue vase, holding a single tulip, rested in the top window above. Smoke trickled from the chimney, and lights on the first and third floors verified its occupancy. Getting in would be difficult. Scanning the sloped rooftop, only inches away from its neighbor, Ahren knew what he needed to do.

He circled the block trying to find a stairway or other means to reach the roofs but found none. Following the road, he came to an alley three streets further with an outside entrance to the top floor.

The worn steps creaked as he followed them to the top, then climbed up onto the landing rail. Stretching, he grabbed the overhanging eaves and pulled himself up.

Salt wind from the harbor greeted him as he crawled up onto the wood-shingled roof; a refreshing change from the city's foul stagnant air. The tightly packed buildings were much closer at the top than on the streets. Their overhanging roofs hindered almost any air flow below. Rising to his feet, Ahren looked out across a wide sea of rooftops and smoking chimneys illuminated by the pale moonlight. Blocks away, he could see the towers along the city walls as silhouetted guards patrolled the parapets. Staying low so no one might see him, Ahren headed back toward Widow Dinstet's home.

It was said a man could travel the length of the city without ever touching the ground. Ahren had never tried it, but had on several occasions traveled the shingle highway to enter upper windows or escape the city guards. Other thieves swore by the tunnel roads within Lichthafen's vast sewers, but the dark and dangerous maze-work never appealed to him. Many of the daring souls who entered the tunnels never returned.

Following the easiest path between buildings, Ahren circled around the block before finally nearing the widow's house. Careful not to slip on loose shingles, he hopped onto one of the adjoining rooftops then froze.

Katze stood on the roof before him, her dark cloak blowing in the breeze. Smiling, she held up the vase in her hand.

Bitterly, he nodded back.

A shadow moved on the rooftop beside her. Marten stepped out from behind a chimney clutching a thick-bladed knife. Another man rose from behind a peaked rooftop holding a cudgel. Katze whistled and the two men charged toward him.

Spinning around, Ahren retreated in the other direction. Katze might have agreed not to kill him, but her thugs had made no promise. He raced down a steep rooftop and leaped across to the neighboring building.

Footsteps pounded wooden shingles behind him, racing to catch up. The heavy satchels jostled Ahren's hips as he ran. He jumped down onto a lower roof and hurried along the slender peak stretching to the neighboring block. A wide canyon opened before him, dropping four stories to the street below. He glanced back, finding his two pursuers not fifty feet behind him. Ahren took a breath, and leapt across.

A loose shingle slipped under his foot, nearly toppling him over the side. Lunging forward, Ahren rolled onto the slanted roof and raced to the other side. Finding no windows or access to the street, he pulled himself up onto a decrepit apartment building. Scanning the roof's edge, he spied a dilapidated balcony. He ran to it and dropped. Gray boards cracked loudly and sagged under his feet.

"What in Saint Vishtin's name—" a wide-eyed man shouted, stumbling back against the railing.

Ahren shot down the steep stairs two at a time to an alley below. Looking back, he spied the men on the roof above. He turned and raced along the narrow lane.

A maze-work of cluttered and cramped alleyways opened before him. Taking one, he followed it around a corner until coming to a dead end. With nowhere to hide, he doubled back and followed another one. The men's shouting echoed behind him.

"Where is he?"

"Check down there!"

Panting, Ahren turned a corner only to find an eight-foot wall blocking his way to the street beyond. He jumped as a gravelly voice rose from the shadows beside him.

"Spare a coin?" A white-haired beggar extended his hand, his mouth filled with blackened teeth. Two more sallow and ragged men huddled beside him next to a broken barrel.

"This way," he heard Marten shout.

Ahren reached into his pouch and removed two gold dreins. The beggars all sat up, their eyes fixated on the coins.

"There are two men following me," Ahren said. "Make sure they don't leave this alley."

The men fervently nodded and Ahren dropped a single gold into the beggar's filthy hand. "You'll get the other one once you've won it." He turned and jogged to the brick wall blocking the passage.

"There you are, Ahren." Marten stepped into the alleyway behind him; his face beaded with sweat. "I thought we might have lost you." His accomplice moved up beside him, still clutching his wooden club.

"I don't want to hurt you." Marten drew his bone-handled knife. "So give me the bags and we'll call it even, for an old friend's sake."

Ahren said nothing.

A half-smile curled on Marten's weaselish face. "Very well." Holding the blade out front, he and his thug stepped into the alley. "I didn't want to hurt you. Not after what happened to Tretan. But business is—"

A broken brick smashed into Marten's arm as the three beggars leaped like hungry wolves. One jumped onto the other man's back, striking him again and again with boney fists. Screaming, the two men staggered back fighting off their sudden attackers. Turning, Ahren grabbed onto the rough-mortared wall and clambered up. Before dropping over the side, he tossed the second coin back into the alley.

Leaving the shouts and cries behind him, he trotted down the street and pulled the list from his pouch. He had eighteen points. Katze had at least ten that he knew of. She probably had twice that, if not more. He scanned the page, searching for the more valuable items, the most difficult. He bypassed the highest, wondering if it had graced every Thieves Duel list in the past decade, or if Griggs just put it there as a sick joke. He stopped just below it. Artisan's Row lay only a few blocks away; a short jog for fifteen points. Returning the list to his satchel, he hurried toward Flagref's Anvil.

The nighttime street grew busier as he neared the market area. Soldiers in chain shirts and private guards in hardened leather vests patrolled the rich shops lining the avenue. Gold and sparkling jewelry glistened from behind iron-barred windows. Turning down a wide lane Ahren passed white marble statues and the colorful pottery shops along Artisans Row. Ahead, a rhythmic ring echoed from a wide two-story shop. An armored guard dressed in a gleaming breastplate etched in spiraling designs stood beside the door. The hand at his belt rested beside a white inlaid sword grip accented with bronze.

He gave a stiff nod as Ahren entered. Waves of warmth flooded the stone building from the massive forge resting behind a half-wall in the back. A soot-faced man worked a huge suspended bellows beside the fire while another in a leather apron struck a glowing red wedge of iron on the anvil. Sparks rained to the floor with every pound from his hammer. Hanging lanterns filled the shop, casting everything in an orange light. Blades of every variety jutted lengthwise from the tiered rows of racks along the shop's walls. Helms and breastplates dressed crude wooden dummies lined like a formation of soldiers behind the sweeping counter almost encircling the room. Decorative hinges, spurs, and other merchandise filled the cases and shelves displayed on the countertop.

"Welcome," said a man behind the counter. "Can I help you?" His thick moustache traced down to his stubbled chin. A second employee worked with another customer looking at door knockers.

"Ah," Ahren said, feigning interest in a pair of blackened gauntlets trimmed with brass. "I am looking for a good knife. Something small but functional with a keen edge."

The man smiled, but not before his eyes scanned Ahren's simple clothes and disheveled hair. He removed a short, hooked blade from the rack. "This will cut ropes and whatever you need."

Ahren took the simple blade and inspected it. The smooth wooden grip and black hand guard held no ornamentation but a small insignia of a star and anvil. "This is fine," he said brushing his finger lightly across the sharp blade. "But I'm thinking of something a little larger. More impressive, if you get my mind." He gestured to one of the ivory-handled daggers along the display. "Like that."

The man returned the knife to the rack and fetched Ahren the thin-bladed dagger. "This is a fine piece. But a bit more costly."

Ahren flipped the blade over in his hand. A graven whale decorated the white grip. "Very nice," he said checking the balance. "I like the weight, but do you have any with a thicker handle?"

The man's tongue ran along the back his teeth. "It depends," he sighed, "on how much you're willing to pay. Any smith will sell you a knife, but Flagref's blades are the finest."

Ahren shrugged and laid the dagger on the counter between them. "A captain in Lunnisburg showed me his once." He set a gold coin on the counter. "He said they were all works of art." Ahren stacked a second coin on top of it. "That was seven years ago." He stacked a third coin. "When I received my commission four years later, I vowed I too would wear one of your blades. And I know what it'll cost me." He added four more coins.

Apprehension melted from the man's face. "I see. My name is Ivo. Please, let me show you our other pieces." He turned, leaving the knife on the table, and fetched two more blades.

Ahren slid the coins back into his purse.

"This is one of Flagref's favorites." Ivo offered an etched dagger with a bronze fox head pommel.

Ahren examined the well-balanced blade. "This is nice. Do you have any with a different design?" He laid it on the table beside the ivory dagger.

"Of course." He handed a curved knife with silver accents and a ship's image carved into the handle. "This is a design most sailors prefer."

"Beautiful. How much is this one?"

"That blade is five dreins."

Ahren nodded, clutching the knife in his hand while miming simple moves. "A good price. What else do you have?"

Ivo brought more blades for Ahren's inspection. Many were returned to the racks once rejected, but several more lay across the table. Despite the constraints, Ahren took his time. He'd always coveted Flagref's fine blades. It was said the bones of any trying to steal one burned in the blacksmiths great forge.

"This is the most magnificent I've ever held," Ahren said, holding a gold and pearl encrusted dagger. "I fear to ask how much."

Ivo smiled. "Fifty dreins."

"And worth every bit. This is the blade of a Kaiser." With a reverent gesture, he offered the dagger back. "Someday I hope to hold that again. Thank you for entertaining me with that." He pointed to a bronze and leather-wrapped handle sticking up from one of the racks. "May I see that one?"

"Of course." Returning the rich dagger to its prominent display, Ivo stretched to reach the blade Ahren had requested. After a casual glance to be sure no one was watching, Ahren slid the fox-headed dagger from the table and slipped it into his satchel.

"Here you are," Ivo said, returning with the dagger. "Practical, yet demanding attention."

"I will agree," Ahren said, taking the blade. "A man wearing this says he knows how to use it." He twirled it around in his fingers. "Excellent balance. I like it. How much?"

"Fifteen dreins."

Ahren examined it closely. "Fifteen?" He licked his lips. "I have but twelve with me. Would you take that?"

"Master Flagref does not haggle his blades. Negotiation means they are not worth what he asks."

Ahren sighed. "Then it's worth fifteen. Tomorrow I'll receive payment for my goods. Can you hold it until then?"

Ivo nodded. "Of course, Captain …"

"Jreksteir," Ahren replied, offering his hand.

"Then I will see you tomorrow night, Captain."

"I look forward to it. Thanks for your help." He bowed then left the shop.

Slipping through the small crowd wandering the shops, Ahren secured the dagger in his pouch so the sharp blade wouldn't puncture the side. He ducked down a dim alley and reached for the list in his satchel when a shadow moved behind him. Ahren wheeled around to dodge a blurring blade. Staggering back, a hard fist smashed into his mouth.

"Found you," Marten growled. Smeared blood coated his cheek beneath a purple, swollen eye. Thrusting the knife, he lunged.

Ahren sidestepped and drew one of the daggers at his waist just in time to parry another attack. Marten circled to the right, pushing Ahren against the alley wall. He stabbed his dagger again, but Ahren spun out of the way and grabbed the man's wrist. Marten's elbow flew back and drove into Ahren's stomach. Bringing his blade up, Ahren slashed the man's forearm. Screaming in pain, Marten slammed his body back, knocking Ahren over a stack of empty chicken cages, and sending them both crashing to the ground.

Glass crunched inside Ahren's satchel and cold wine spilled everywhere. Flipping around, Marten leaped to his feet. He kicked Ahren's hand with a hard boot, sending the dagger skittering away.

"Give me the items," Marten spat, pointing his blade at Ahren's face.

With an angry sigh, Ahren reached for the soaking satchel. His fingers lingered near the sheathed dagger still at his waist.

"Don't try it."

Begrudgingly, Ahren removed the dripping bag and held it up.

Marten snatched it with his bloodied hand. "Now the other one."

Ahren slid off his other satchel. As Marten reached for it, Ahren swept his leg, knocking the man to the ground. Drawing the knife hidden in his boot, Ahren scrambled to his feet.

"What's going on?" a voice shouted. A city guard stood silhouetted in the alley entrance. Metal rasped as he drew his sword. "Stop where you are." A second guard stepped up behind him.

Ahren moved toward the wine-soaked satchel still in Marten's hand, but the two guards charged into the alleyway.

"Halt!"

Turning, Ahren fled down the passage with Marten close behind. The guards' chain shirts chinked as they gave chase. Marten darted down the first narrow alley and one of the guards followed him. Veering onto an empty side street, Ahren raced faster and slid behind a closed fruit stand before the pursuing guard reached the lane. Clomping bootsteps hurried past, and Ahren let out a deep breath.

Still crouched in his hiding place, he returned the boot knife to its sheath and opened the remaining satchel. The silver lock and Flagref's dagger were still inside. His picks and small lopiune vial were all that remained of his gear. Marten had the candlestick, the broken wine bottle, seven remaining gold coins, and most importantly, the list.

His head slumped into the brick shop front behind him. Winning now was near impossible. The items he could still recall from the list wouldn't even match what Katze already had. All but one. One hundred points would ensure her failure. Ahren only wished there was another way. He sighed, then slid Flagref's dagger into his empty belt sheath and hurried away.

Mritlek the Jeweler had been Lichthafen's greatest. Lords, Kaisers, and even the Hierophant were among his clientele. Known for its unparalleled beauty and craftsmanship, his jewelry was the most coveted in all of Delakurn. The Grysiem Tigress was his final masterpiece. While the rest of his magnificent creations rested safely locked in treasure rooms, the Tigress resided in the house of Count Resuom, the man Ahren considered the evilest man in the world.

Stopping at a butcher's shop before it closed, Ahren traded his boot knife for two pounds of fresh goat's meat, an arrangement the tired butcher had been eager to accept. Ahren dropped the cloth-wrapped ball of meat in his satchel and headed toward the Nobles District.

The tightly packed buildings grew further apart, allowing soft wind and crisp moonlight to pour across the cobbled streets. A knot tightened in his gut as Ahren passed the large, rich homes, many of which hid behind smooth stone walls and arched gates. Soldiers in black and golden tabards patrolled the quiet streets.

Ahren stopped beneath a slender flowering tree and stared across the lane. A blockish house sat alone behind a five-foot wall capped with a spiked wrought iron fence. Light peeked from behind its barred windows and four-story tower rising slightly above the building's flat roof. It appeared exactly as it had ten years ago; the night Tretan died.

Scarcely a day passed that Ahren had not thought of his old friend. Growing up in the foul city streets had made them closer than any real brothers could ever be. Tretan had the ability to make anyone like him. Between his smooth allure and Ahren's nimble quickness, they were the best pickpockets Griggs had ever seen.

But Tretan wanted to be more than an Alley Cat. To gain respect, he challenged the then Master of Thieves to a duel. When Tretan saw the Grysiem Tigress on the list, he ignored everything else. They'd always heard the rumors and tales that the count was a demon-worshiper and murderer of children, but Tretan wasn't afraid. Ahren came along as a lookout while his friend broke into the house. From atop the wall, he'd watched Tretan sneak into the near-impregnable mansion. He remembered the shouts and commotion from inside. He remembered Tretan's terrified face as he raced back across the yard, cradling a wooden box, and Count Resuom's marsh tiger chasing him down. He could still hear the screams.

A dark coach rumbled up the street and stopped before the oaken gate. A cloaked figure in a wide hat stepped from the carriage and clacked a brass knocker on the door. It creaked open and the man slipped inside. Ahren spied a hooded man on the dark lawn before the gate door closed. The count was entertaining company. At least the tigers would be in their pen.

After the coach drove away, Ahren darted across the street and circled the wall into a shallow alley. Peeking over the stone top, the small grounds appeared empty. Short hedges lined the simple yard. Wide steps rose to the house's main door. The sturdy bars across the windows left the rear servants' door the only other entrance. An old twisted oak tree grew up beside the house, casting shade over half the property. Near the rear of the house, a pair of marsh tigers impatiently paced back and forth in an iron cage.

Removing the bloody bundle from his bag Ahren unstoppered the vial of lopiune and poured it into the meat. Still watching the grounds, he massaged the drug into the cold flesh through the cloth, careful not to let it touch his hands. A single draught of the potent philter could render a man unconscious for hours. Ahren hoped he had enough.

Once sure no one could see him, he climbed the wall and over the spiked fence. Keeping to the shadows, he crept closer to the tigers' cage. A low growl resonated as the huge cats watched him with hungry green eyes. Ahren studied the cage door as he neared. A flat metal arm arched from the iron door to the house, allowing the count to open it from inside. Crouching several feet outside the bars, Ahren tore the chunk of meat in two and tossed the pieces into opposite ends of the cage. With quick snarls, the beasts gobbled them up.

Staying low, Ahren circled back to the lone tree and climbed the thick trunk. Pulling himself onto a sturdy branch, he crawled up and onto a second-floor balcony. He knelt behind the stone railing and quickly picked the lock. Carefully, he creaked the double-door open and peeked inside. A massive stuffed bear stood in the corner, its mouth open in a fearsome growl. He slipped through and shut the door behind him.

Ahren crept across the thick rug to the door across the room and listened. Distant voices murmured on the other side. He peered through the keyhole to see an empty hallway. Holding his breath, he cracked open the door.

His chest tightened in panic to see a face staring back at him. A huge, ornately framed mirror hung along the back of the hall. Letting out a sigh, Ahren searched the reflection of the hall behind him. The passage continued another twenty feet before stopping at a carved door. A wooden railing ran the length of the right side, broken only by a stairway leading up and another down to a large open chamber. The soft chanting of multiple male voices rose from the room below as their upcast shadows danced upon the dark-paneled walls through a gray haze of incense.

Quietly, Ahren slithered out into the hall and toward the door, staying low so no one on the first floor might see him.

"I heard something," said a voice from the room below.

Ahren froze. His fingers dug into the jade carpet.

"I heard it too," another replied. "Could it be Farehf and Ulka?"

"No. They're in their cage. Go. See what it is."

A cold layer of sweat formed along Ahren's palms. He scurried across the hallway and slipped through the ornate door as he heard the men below spread out.

Shutting the door behind him, Ahren found himself in a small room. A lit candelabrum rested atop a massive table draped in rich velvet. A carved white skull rested on a shelf beneath a mounted tiger's head. Across the room, a slender pair of double doors opened to a round balcony over the chamber below. Ahren's eyes locked onto a small wooden box accented with gold inside a niche along the wall.

Rising to his feet, Ahren approached the familiar box when he heard footsteps at the door behind him. He dove and hid beneath the table just before the creaking door burst open. Peering through the gap beneath the tablecloth he could see a pair of brown shoes beneath gold and emerald robes. Ahren's hand slid to his dagger as the feet approached, stopping inches from him.

Shouts and hoots erupted from downstairs.

"Halred," someone yelled. "Get down here."

The feet whirled around and ran out of the room. Ahren glimpsed a hooded man holding a pronged knife hurry down the stairs, leaving the door open behind him.

Something smashed downstairs, followed by more cries and cursing. Ahren reached for the box, but stopped. It was too easy.

Ignoring the growing commotion, he studied the small alcove containing the casket. He saw no trigger pin or wires, but as he ran his fingers along the wood, he felt a narrow slit across the top, running behind a small lip along the front. It was a trap.

Removing a thick leather-bound journal from a nearby shelf, Ahren jammed it upright in the alcove to catch any dropping blades. Blindly, he felt along the rear of the box and found a notched wooden peg jutting from the niche's back wall. Hooking his thumbnail under the peg he carefully slid it back into the wall until it caught on the notch and stayed in place. He licked his lips, then gently removed the box and set it on the floor.

The racket downstairs grew louder as glass shattered somewhere in the house followed by hoots and running footsteps. Staying wary of the open doorway, Ahren removed his picks. Sweat beaded along his brow and ran into his eyes as he desperately tried to unlock the box.

"What have we here?" someone shouted with a laugh.

"Clear the table!"

The lock clicked and Ahren opened the lid with trembling hands. A gold and jeweled figure of a tiger-headed woman nestled inside a velvet cushion.

"Let me go!" a woman screamed.

Ahren's head snapped up as he recognized Katze's voice.

"Hold her still!"

The lock clicked shut as Ahren closed the casket, and left it on the floor. He crept to the balcony overlooking the room below. Five hooded figures in green robes wrestled Katze onto a wide marble table while two more tied her down. She thrashed and fought, driving her heel into an attacker's chin before they managed to tighten her ropes.

"What has the Huntress brought us?" asked a hooded man in a tiger mask; the only figure in the room not restraining the woman. He pulled a golden candlestick from Katze's bag. "A thief. A greedy rat in the house of cats."

"Let me go, you bastard," she spat through clenched teeth.

Ahren couldn't help a rise of satisfaction in seeing Katze caught and bound. His eyes widened in horror as the masked man unsheathed a leaf-bladed dagger.

"It has been a long time since our altar tasted blood. Truly the Goddess has given us a gift."

Katze froze staring at the polished blade, then erupted in a wave of fierce thrashing as the man raised his arms.

Ahren's breathing quickened as the eight hooded men circled the altar table.

Their leader stood above her head and lowered his dagger straight in front of him. "I give you to Tsarasch, Maiden of the Hunt and Tiger Queen." The other worshipers joined in a low drone that rose higher as their masked leader drew the blade toward her throat.

Ripping his dagger from its sheath, Ahren swung over the railing and leaped into the chamber. The man below him screamed, bones cracking as Ahren drove his feet into the devotee's back. Landing atop the crumpled body, Ahren slashed his dagger, slicing the masked leader's hand and knocking his blade across the room.

Stumbling back, the leader's mask slipped, revealing Count Resuom's withered face. "Stop him!"

The green-cloaked men on either side of Ahren ripped curved, double-bladed knives from their sheaths and lunged. Twisting his body back, Ahren grabbed the first man's extended arm and jerked him across to the other side and into the other attacker's claw-like blade. Ahren shoved the men away and leapt up onto the altar table astride Katze.

"Behind you!" she cried.

Ahren kicked the attacker behind him then slashed the ropes binding Katze's wrists. "Get out of here!" He slipped his dagger into her freed hand and rolled off the marble table in time to punch one of the charging worshipers. Drawing Flagref's dagger from his belt he parried the man's next attack.

Katze cut her ankles free and jumped off the altar.

A ringed fist smashed into Ahren's mouth. Stumbling back, he managed to dodge a blurring blade. Swinging his dagger upward, he drove it deep into the man's gut. Hot blood burst over his hand.

Footsteps raced from behind him. Ahren turned to see a worshiper closing in with a raised scimitar. Ahren pressed against the table, unable to get away in time.

A slender leg swept the charging man's feet, sending him to the floor. Katze sprang on top of him and sliced his throat.

Ripping a spear from the wall, another zealot charged screaming into the room. Ahren grabbed a lamp from a shelf beside him and hurled it at the attacker's feet. Glass shattered and flaming oil exploded across the floor, setting the man's clothes ablaze. Fire licked up a hanging tapestry and spread along the lushly rugged floor.

"Come on," Ahren shouted to Katze, motioning to the stairs. "Let's get out of here."

Billowing black smoke filled the room as they raced to the second floor. Ahren turned left and hurried down the hallway to the room from which he'd entered. He threw open the balcony doors and turned, but Katze was gone.

He ran back to the hall to see Katze in the other room picking the ornate box up from the floor. "What are you doing?" he yelled. "Leave it!"

An amused grin spread across her lips. She cradled the box in her arms and ran toward him.

Count Resuom charged up the steps with a loaded crossbow in his bloodied hand. Lowering the weapon, he aimed as Katze raced past.

"Katze!" Ahren screamed. He hurled Flagref's blade past Katze's head and into the old man's chest. Dropping the crossbow, the count staggered into the railing to catch himself. Wood creaked then broke under his sudden weight, sending the count over the side and into the flames below.

Together Ahren and Katze raced to the balcony. Two bloodied and hooded devotees rushed after them. Ahren slammed the balcony doors shut and pushed his weight against the men's angry pounding.

"They're getting away!" one of them screamed from the other side. "Release the tigers!"

"What do we do?" Katze hissed, bracing her shoulder against the violent door.

"Hold on." Bracing his leg against the stone railing, Ahren pressed his back to the door and pulled the silver padlock from his bag. He hooked the shackle through the door's handles and clicked the lock closed. "Now go!"

Still holding the awkward box under one arm, Katze lowered herself over the railing and dropped to the bushes below. The door behind him rattled and shook, but held fast. With a grin, Ahren swung over the rail and dropped to the hedge beside Katze.

The tigers' cage door squeaked open. Ahren turned to see the two beasts lying on their sides watching him with careless eyes. Rolling to his feet, he pulled Katze from the thick bushes and they ran to the outer wall.

Shouts and cries echoed from inside the house. Smoke trickled from several windows as orange light flickered from behind the shutters. Panicked guards called "Fire!" from the streets outside as Ahren and Katze scaled the wrought iron fence and hurried away through the alleys. Alarm bells chased them from the Nobles District.

"Thank you for saving me," Katze said as they neared Griggs' tavern. She still held the heavy box under her cloaked arm opposite Ahren.

"I couldn't let those bastards take you away like they did Tretan."

She swallowed. "But you gave up the duel for it."

He sighed but said nothing.

"I saw the dagger you used to kill the count. I know what it was worth. You even used Hetstier's lock so we could get away."

Ahren grinned. "I was hoping to keep that dagger," he chuckled.

They continued down the narrow streets in silence until reaching the tavern. A roar of cheers and applause erupted as they stepped into a small room through the back door.

Griggs set a handful of cards on a table, his eyes barely concealing his relief. "Welcome back."

Katze held the gold-trimmed box above her head. "I have it!" she declared and plopped it hard onto the table.

Griggs nodded in approval. "Ahren, what have you brought?"

Ahren chewed his lip. "That's it," he said, holding out empty hands and motioning to Katze.

Boos and chuckles poured from the half-dozen thieves packed into the backroom.

Katze worked a pair of wire picks into the lock. "Ahren forfeited to save my life. I share this with him." The lock clicked and she opened the box. "This is *our* victory."

The cramped room went silent. A single black feather rested on the velvet cushion inside. Katze turned to Ahren, her mouth open in puzzled disbelief.

A wide smile stretched across Ahren's lips. "I'm happy to hear that." He removed the jeweled figure from his satchel and set it on the countertop. "And the new Master of Thieves doesn't mind sharing."

Shouts and laughs exploded as lost bets were reclaimed and coins changed hands. Raised mugs toasted the new Master of Thieves. Ahren slipped through a gauntlet of praise and jokes and entered the barroom where he took an empty booth in the back.

Katze slid in beside him, carrying a pair of drinks. "Very clever," she said, offering him a stein.

He smiled and raised his tankard. "To the Mistress of Thieves, may she find it in her heart to forgive me."

She squeezed his arm. "I never did welcome you home."

Ahren met her soft black eyes. "I missed you too."

The Seventh General

Squawking gulls circled over the bustling Lichthafen harbor. As the fading sun retreated far to the west, stars twinkled on the horizon. Cool air wafted from the sea, carrying the stink of mildew and dead fish. Ahren peered through the chipped arrow slits of one of the towers along the harbor walls at a sleek, freshly docked ship. The tied, sky-blue sails announced it had come from Porvov, the great city in distant Rhomanny, seat of the Holy Church of Arieth, Crown Jewel of Delakurn, and—to a known few—headquarters of the Tyenee.

Narrowing his eyes against the failing light, Ahren studied the passengers descending the gangplank; their dress, their age, and above all, their demeanor. Experience had taught him that generals of the Tyenee were as diverse as the cities they manipulated from the shadows. Yet even the friendliest of their faces held the same flicker of ruthlessness. So far, among the fops, skittish merchants, and noisy families, no one had met the qualifications.

A hefty-set man in dark green marched confidently from the ship. Copper buttons glinted from his heavy brocade doublet, and the twisted steel of his basket hilt rapier hinted that the ornate weapon was intended for more than just show. It had to be him.

"My shift's almost done," Josik whispered. "You'll need to be out of here before my relief comes, or it's both our heads."

Ahren turned to the gangly guard beside him. His short brown beard almost concealed the sunken cheek from which it grew. "Don't worry."

Josik snorted. "I've got three daughters and an expecting wife; don't talk to me about worrying."

"Fair." Ahren shrugged, and handed the soldier five silver coins. "Maybe this will ease your heart. I'm done here anyway."

"Thanks." Josik dropped the coins into a rawhide pouch and gestured down the winding stairs. "Always a pleasure, my friend." They hurried down the tower steps to an iron-bound door. The guard peered outside, then motioned it was clear.

"When is number four due?" Ahren asked, stepping out into the dark city streets.

"Two months. The midwife predicts it'll be a girl."

"Four daughters," Ahren laughed. "May Arieth have mercy on you." He winked to the despondent guard and headed down the street.

"May you pass safely through the mist," Josik called behind him.

"Did you see him?" Katze asked, stepping from an alleyway.

Ahren brushed the dark curls from Katze's face and kissed her. "I think so. How's your father?"

"Nervous. He finally finished cleaning the bar and then started all over again just before I left. This will be his seventh general to serve in twenty years. Nine of which were without a one at all. Hopefully this one will outlive the others."

"Hopefully." The apparent curse besetting any Tyenee generals assigned to Lichthafen for the past two centuries was well known among its members. The last one, sent three years ago, hadn't even lasted an hour before shoddy scaffolding collapsed in the street, killing him and two others. Since then, no one was willing to try their luck, leaving Griggs, a mere lieutenant, master of the city's underworld. Now, with a new boss looking over his shoulder, Griggs was terrified of what might happen. Even though he'd served his masters well, a new commander could find his established order and connections as a threat. Griggs was afraid, and Ahren afraid for him.

They followed the winding lanes lit beneath the dim glow of wrought iron lamps. Bearded beggars leered from the shadows as they passed and tight-bodiced whores stepped onto the cobbled streets to begin their night's work. Bell-ringing hawkers called to them as Ahren and Katze turned down a dingy street and headed to Griggs' Inn.

A tiny bell above the door rang as they stepped inside the narrow tavern. The familiar layer of dirt and scum accenting the floor and tables was gone. Fresh tapers burned from the holders mounted around the room, most of which Ahren had never seen used before. A few patrons talked and ate, yet the more unkempt and seedy regulars were noticeably absent.

"There you are," Griggs said from behind the counter. "Sit. Let me get you something to eat." The square-jawed man filled two bowls from a stew pot above the fire and set them down on the table. "So?" he whispered. "Recognize him?"

Ahren shrugged. "Don't know."

The thief king ran his fingers through his graying temples. "Guess it don't matter. We'll see him soon enough." A table of customers rose to leave and he hurried off to fetch their dirty plates.

The bell tinkled again as a man with thinning gray hair walked inside. Ahren watched, wondering if this was the new boss. With a gruff order, the man ordered his drink and invited himself to a backgammon game at the far table. Ahren shrugged and returned to his meal. He finished just as a young gentleman with a polished rapier glinting at his waist strode inside. The newcomer scanned the tavern once, reminiscent of a captain surveying his ship after a storm.

"Greeting, sir," Griggs said, stepping behind the bar. "What can I get you?"

"I'm looking for a man named Griggs," the man replied, brushing back a lock of blond hair with a gloved hand.

Ahren turned his head for a better look. *Surely this dandy isn't the general.*

The barkeeper's brow furrowed. "I am he."

The man pulled his shirt open slightly and Griggs' flush face paled. "Then let us retire somewhere quiet. There's much to discuss."

Ahren held his second beer since the two men had entered the back room before Griggs cracked the door open and motioned for him and Katze. They stepped through the thick door into the large yet mostly empty storeroom.

"Master Skeroff, I want you to meet my daughter, Katze."

The general rose from his chair at a pair of tables and took Katze's hand. "It is a pleasure." He gently kissed her long fingers. "I've heard of your exploits in your father's reports. He failed to mention your beauty as well. An oversight, I'm sure."

Ahren forced a smile, surprised by his threatened twinge at the attractive man.

"And this is Ahren," Griggs continued, seeming to ignore the general's advances. "The Black Raven. This is Skeroff, General of the Tyenee and the new Master of Lichthafen."

"The Black Raven." Skeroff smiled broadly. "I've been looking forward to meeting you for some time." He shook Ahren's hand and gestured to the table. "Sit down, both of you. Griggs, bring us some more wine."

Ahren sat, casually examining the young general. He couldn't be more than thirty, if even that. "So will you be staying here?"

"For now," Skeroff replied. "Once my wares arrive in a month, I'll move everything over to my tailor shop. This bar has served as the hub far too long. I'm certain it's already drawn too much unwanted attention. Moving the operation somewhere new only solidifies people's understanding of a new regime." He glanced up at Griggs, pouring cups of wine. "I'm sure you can find a suitable location. It needs to be central. In a location where both peasant and merchant might visit."

He sipped the dark wine. "Until then, there's much to do. Griggs has informed me that over twenty gangs operate in the city, and while he's at least kept them from growing too powerful, the power between them is too much. In two weeks I want half of them gone."

Katze's face flashed with disbelief. She opened her mouth to speak, but Ahren cut her off.

"That's no easy task. How do you wish us to do that?"

Skeroff smiled. "I'll weigh their strengths. Those with the most useful and malleable talent will be melded into our ranks. Others will be pitted against each other one by one, until all are too weak to continue. A few Porvov Switches and assassinations will handle the rest. After that, the rest will fall into order. For that, I'll need you."

"Understood." Ahren lifted the wine to his lips to conceal his growing dread. Gang wars were never easy, and he knew some of the people whom Skeroff would want eliminated.

"Then tomorrow we'll start." Griggs raised his clay goblet. "To Skeroff, the new Lord of Lichthafen."

"Please, Ahren, you know I can't." The bearded man swept his arm across the furniture shop. "All my money is in this. I can't pay that much."

"You had enough to spend last week in Darian's gambling hall," Ahren replied coolly. "Now I need to collect what's mine."

Bernhard ran his hand over his mouth. "No one told me you were going to be doubling the price. I can pay what I have, and if you give me a couple weeks, I can pay the rest. Griggs would understand."

Ahren drew a breath. Bernhard was right. "Griggs needs the money now. Not later."

Bernhard gave a nervous laugh. "Please, Ahren. I'm begging you. I can't pay that right now. Trust me, I would, but I can't."

"I'm not leaving until I have it." He picked up a white and red vase painted with the image of a girl and a dog. "So give me the silver, and I'll leave."

"I told you—"

"I don't care what you told me!" Ahren yelled. He poised the heavy vase, ready to smash it, but hesitated. His gaze flickered to his reflection in the mirror behind the shop owner. There the Black Raven stood. The extortionist. The bully. Everything Ahren had vowed never to be.

"It's that new guy isn't it?" Bernhard asked. "I've heard about him. People talk."

Ahren didn't answer.

He sighed. "I can pay the ten I owe you, plus six more. I'll get you the rest as soon as I can, I swear."

"Fine." Ahren set the vase back onto the counter.

"Arieth bless you." The shop owner opened a wooden box from behind the counter and poured out the additional coins.

"Don't disappoint me." Ahren scooped up the silver. "I'll be back in a few days." Glimpsing his shameful reflection again, Ahren turned and quickly retreated. He let out a long sigh as he stepped out onto the street and headed back to Griggs' tavern.

How did this happen? The Black Raven, the greatest thief and burglar in the Tyenee, reduced to a thug.

Shop owners and peddlers called to him as he passed. Their new-found enthusiasm wasn't respect, but fear. Once he blended in.

Known only to those who needed to. His anonymity was slipping.

He knocked once before stepping through the alleyway door into the tavern's back room. Bolts of fabric and oaken chests lined the walls. The scent of wood and spices overshadowed the familiar smell of dust and ale.

"Ah, Black Raven," Skeroff said, peering over a log book. "Good. We'll need to evacuate this merchandise before it draws any more attention. Griggs' inadequate storehouses are already full."

"We can do it tonight." Ahren tossed down the collected silver and gold, plus some of his own to conceal Bernhard's shortage.

"Excellent." The young thief master counted the coins and dropped them into a dingy leather bag. "Who didn't pay?"

Ahren poured a tankard of water and sat. "The Blue Dogs didn't have enough, but promise to bring it next week. Also, Flerin the butcher will bring his in two days."

"Did you agree?"

"They're good for it."

"And if they don't have it then?"

Ahren shrugged. "Depends on the reason."

"Ahren, don't be soft," he chuckled. "Accepting excuses means they'll only make more. Griggs allowed excuses. This city should be yielding twice what it has." Skeroff chewed his lip. "I'm the youngest general in the history of our order. Do you know how I did that?"

Ahren shook his head.

Skeroff held up a finger. "Never compromising. That's it. You're the greatest talent in the Tyenee in generations. Just imagine what we could accomplish together. All you need do is take heed to my advice."

"I will," Ahren said. "Thanks."

"Superb. This is the greatest city in Mordakland. With your help, we'll make Lichthafen the most bountiful city the Tyenee has ever had."

Yellow cascades of hardened wax hung from the burned-out candle holders as Ahren stepped into the bar. A few patrons still lingered in the common area. He winked to Katze, who was cleaning up the already empty tables, then limped up the stairs to the second floor. A charging guard dog had forced him out a different window than he'd wanted, and the three-story fall hadn't been kind. Ahren only hoped it would be better by morning. At least he was back doing something active.

He composed himself and knocked on the door to one of Griggs' nice rooms. Moments passed. Then Clauser, another former Alley Cat and now one of the city's more successful fences, marched into the hall, cursing under his breath. He ducked his head from Ahren's questioning glance and quickly slunk down the stairs.

"Ah Ahren," Skeroff said, pushing several rolled parchments aside. "Come in." Trying to hide his injury, Ahren walked over and took the seat opposite the young general

"Are you hurt?" Griggs asked. He sat in the corner, his hand resting on the neighboring table, clutching a drink. The thief master's ability to see every detail bordered on the magical.

"It's nothing." Ahren removed a bundle from his satchel and unfolded it across the table, revealing an assortment of gem-encrusted treasures.

"Excellent." Skeroff selected a gold comb and held it up. The small emeralds and diamonds along its side sparkled in the lamplight. He took a star-shaped broach and a pearl bracelet and set them aside. "Hide these in Kherisdat Bakery. We'll send word that Erik orchestrated the jeweler's theft. Once the guards find these, he'll be gone. His smuggling operation has lasted too long."

Ahren nodded. "I'll do it first thing tomorrow."

"No. Katze can do it tonight. Tomorrow we'll send the rest to Fritz in Lunnisburg. He should get a good price." He folded the remaining jewelry back into the cloth and set it aside. "You did good, Black Raven."

"Thank you."

Skeroff opened a tiny box and removed a bronze medallion on a copper chain. "The Tyenee rewards those who serve us, and this is long overdue. Congratulations, Lieutenant."

Stunned, Ahren took the round pendant. A mountain of upturned daggers, the glyph of the Tyenee, adorned the face. A shallow engraving of a raven marked the back. "I don't know what to say." He glanced nervously at Griggs, who gave an emotionless smile. Ahren was now the same rank as his former mentor and father of his love.

"There's nothing to say," Skeroff said, amused. He handed Ahren a filled goblet. "The days of the Black Raven breaking into every little house and shop are over. But don't think the risks are done; they've only changed."

Ahren's heart pounded. He'd never heard of a lieutenant working jobs. They served as a general's second, usually stationed in a city, orchestrating crimes they'd never perform. They grew fat. Bald. The joy faded from their eyes. Ahren looked down at the medallion growing heavy in his hand. They'd clipped his wings.

Skeroff raised his glass in salute and drank. "I'll want you with me for the next couple days. There's much to be done, and for you to learn."

"I look forward to it," he replied through a forced smile. He needed to talk to someone. Katze would understand. She could comfort him. He finished his wine and rose. "Now if you excuse me, I'll be heading to bed."

"Fine." Skeroff gestured to the broach and necklace still on the table. "Take these to Katze and tell her what to do, Lieutenant."

"F-f-fi-fifty?" Clauser stuttered. "I c-c-ca-can't pay that much g-g-gold."

Skeroff squeezed his gloved hands together. "You fenced over two hundred dreins worth of goods for Griggs last month. I know he hasn't been your only client. Erik used you frequently, before the city guards caught him. All I'm asking is a fair share of what you've been skimming off the top."

Ahren stood in the back of the storeroom, cleaning his fingernails with a wooden splinter as the two men talked. He rarely spoke during these meetings and had nothing to add when he did. His job was merely to observe, learn how it was done—and serve as intimidation for Skeroff's guests.

"B-b-but I-I never made that much for m-my-self," Clauser protested. He pulled at his aged and dingy suede doublet. "Would I d-dress like this if I d-d-did?"

"I said you were skimming. I never implied you were stupid. Showing off profits would be too noticeable for any fence." The thief master opened a stained logbook and flipped through pages of scrawled entries. "Griggs kept records of what business he gave you and what profit he made. You must think me as big a fool as him if you're saying you only kept five percent."

The fence turned to Ahren. "You-you know me Ahren. T-te-tell him. I'd never s-st-steal from Griggs."

Ahren shrugged. They'd known each other since they were children, stealing and spying together for Griggs. He was like a father to them. Clauser might not be smart, but he was loyal.

"Yes, Ahren," Skeroff said through a smile, "tell me." It was a threat. Undermining the general's argument would only make things worse. The point was to scare Clauser. Make him negotiate a lower amount or agree to some future favor and feel better for it in the end.

"Everyone knows you pocket more than you say." Ahren flicked the splinter into the corner. "Griggs, Katze, me; we all know it. That's just an unspoken fact. We also know you don't keep as much from us as you do your other clients. Of which there are plenty. With us, you'll still make more than you did before."

"Ah-ah-Ahren, I swear I never s-st-stole from him!" Clauser blurted, his face paling except for the purple scar along his cheek.

"Enough." Skeroff slammed his hand onto the table. "Your past with Griggs doesn't interest me. What does is the fifty gold dreins I estimate you stole from your clients. Will you pay it or not?"

"I c-ca-can't. I can p-p-pay f-five."

Pursing his lips, Ahren cursed the stuttering fence for offering so low. He'd have been better to offer nothing.

"Five?" Skeroff balled his fist and pressed it to his mouth. "Five? What in Saint Vishtin's name do you take me for?"

"F-five is still good money. M-more than y-y-you deserve."

The crime boss' eyes narrowed to dark slits. "What does that mean?"

"I know y-y-you s-se-setup Erik and had U-Ulrein killed. You can't just sh-show up and ex-expect to force change on everyone. At this r-ra-rate you'll be d-d-dead in a m-month."

"Dead? Dead!" Skeroff jumped to his feet, knocking his chair back across the wooden floor. His hand clutched the sword at his side. "How dare you threaten me!"

Stunned, Ahren watched Clauser gulp and hold out his hands. How had this happened?

"P-p-please, I-I wa-wasn't threatening you. I-I meant—"

"Enough!" Skeroff snapped. "Ahren. Kill this man."

Terror seized Ahren's gut. His mouth hung open in disbelief. "Master Skeroff …"

"P-please, I b-be-beg you!"

The general's face warped with fury. He ripped his rapier from its sheath and plunged it into the seated man's throat. Blood gurgled from Clauser's mouth as his chair fell back, spilling him at Ahren's feet.

"I gave you an order," Skeroff growled, ignoring the dying man's gasps.

"But he misspoke," Ahren blurted. "Clauser does that."

"That doesn't matter." Skeroff marched around the table and yanked the sword from the man's neck. Blood belched across the storeroom floor. "I gave you an order. You hesitated."

Eyeing the red-stained blade in the man's hand, Ahren drew a breath. "I … apologize. I just thought—"

"No. You questioned me. What do you think would happen if by some miracle you had persuaded me to let him live? Everyone would hear. That would destroy us." The rage calmed in the man's pale eyes. Turning, he tossed the sword onto the table. "You're weak. Maybe I misjudged you."

Ahren glanced down at his childhood friend, still twitching in a crimson pool. "Forgive me."

"Leave me." Skeroff knocked back his cup of wine. "And send someone to clean this up."

Oily smoke hung in the tavern air like mist, giving spectral halos to the candle-silhouetted patrons. Katze sat in a far booth near the stairs, absently watching a card game at a nearby table. All three players were cheating. Her gaze lifted as Ahren started down the steps from his room above. His empty canvas satchel bounced against his hip beneath the gray cloak.

"Are you ready?" she asked, standing to greet him.

His delicate blue eyes shimmered with excitement. She always loved his eyes right before a run. "Quite." He kissed her, pulling her close against his chest. "I wish you were coming with me."

"Marten will take care of you. You're not still angry with him for our Thieves Duel, are you?"

"Not at all. I'd just prefer you."

She kissed him again. "Father said I have to do something for him. Once I'm done, I'll watch you from the rooftops."

"Just be careful."

"Me?" She slapped him playfully on the chest. "These are my streets more than yours. I'll be fine."

Marten stepped into the bar, rubbed his hand across his stubbled chin, then headed to where Ahren and Katze stood. "Are you ready?"

Ahren gently kissed Katze's forehead before turning to the weasel-faced man. "Yeah."

Marten adjusted a coiled rope hidden beneath his loose cloak. "Let's go."

Katze watched the two thieves head into the night streets. The bell tinkled as the door closed behind them, and she turned to where her father cleaned the bar. "You wanted to speak with me?"

Griggs didn't look up as he scrubbed a stain caked onto the wooden counter. "Yeah. I'll need to report that Ahren and Marten left, shortly."

Her brow rose. "All right. But what did you need to talk to me about?"

"Tonight is important. But it's nothing we can discuss right now." Griggs finished his cleaning and tossed the frayed rag over his shoulder. "Have you ever paid attention to the view from the safe room?" Without waiting for a reply, he turned and walked around the counter to wait on a table of customers across the room.

Confused, Katze glanced over to the low hidden door behind the counter. The heavy cask normally blocking the entrance had been moved aside. The room was used for hiding merchandise or thieves trying to avoid chasing guards. The barrel was always left in front of the door unless someone was going in or out. She looked back to see her father leaning over the crowded table, his back toward her. Still puzzled, she followed his hint, weaving behind the tall counter and crouching at the gap between the barrels. She hooked her finger through a tight knothole, pulled the hidden door open, and crawled inside.

A hanging weight on a pulley closed the door behind her,

plunging her into near darkness. The crevice was no more than two feet wide, but stretched the length of the building. Strips of thin light shone between the wall slats of the neighboring back room. The heavy stink of mildew and dust filled the uncomfortable crevice. Careful not to brush the walls, Katze rose to her feet and peered through one of the narrow cracks into the adjoining room.

Skeroff sat alone at his table, muttering silent words before scrawling his quill over a parchment. A knock rattled the door and Griggs stepped inside.

"Ah." Skeroff stabbed his quill back into the inkpot. "I was just finishing your letter of recommendation. Once the Masters read my report, I'm sure they will follow my advice."

"Thank you, Skeroff." Griggs sat down and poured himself a healthy drink. "You're too kind."

"Rewarding those who prove themselves is essential. You've earned a generalship. I only hope whatever city you're assigned will be useful for moving merchandise." He handed the parchment to the barkeep.

Generalship? Father's always said he would never leave Lichthafen. Does he really hate Skeroff that much? She shifted closer to hear them better.

Griggs scanned the letter before handing it back. "I came to tell you Marten and Ahren just left for the moneylender's house."

"Excellent. Once Marten has proved his loyalty, he will make a fine addition to the Tyenee. Your recommendation was critical in his choosing."

The Tyenee already has enough members in this city. And Father's never completely trusted him. Why not choose Jan or Adolph instead?

Griggs knocked back his cup. "He's a good man."

"And you're sure he knows what to do?"

"I was very specific. I wish it didn't have to come to this, though." He glanced over to the exact spot Katze was hiding.

The handsome general brushed back his blond hair and sipped his drink. "Neither do I. But defiance cannot be tolerated. Ahren has much respect and influence in more than just Lichthafen. If he questions his master, his peers will follow."

"I understand. We agreed." Griggs poured another drink. "Ahren must die."

Katze's chest tightened. *How?* She couldn't breathe for fear of letting out a cry. *How could Father say that?*

Skeroff gave an approving smile. "Good. Once Marten returns with word that he's dead, we will hold a wake in his honor and I will send word to Porvov of his fate. Then we will speak of it no more."

"Some of the other generals won't be happy to hear of his assassination."

Skeroff nodded. "Sentimentality can outweigh judgment. I'll say he died on the job. No one needs to know the truth and the Black Raven's legend will be forever unmarred."

Griggs took a long sigh. He turned his head toward the wall behind which Katze hid, looking straight into her eyes. "You know what is right."

Katze felt his words. Ahren was in danger and she had to save him. Quietly, she crept back to the hidden door.

Loud snores resonated beyond the closed bedroom door as Ahren worked his picks on the iron strongbox. Clouds sailed briskly along the heavens outside, occasionally shielding the moonlight from the open window. The lock clicked and Ahren returned his tools to their soft leather pouch. Hinges squeaked as he lifted the lid, revealing three bulging sacks crammed inside.

Careful not to spill any of the coins, Ahren lifted the first heavy bag and peeked inside to find it filled with silver sasiks. The next bag held copper and the final one gold. A leather book rested at the chest's bottom. A quick flip under the pale moonlight revealed the names and debts of Vizeil's clients. The moneylender's records could prove even more valuable than the healthy treasure. Ahren slipped the journal into his satchel then placed a single raven's quill into the empty box. With a small smirk of satisfaction, he lifted the now lighter chest and returned it to a niche in the wall beside the fireplace. The hole only half concealed the strongbox. Ahren then carefully set a leather stool before the spot. While the box was still technically exposed, the stool's placement gave a near perfect illusion of nothing but a solid wood wall behind it.

Ahren crept to the open window and peeked outside. The dark streets lay empty. He scanned the rooftops, hoping Katze might have come, but didn't see her. Disappointed, he stuck his hand outside and fluttered his fingers. Marten slinked from the shadows and stopped just below the window.

Ahren heaved the first bag outside and lowered it as far as he could before letting it fall. The slender man caught it and set it on the ground beside him. Ahren dropped the other two sacks the same way before crawling out onto the sill and scaling the two floors to the street below.

Marten was already gone when he reached the bottom. Ahren quickly grabbed the remaining bag and hurried to the edge of the street where his partner was already loading their treasure into a barrel lying on a small cart.

"Everything go all right?" Marten glanced out over the streets behind them.

Ahren stooped to push his bag into the straw nest inside the barrel. "Flawless." He set the lid over the top and began tying the barrel firmly down. "Let's go."

"There's just one thing," Marten said, stepping closer behind Ahren.

"What's that?" Ahren asked, still cinching the knot.

A hard *thwack* came from behind him. He whirled around to find Marten standing just inches away, holding a long knife. Confusion glazed over the thief's eyes.

"Marten, what are you doing?"

Another *thwack* sounded and the blade fell from the weaselish man's hand and clattered on the cobblestones. He staggered and fell. Ahren caught him, then saw the two arrows jutting from Marten's back.

Horrified, he looked up to see Katze crouched on a nearby rooftop, clutching her bow. *Why?* Marten's knife lay at his feet. *They'd ordered my execution.*

Ahren looked back up to Katze watching him from the rooftop. A soft wind pulled at her black curls and billowed her cloak. The relief on her face washed away to rage. She spun around and ran across the rooftops toward Griggs' tavern.

He let Marten's body fall, grabbed the wagon cart handles and ran. Her eyes said it all. She wanted blood. The rooftops didn't lead straight there. He could beat her.

The wooden wheels squeaked and rumbled across the uneven stones as he raced through the empty back streets. *How could Skeroff do this? Did Griggs know? Could he have ordered it?* Anger welled, driving him faster. The cumbersome cart only slowed him. He left it in a narrow alley. He'd come for it later. If the Tyenee were truly after him, he'd need every bit of the money to keep Katze and him safe.

Sweat ran down his face as he reached the bar. Several young men stood by the door, enamored in their own drunken chatter. Ahren darted through the neighboring alley and headed to the rear entrance. Panting, he drew his dagger and clutched the leather grip as he threw open the door to Skeroff's meeting room.

The young general sat slumped in his chair, his blond locks spilled over his face. Crimson blood spread across his open doublet and silk shirt. A single arrow protruded from his heart.

"He ordered your death," Katze said from beside the open doorway. "I heard him." She turned to Ahren, tears creeping into her eyes. "He sent Marten to kill you."

Ahren pulled her to his chest and held her tight. "You saved me."

"I love you, Ahren," she sobbed. "I love you."

"I love you too." He hugged her and kissed her head. "Katze, did your father know about this?"

She didn't answer.

"Katze, did Griggs know?"

The door to the barroom opened and Griggs walked in, holding a bottle and three tankards. "Saint Vishtin," he breathed, staring at Skeroff's body.

Ahren pulled Katze back, and squeezed the dagger still in his hand.

"Someone killed him?" Griggs said. "Thank Arieth you two are all right. Did you see who it was?"

"No," Ahren cautiously replied.

Griggs sighed and set the cups down on the table. "It must have been Marten. I figured that bastard might try something after Clauser's death. The Tyenee will expect vengeance, of course."

Katze stepped around Ahren and closed the still open door. "Marten is dead, Father. I shot him as he tried to kill Ahren."

"Oh my," Griggs replied with mocking surprise. He uncorked the bottle and poured a heavy dose of Rhomanic vodka into the tankards. "Are you hurt, my boy?"

Ahren shook his head. "I'm fine." He watched as Katze set her bow aside and took a cup from her father's extended hand.

"It's a pity." Griggs plopped into one of the wooden chairs and eyed the corpse. "We got along so well. Skeroff's final letter to Porvov was a request to give me my own city. Me, a general." He raised his tankard in salute to the dead man slouched across from him. He took a long drink then stopped. "Ahren, did you get the money from Vizeil's?"

"It's a few blocks back. I left it … when I heard what happened."

"Then bring it here. I'll send part of it, along with Skeroff's letter to Porvov, on tomorrow's ship. I suppose I'll wait until the next one to tell them about his assassination. Might make the Lords of the Tyenee suspicious if they received such news on the same day."

"What are you going to tell them?" Ahren asked.

"The truth of course." Griggs chuckled. "The curse of Lichthafen has taken yet another general. Katze, my wonderful daughter, avenged Skeroff's murder. What else is there?"

A cool smile crept along Ahren's face. "Nothing. With luck, the Tyenee will assign you here. Since no one else seems to want the job."

Griggs took another drink. "I'm counting on it."

Shadows Beneath the City

A hren braced himself inside the coffin-like box.
"Saint Vishtin, this thing is heavy," a guard grunted, carrying one end of the long, brass-bound crate.

"Put it over there," his deep-voiced partner said.

The men carried it several feet before setting it down with a careless thud. Listening to the two men shuffle back and forth, Ahren remained still, suppressing his urge to peek outside. Katze never ceased to laugh that the Black Raven, the greatest thief in Delakurn, didn't like the dark. He had told her the story of Dolch, the thief master with the powers of demonic darkness whom he had crossed years before, but Katze had waved it off as silly paranoia. Reluctantly Ahren succumbed to her pleas to extinguish the lamp he burned beside their bed at night.

Muted thunder echoed outside.

"Damn it," one of the guards growled as they slid another crate on top of Ahren's.

"Hurry up and get the rest before it starts raining."

Ahren's pulse quickened as the men worked. The hair on his legs tingled as if the blackness was slithering along him, smothering him. A thud came from outside as another crate was unloaded followed by several smaller boxes.

"That's it. Let's go." The heavy warehouse door groaned shut and the men's wagon squeaked away.

Ahren slid a latch beside his head and peered out a tiny hole. A wooden box rested inches beside his, preventing him from opening the side door to his crate. Turning over, he checked the peephole on the other side and found a support pillar standing beside him. There was no way he could open the door with enough room to escape. He rolled onto his sweating palms and peeked out the hole at his head to find it clear. Holding the leather strap so the door wouldn't fall open, he unlatched the small door and lowered it quietly to the floor.

Lightning erupted outside through the narrow windows, filling the huge room with fleeting light. Shadows flickered along rows of crates and stacked barrels. A loud crash of thunder shook stone walls.

He peered around to ensure he was alone, and then slid from the confining box that had held him for six dreadful hours. Stretching his legs and back, Ahren surveyed the massive room. No thief in over two centuries had successfully entered the Royal Warehouses. Carved, emotionless faces stared down at him from the tops of the stone columns, cast orange from torches beside the main door. Wavy, leaded glass sealed the windows along the upper walls. Nobles and wealthy merchants paid too high a price for housing their goods only to have them spoiled by the elements.

Soft taps drummed the ceiling above as rain began to fall.

Squinting in the dim light, Ahren walked the aisles between stacks of crates, and bolts of fabric. He wished he could carry one of the burning torches, but the moving light in the windows could alert one of the guards along the palisade outside. Dark shadows seemed to move and flood around him as he searched. Another flash of lightning burst, sending the shadows scurrying away. Gold glinted on the second-floor loft. Ahren made his way to a steep stairway and hurried to the top.

Dim light, cast through the narrow, arched windows circling the second floor, made it much easier to see. Pulses flashed through the cloudy skies outside, illuminating the other warehouses crowded within the fortified walls.

A small gilded chest rested atop a stack of large polished trunks. Lifting the heavy box, Ahren set it on the floor and removed the tools from his pouch. He slipped the wire picks into the gold-trimmed lock and worked. The closing shadows crept nearer as if curious. The growing patter of rain on the roof nearly drowned out the click as the lock opened.

Carefully, Ahren opened both sides of the rounded lid. A black leather bag, stitched with gold thread, rested inside. Its contents softly clacked as he lifted it out. Squeezing the soft calfskin, he felt six distinct round lumps like acorns. The buyer said there were to be five. Ahren untied the golden cord holding the bag shut and slowly pulled it open. A bright beam of light peeked out the tiny opening. Quickly, he drew it closed. The gems were definitely inside. But he couldn't open the bag in view of the windows. With a smile, Ahren drew out a long raven's quill from his pouch, dropped it into the empty chest, and relocked it before returning the box atop the trunks.

A deafening boom of thunder rattled the window panes as Ahren slinked back down the stairs. Wind whistled outside as the rain grew harder. Clutching the leather bag, he crawled back into the crate and pulled the trapdoor shut. The unsettling darkness immediately closed in; Ahren opened the leather pouch.

Iridescent rays of light burst from the pouch, flooding the wooden box, scattering the shadows. Ahren reached inside the soft leather and drew out a faceted gemstone. Light, equivalent to a single candle, glowed within the crystal's walls, bursting from each of its many faces like a prism in the sun. Squinting, he peered into the bag to see five more brilliant gems resting within the black velvet lining.

The extra plamya stone was an unexpected surprise. A burglar could find many uses for a light without flame. It would make a fine gift for Katze.

Ahren dropped the gem back into the bag and cinched it before opening the crate. He knelt beside one of the other boxes from the shipment he arrived in, and unlocked it. The gray uniform of a Lichthafen guard lay tightly folded inside. Bright bursts of lightning erupted outside as Ahren stripped off his clothes and dressed in the cold, heavy chain mail and hard boots. He cinched a sword belt around his waist, then stuffed his clothes into the box and locked it.

Pulling the heavy guard's helmet over his head, he headed back upstairs. The hard boots clonked across the wooden floor as he approached the back window. He peered through the streaked, wavy glass to see dark rooftops silhouetted behind the perimeter wall. A single guard stood huddled out of the rain, beneath one of the tower overhangs. The grounds below appeared empty of patrols. Ahren waited until the guard turned his attention out toward the city, then opened and closed the leather bag of plamya stones. Somewhere on the seemingly empty rooftops Katze would have seen his signal.

He slipped the bag beneath his dingy tabard and headed downstairs. One of the flickering torches waned, then burnt out, sending up wisps of gray smoke. Shadows encroached inward, patiently anticipating the other flame's impending departure. The patter of rain on the roof came in waves with the wind.

Ahren waited.

Weak blue flames clung to the dying second torch as a bell outside tolled three times in the yard. Ahren extinguished the light, then cracked open the warehouse door. The grounds were mostly empty. A pair of drenched soldiers hurried past, toward the front gate for the shift change. Ahren took a breath, then slipped outside.

Cold rain pelted his face. A cascade of water fell beside him from the slated roof, splattering off the dark cobblestones. Stepping beneath the pouring water, Ahren drenched himself, giving the appearance that he too had been standing in the rain.

Casually, he strolled between the towering warehouses and silos, slowly making his way toward the front gate. He crossed the open courtyard past a stone well when he noticed a group of fresh soldiers standing beneath the covered awning before the gate. An officer in a trimmed and embroidered cloak nailed a poster to the wall.

"Keep your eye out," he said. "He's here somewhere."

Squinting, Ahren could see his own face sketched on the tan parchment, "WANTED: The Black Raven" boldly lettered above it. Lowering his face, Ahren feigned scratching his eyebrow as he turned and headed back.

The weight of paranoia settled in his chest. *Who had tipped the guards? How did they even know I was here?* Only the buyer, Katze, and Griggs, her father and Thief King, knew where he was. None of them would have betrayed him. He took a long breath to calm himself, then nonchalantly strolled toward the outer wall.

"Hey you," a graying soldier said. "There's a thief about. Keep on the lookout."

Ahren nodded, and then hurried up the stone steps along the outer wall. The strong wind blew harder as he reached the top. Lightning cracked the sky, briefly illuminating the rooftops and stormy sea outside the city. Keeping his head low, as if to shield it from rain, he followed the narrow walkway around to the rear side.

The sentry standing below the tower overhang left his position as Ahren approached. "Have fun," he chuckled, mistaking Ahren for his replacement.

Ahren smiled as he passed.

"Halt!" someone yelled from the courtyard.

Ahren pretended not to hear.

"I said, halt!"

Ahren stopped beside a spot where the roof of an outside building leaned out over the neighboring street, just a few feet from the wall. He turned to see the officer and a trio of soldiers standing in the courtyard glaring up at him. The freshly relieved sentry stood not fifteen feet away with a confused expression.

"Who are you?" the officer asked.

"Fritz," Ahren replied.

The officer's eyes narrowed. "Stay right there." His hand moved to his sword as he marched toward the wall's steps. Two other soldiers hurried to the stairs on the wall behind him. The guard on the wall reached for his sword.

Ahren raised his hand high above his head in a tight fist.

The sentry stepped closer. "I don't know you."

Ahren opened and closed his fist three times.

An arrow flew from the darkened rooftops and pierced the guard's arm. The sword fell from his hand as he dropped to the stones with a cry.

"Archer!" someone shouted.

Wheeling around, Ahren ran and leaped across the chasm to the nearby rooftop. The heavy mail shirt pulled him down, but he managed to catch the edge and roll onto the wet shingles. Guards screamed in alarm as he scrambled to his feet and ran. Arrows whistled past, covering Ahren's retreat.

Thunder boomed as Ahren jumped to a neighboring rooftop. His hard boots slid on the slick incline, sending him over the edge. He grabbed hold of the wooden eaves and caught himself before he fell to the cobblestones three stories below.

"There he is!" a guard cried.

Ahren pulled himself up and swung his leg onto the roof. He

turned to see several soldiers leap from the wall onto the building behind him. *Why did Katze stop shooting?*

Rolling to his feet, Ahren ran as the soldiers gave chase. He raced past chimneys and scrambled up onto a higher building, desperate to reach her. The warehouse alarm bells had alerted the city guards, who scurried through the streets below trying to find him. Ahren jumped to a flat rooftop and froze.

Katze stood on the opposite end, her eyes wide in terror. Her bow lay at her feet. Black strands of wet hair clung to her face. A shadow moved behind her and a wavy dark blade formed at Katze's neck.

A pale man with jet hair emerged from the darkness. A long scar ran down his face across a milky eyeball; the remnants from the last time they had met. "Good to see you again, Black Raven," Dolch sneered.

"Ah … Ahren," Katze whimpered.

"Let her go," Ahren growled.

An amused smile curled across Dolch's lips. He jerked the blade and blood burst from Katze's throat.

Screaming, Ahren ripped his sword from its sheath and charged as Katze's body fell. Black flames erupted in Dolch's hand. He hurled the fiery ball across the rooftop.

Ahren sprang to the side. The demonic flames hit a chimney behind him and crackling ice spread over the wet bricks. He jumped and rolled back just as another ball of black fire hit where he had been. Squeezing the sword handle, Ahren lunged.

An echoey laugh escaped the demon-man's lips. He leaped back onto the low wall surrounding the roof, and then jumped over the side.

Ahren dropped to his knee and lifted Katze's crumpled body. Her dark eyes stared dreamily up at him, and then faded. Running his fingers across her soft face, he brushed back her black hair and closed her eyes. She lay still, as though calmly sleeping in his arms. Pink smears stained the colorless skin around the deep wound. Streams of diluted blood coursed along the wet rooftop and funneled out the drain to the streets below. "Katze," he wept, pulling her close. Tears ran down his rain-spattered face. He squeezed her tight. "I'm sorry."

"There he is!" someone shouted.

Glancing up, Ahren spied a pair of soldiers racing from the neighboring rooftop. Sadness melted into rage. Heat poured through his veins. He laid her body at his feet and stood.

"He's killed someone," one of them cried.

"Halt!"

Ignoring his pursuers, Ahren peered over the wall which Dolch had jumped. Lightning erupted above. Four stories below, the demon-man stood in a narrow alleyway looking up at him.

"Here I am, Black Raven," he laughed. "Come on."

Ahren jumped to the neighboring building and slid down the steep rooftop.

"He's getting away," the soldier shouted. "He's going down to the street!"

Ahren dropped onto a small balcony and swung over the side to the railing of the floor below. Clutching the edge, he dropped to the filthy alley floor. He charged along the passage back to where he'd last seen his foe standing.

Turning a corner, he ducked as another ball of cursed fire flew past him. Black flames licked up the wall of a wooden shop, chewing into the wet timbers coating them in crackling ice. Undaunted, Ahren clutched his sword and moved into the alley. With an evil smile, Dolch reached down and tore a square iron sewer grate from the ground.

Jingling mail and clomping boots sped up the passageway from the far side.

A young soldier hurried around the corner, followed close behind by his partner. "Halt!"

Wheeling around, Dolch hurled the massive grate across the passage. It slammed into the soldier's body, knocking him into a stone wall with a terrible clatter, nearly pinching him in half. Blood and broken chips of rock exploded across the walls. With Dolch's back turned, Ahren charged. He swiped his sword through air as the demon-man jumped into the sewers.

Shouts and thundering boot steps raced from both ends of the alley. Crouching low, Ahren lowered himself down the wooden ladder into the black hole.

Sounds of pouring water reverberated through the dark tunnel.

Lightning burst outside, momentarily flashing down the entrance shaft and a second grate forty feet up the passage. A walkway stretched between them, running alongside a muddy, fast-moving stream. Cascades of water gushed from small openings spaced along the upper wall, feeding the rushing sewer.

"He went down there," someone cried from above.

"Fetch torches," another voice barked. "Alert the others to flush him out. That bastard won't get away."

Adjusting to the near darkness, Ahren peered up and down the passage. Fear balled in his gut as he imagined silky fingers of shadow entwining around his throat.

A low voice whispered from the shadows behind him. *I see you, Black Raven.*

Clutching his sword, Ahren spun to face his enemy.

Are you afraid? The voice came from above.

Ahren shot his hand beneath his soaking tabard and pulled a plamya stone from the leather bag. Thin beams of prismatic light shone from the small crystal, pushing the darkness back. Ahren looked all around him, but saw no trace of the demon-man.

You should be. The voice echoed from the passage ahead. *I'm not through with you.*

Slick grime coated the narrow walkway alongside the sewer reservoir. Sticking close to the wall, Ahren followed the tunnel to where the voice had come. He held the magical stone low, trying to keep from ruining his night vision. Brown insects scuttled along the path, retreating from the rising water. Horizontal lines of leaves and debris along the walls verified the tunnels' history of flooding.

The sewer curved then narrowed to a low tunnel. Stooping, Ahren peered into the long passage. A pointed arch roof, four feet at its peak, extended the length of the tunnel. A narrow crawlway ran along the side, not more than a foot across.

Did the mighty Black Raven think I would never find him? Did you believe I'd forget you, forget what you did to me?

Lowering to his knees, Ahren crawled into the narrow passage. Swift, foul water rushed only inches away. Pungent slime gripped the walls, reeking of filth and rot. Fresh prints from soft leather soles ran down the walkway. Curling his nose from the overwhelming stink, Ahren followed the path until coming to a set of rusted iron bars across the tunnel. Their attempt to block anyone's passage had been thwarted by saws decades before, leaving the jagged remnants hanging from the ceiling like sinister teeth. A chamber opened up beyond it, filled with a wide lagoon. Ahren's small light failed to reach the walls. Crawling under the bars into the room would leave him too vulnerable if Dolch were waiting inside.

Removing a second gem from his bag, Ahren tossed it as far as he could into the chamber. He risked cracking the gem, releasing its magic, but Ahren no longer cared about the client's prize. The glow of the light spun across the stone walls as it sailed past to finally bounce to a stop just short of the far side thirty feet away. Three tunnels fed into the chamber lagoon which emptied out Ahren's passage and another just like it. Arched bridges linked the wide walkway circling the room. In one quick move, Ahren slipped through the cut bars and into the chamber, ready to defend himself.

Keeping on guard, he circled the room to retrieve the glowing stone. As he knelt to pick it up, voices came from the passage beside him.

"There's a light down there."

"It could be him. Be careful." Orange torch light flickered from the hall.

Closing his fist around the glowing gemstone, Ahren hurried into an adjoining passage. Crouching in the shadows, he peered back to see five Lichthafen soldiers carrying torches emerge into the large room.

"He couldn't have made it far," their leader said. He motioned to one of the passages. "Jan, Bemot, you take that way. The rest, follow me." He and two of his men turned and quickly marched toward the tunnel in which Ahren hid.

Still clutching the stone, Ahren hurried along the dark passage, trying to keep ahead of the soldiers' torchlight. The tunnel turned unexpectedly and Ahren nearly slipped into the raging current. The marching guards drew closer. Keeping his hand against the wall for guidance, he rushed through the black passage as fast as he could manage.

Lightning flickered through a sewer grate ahead, momentarily illuminating the long tunnel. Gushing water poured from a rectangular hole near the ceiling ahead. There were no side passages or alcoves for him to hide. The flickering lights grew brighter as the soldiers neared. Before they turned down the passage, Ahren raced to the cascading waterfall and pressed himself against the wall behind it. The cold water, polluted with filth from the city streets, flowed over his body.

"He must be close," one of them said as they neared.

Ahren held his breath. He could barely hear past the sound of running water.

"Be careful," the officer said, walking past the cascade. "He killed a girl and one of our men already."

"What does he look like?" a whiney-voiced soldier asked.

"He was dressed as a guard when he fled the warehouses, but now he's changed into all black."

"When we find him, I'm …"

Ahren waited for his pursuers to turn down the far side before emerging from the rank water. He loosened his grip from the gem, spilling out light, and hurried back the other way. Torchlight from the other two soldiers still lingered in the far passage. He started toward the tunnel from which the guards had come, when he heard Dolch's voice behind him.

Wrong way, Black Raven.

He whirled but found no one there. Across the room, the shadows within the second exiting tunnel seemed unnaturally thick. Opening his hand more, rays of light sprung from between his fingers and pierced the inky darkness.

Nothing.

He crossed the bridges over the canals and crept closer to the low exiting tunnel. Like its companion, the rusted iron bars meant to block passage had long been cut. Keeping his grip tight on his sword, Ahren carefully maneuvered through the jagged hole and onto the narrow crawlway inside.

The torrential water had risen to just inches below the pathway. The current's echoing roar filled the tunnel. Knotted strands of moss hung from the dripping stones above and brushed along Ahren's neck and back as he crawled as fast as he safely could. The tunnel opened into a wide, arched passage.

Squinting, he tried to see into the dark walkway, but the gem's meager light provided little help. He tossed the plamya stone ahead.

The light skipped off the filthy floor, illuminating the mortared brick side tunnels as it passed. The stone skittered, about to stop, then vanished, plunging the passage in blackness.

Panicked, Ahren drove his hand under his tabard. The soaked leather bag had swollen, making it difficult to uncinch. Blindly, he managed a finger inside the pouch and pulled out another gem.

He held it out, expecting to see the demon-man before him, but the shadows were empty. Still cautious, he crawled from the tight passage and stepped onto the wider pathway. Bits of refuse and moldy rat bones littered the ground. Creeping closer to where the last stone had disappeared, he saw that the walkway ended where a second stream cut through, intersecting with the large sewer. He peered into the dingy, brown-foamed water, hoping to spot the glow of the plamya stone beneath the waves, but saw nothing. The current had swept it away.

Lose something, Raven? Dolch's voice chuckled. *Tell me, is it the treasure or the woman that you mourn the most?*

Ahren's knuckles tightened around the sword handle. Holding out his light he scanned the passageway. He saw no sign of his quarry, but the rib-like arches lining the tunnel left dozens of dark hiding places. Something moved in the shadowy distance down the hall. Ahren turned in time to see Dolch step from an alcove and hurl a fistful of stygian fire.

Ahren leaped down the side passage just as the black flames exploded against the stones behind him. A hard wave of cold hit him as frost sheeted across the wall. Glancing back, he saw his attacker flee down the passage.

Rolling to his feet, Ahren hopped across the open canal and gave chase. The tunnel snaked from side to side, broken by iron grates pouring water from the streets above. He turned a corner and found himself in a wide chamber where two surging streams joined.

"Halt!"

Ahren jumped to see a soaked soldier carrying a lantern hurrying up the other passage toward him.

"Where did you get that?" the man asked, pointing his sword at the plamya stone in Ahren's hand.

"Back there," Ahren replied. "The thief must have dropped it."

"You're with the warehouse guards," he said stepping closer. "Where's the rest of your men?"

"We got separated."

The soldier nodded. "Me too. Have you seen ..." He stopped. "What's that?" Holding his lantern high, he aimed the light across the rapid water. The yellow glow swept across the gray stones then froze.

Dolch crouched against the upper far wall like a spider, clutching a black wriggling blade of solid shadow. His single blue eye glinted as inky flame erupted in his other hand, dripping hissing drops between his curled fingers.

Staggering back, the terrified soldier cried out as Dolch hurled his evil magic. The black fire burst, engulfing the soldier in dark flames, extinguishing his lantern. Cracks spider-webbed across his screaming face and chunks of icy flesh broke off. Slapping at the cursed flames, he fell face first, sizzling to the ground.

Ahren sprang to the side as another fistful of fire flew from the demon-man's hand. The frigid blast hurled him forward, knocking the glowing stone from his hand. The ground slid away as Ahren fell into the rushing water.

The cold sewage slammed into him, rolling him end over end. His steel helmet fell off, but the heavy chain shirt dragged him down. Chunks of sweeping debris smashed into his fingers as he blindly struggled to grab hold of anything. He slid across the sewer floor, pounding into the hard walls and tumbling back every time he tried to reach the surface. His lungs burned for air. Foul water pushed its way through his tight lips and up his nostrils.

His battered hands managed to grab hold of a loosened stone along the wall. Fighting the torrential surge, he managed to pull his head above the waves long enough to gasp a short breath before the current yanked him away. He struggled to remove the chain mail shirt, but to no success. His strength waned and he felt euphoria wash away his panic as he began to drown.

He slammed into something hard. Water rushed around him, pinning him to a set of iron bars stretched across the canal. Chunks of wood, torn cloth and other refuse clung to the rusted bars. Grabbing hold of the sharp, slimy metal he pulled himself to the surface. Coughing and sputtering, Ahren found the walkway embankment and crawled onto the filthy stone. His stomach heaved and he vomited putrid water.

Still panting, Ahren rolled onto his back. His fingers felt along his stomach, finding the plamya bag still tucked beneath his drenched tabard. He had light, but his sword lay somewhere at the bottom of the canal. Removing one of the glowing gems would help him see, but leave him exposed. If Dolch or any of the soldiers scouring the labyrinth found him, it was over.

Taking a deep breath, Ahren rose to his feet. His hand moved along the smooth stone wall beside him as he blindly followed the passage. The roar of rushing water filled the darkness, but Ahren focused his ears, listening for the faintest sounds buried beneath.

Lightning flickered through the street grates above, momentarily illuminating the tunnel ahead. The arched passage appeared empty save a pair of black rats fleeing the rising water. He continued onward.

The passage sloped slightly upward as it turned. Torchlight flickered ahead and Ahren crouched in the corner. A pair of armed soldiers marched toward him. Ahren's disguise had worked before, but he knew not to risk it. He inched back, ready to retreat, but they turned into a side passage instead. Ahren waited for their light to move away before hurrying past and continuing on.

Lightning pulsed above, briefly showing the tunnel split just ahead of him. Sticking to the left side, he made his way carefully toward the divide when another flash lit the tunnels. Dolch moved from a nook in the shadows.

Fear lurched inside Ahren's gut. He dropped lower, readying for an unseen attack. Another flickering pulse flashed from above, lighting the tunnel long enough for him to see the demon-man heading toward the right passage.

Ahren waited several long breaths before moving from his place. Carefully, he followed the walkway toward the left tunnel. Again the passage veered to the side, and he spied a colorful glow through a low passage ahead.

Water overflowed from the canal, and now splashed under his feet as he hurried toward the plamya stone's glow. Dropping to his knees, he crawled quickly through a cramped tunnel, before emerging in the passage.

The soldier's body still lay face down on the stone, his extended hand inches from his fallen sword. Rainbow hues shone from the glowing gem resting only a few feet away. Its narrow prismatic beams danced off the encroaching water and reflected across the chamber walls.

Ahren scanned the rest of the passage to be certain he was alone, and then hurried from the low tunnel to the man's sword. He leaned to pick it and the glowing stone up, but stopped.

He rolled the body over. The man's pitted and broken face was beyond recognition. Ahren pulled the now corroded helmet from the dead man's head. Bits of blond hair and scalp peeled off with it. He scraped them away and put the helmet on. Checking the body for anything else, he removed a copper medallion of rank and put it around his neck. The corpse watched him with ruptured and dimpled white eyes. Teeth grinned up from his lipless mouth. Ahren rolled the body into the surging current beside him. Its chain shirt dragged it instantly to the bottom. Ahren looked around one last time, then lay face down on the ground with his outstretched fingers brushing the fallen sword.

A thin film of water ran past his face along the stone, slowly covering the walkway. Ahren remained still. Sneaking up on the demon-man was hopeless, as would be a straight-out fight. Dolch expected him to be irrational. He was counting on Ahren's emotions to weaken him. Ahren had spent much of his life around killers, and the true ones all told him the same thing: emotions got you killed. He had to bury his. Forget the darkness. Forget Katze. Only when it was done could he mourn her.

The water crept higher, past the helmet's nose guard, and flowed against his face. Dancing light across the chamber walls waned as the rising water threatened to consume the half-submerged plamya stone. He'd need to move soon.

He remained still. The rising water touched his lips. Soft tingles moved across Ahren's back and neck. Through the corner of his eye, he spied shadowy tendrils snake across the walls. A faint splash came from behind him and ripples moved past.

Holding his breath, Ahren watched black soft leather boots creep past, only inches from his face. Fear and anger welled inside him, but Ahren suppressed them.

He waited until Dolch had moved past, and then slowly lifted his head. The demon-man's back was to him. Wrapping his fingers around the wooden sword handle, Ahren lifted the blade. Water poured off him as he rose.

Dolch stopped and turned. His one eye widened is surprise, a blade of darkness springing to solidity in his hand.

Clenching his eyes, Ahren raised the soldier's sword and swung, bringing it down hard on the glowing gem lying in the water between them.

A deafening boom erupted, trembling the walls and vibrating the bones in Ahren chest. Hot water splashed across his face as he held tight to keep the sword from flying from his hand. Redness filled his vision behind his tightly closed eyes as the magical gem exploded.

He opened his eyes to see trailing sparks, like miniature comets, shooting across the room, ricocheting off the water and bouncing off the grimy walls. Some sputtered and glowed as they flew burning beneath the muddy waves. A semicircle of hot steel glowed in Ahren's blade where it had struck the gem.

Holding his eye, Dolch staggered back. He screamed in fury and black flames erupted in his open fist.

Ahren surged to his feet and lunged. Blindly, the demon-man threw his cursed fire. Ducking to the side, Ahren swatted it away with his sword. The hot blade steamed and shattered a foot from the hilt.

The bounding sparks began to fade and darkness encroached. Ahren sprang forward. He side-stepped a wild swing of Dolch's black sword and drove the broken blade deep into the man's gut. Blood oozed over the handle and across his fingers. Orange lights grew around them as Ahren stared deep into Dolch's one blue eye and shoved the blade deeper, twisting it upward.

The demon-man's mouth hung open in a shocked stare. The black blade in his grasp wavered then dissipated. He staggered back, the broken sword jutting from his body, and fell into the raging current.

A hand grabbed Ahren's shoulder and he spun around. Three soldiers with torches stood behind him. The leader said something, but Ahren couldn't hear above the ringing in his ears. He shook his head.

"I said, good work," the soldier yelled. "You killed the Black Raven."

Ahren could only stare at him in shock.

"We heard an explosion and got here just in time. Are you okay, sir?"

"I … I killed him," Ahren said, regaining his composure.

The soldier slapped him on the back. "That you did. Come. Let's get out of here before the damned place floods."

Ahren's body ached as the adrenaline wore away. He followed the soldiers down a long passage before coming to a ladder to the surface.

"Good thing we found you," the sergeant said. "What squad are you with, sir?"

"Merchant District," Ahren lied. He pulled himself up the ladder to the raining street above. "Sergeant, how many more men are down there?"

"I don't know." He shrugged. "Maybe a dozen."

"Give me a few minutes to collect myself," Ahren said. "You and your men do a quick sweep. Get our boys out of there before it fills up."

The soldier nodded, and led his men back down into the tunnel. Ahren waited a few moments, enjoying the rain washing away the grime coating his body, then hurried several blocks back toward the Royal Warehouses.

He slowed in an alleyway looking out across the street to the building on which Katze had died. A lone soldier sat on the bench of a horse cart, staring down a narrow passage. A soaked dun tarp lay rolled around a dead body in the back.

Ahren threw his shoulders back and marched toward the cart. "You, what are you doing?"

"Waiting for them to bring the bodies out," the bearded soldier replied.

Ahren jabbed his finger toward the rolled tarp in the back. "Who's that?"

"A girl, sir. The Black Raven murdered her before running into the sewers. He killed a soldier there too."

"Why don't you go help them carry our fallen brother instead of sitting here. Men are dying!"

"B ... but ... the cart, sir," he stammered.

"I'll watch the cart. You go."

The man nodded. "Yes, sir." He scrambled from the bench and hurried down the alley.

Ahren watched him leave, then crawled up onto the bench and drove the cart and Katze's body away.

The next night, Ahren and her father brought Katze outside the city and buried her on a hilltop overlooking the bay. They laid her in her grave dressed in a gown of white, with one of the glowing plamya stones upon her chest. The buyer would have to settle for three of the magical gems instead of five. This one was hers, so the darkness would never touch her again.

Darclyian Circus

"You have blood on these hands," the old woman muttered. Yemda's dry, wrinkled fingers worked their way firmly across Ahren's palms. "Cleaning them is useless. There is more to come."

Wondering if the white-haired crone could hear his thoughts, Ahren's eyes scanned the packed wagon interior around him, trying to think about something other than why he was really there. If she caught so much as a hint about the emerald or the Tyenee, he'd be dead. Unusual baubles lined the narrow shelves beside a white skull above the fold-down bed. Webs of colored glass, bone, and wooden beads draped from the cloth-covered ceiling. Feathers and brass keys hung in a strange pattern above them, giving a vague air of mystery the old witch deliberately sought. Fegmil the circus master stood quietly behind him, and Ahren couldn't help feeling a little discomfort under his unseen gaze.

"What is it you do?" The old woman drew her nail in a pattern through the lines in his palm. "Why are you here?"

"I was a sailor," he answered. "I've traveled the world, but just the coasts. I want to see the land."

Her thin lips seemed to frown at his answer. "Do you speak any tongues other than Mordakish?"

Ahren nodded. "Rhomanic, Mercińan, and a few words of Galestian."

The old woman's eyes narrowed, as if looking through his hands and onto the table beneath. "Mercińan won't really help you since we never leave the mainland."

"That's agreeable with me."

"You fear very little." Yemda tapped below his thumb. "You show loyalty and a need for perfection." She curled Ahren's hands into fists then unfolded them. "You are strong, yet limber. There is grace in you. Tell me Ahren," she said, running her fingers down his, "many people join us because they are running from something. They try to escape, but oft times can bring unwanted danger into our fold. What are you running from?"

Katze's dead face flashed in his mind. "Nothing."

The crone pinched the top digit of his small finger, hard.

She gazed up at Fegmil and nodded.

The circus master squeezed Ahren's shoulder. "Welcome to the Darclyian Circus, my boy."

Ahren turned to face the quellen behind him. Small round mirrors dotted his brightly colored vest and flat-topped cap. "Thank you, Master Fegmil."

The quellen lightly slapped Ahren's arm. "No more of that. Just call me Fegmil." He tugged at the gold hoop dangling from one of his huge, hand-sized ears. "Come, let's introduce you to everyone and find you some work." Pushing through the bead curtain, he opened the wagon door behind him and stepped outside.

"Be careful," Yemda mumbled, "the blood on your hands may soon be your own."

"Thank you." He smiled to the old witch, then set his wide-brimmed hat back on his head and followed the gray haired quellen outside. A ring of brightly painted tents and wagons lay before him. Striped canvas walls stretched between them to keep unpaid visitors from seeing inside. Rows of carts and wagons surrounded the outside and lined the circus entrance. The gray, dingy walls of Lichthafen rose behind them, a stark backdrop to the faire's bright colors.

"No! No! No!" Fegmil yelled to a pair of men hammering tent stakes beside a lashed pig yard. "Put it further down. No one wants to eat beside swine filth." He motioned Ahren to follow and plodded down the muddy lane. "The local idiots are always the same. They travel to be here, arrive two days before we pack up, pay their vending fee, but put absolutely no thought into where they set-up."

Ahren hurried to keep up with the quellen's short legs. They passed vendors selling food and exotic wares from around the world, as well as local farmers and artisans hoping to sell their own goods from small booths.

"Everyone here does their part," Fegmil said. "It's not just the performances, but setting up, maintaining the wagons, feeding and cleaning after the animals." He jabbed a thumb to a group of children pointing at a pair of marsh tigers pacing the bars of their wheeled cage. Bright green Merciñan parrots squawked and hopped around inside the barred wagon beside it. "We also look out for one another. We're a family here."

Ahren followed Fegmil through a flap, and stepped into the inner ring. Rows of benches ran along one side before a straw-strewn track. A pretty blonde girl stood atop a galloping stallion circling the track. Two tall, thick poles rose from inside the ring like ships masts. A shirtless gypsy man and a skinny boy swung across the trapeze between them. A group of sweating workers sat and watched from beside one of the open-sided ale wagons forming the outer wall.

Fegmil marched toward the chattering audience. "I assume everything's ready for tonight?"

"Just about," a greasy-haired man said between his missing front teeth.

The three-foot circus master stopped and flourished his arm up toward Ahren. "Everyone, I want you to meet Ahren. He'll be joining us on the road."

The group nodded in mumbled greetings.

"What do you do, Ahren?" asked a massive Larstlander, his huge muscled arms folded across his chest. Ahren recognized the hulking Northman as Bjornrek, the strongman from the posters outside.

"We're about to find out," Fegmil said. "Drugho!" he shouted up to the gypsy acrobat. "Come here."

The lean gypsy flipped off the trapeze and landed on the taut net stretched between the poles. He grabbed the edge and swung himself down. "What is it?" he asked, tossing his black ponytail over his shoulder.

"This is Ahren. I want to see what you can do with him."

Drugho's brow rose as he inspected Ahren. "Without bending your knees, touch your toes."

Ahren tossed his hat on one of the nearby benches, then bent over and pressed his fists firmly against the ground. Several chuckles came from the men watching.

"That's good," the gypsy said. "Now stand on one foot and hold it."

Ahren did as he was told.

Drugho stood silently watching for over a minute before speaking. "Have you ever worked as an acrobat before?"

"No. But I've worked ship riggings since I was a boy."

The acrobat ran his tongue behind his lower lip. He jabbed his finger at the platform set twenty feet up one of the poles. "Climb up."

Setting his foot down, Ahren crossed the horse track and took hold of the knotted rope hanging from the platform above. He took a breath, then climbed the thick rope to the wooden ledge. As he stood, the pole teetered slightly under his weight. He looked out over the wall surrounding the arena to see the small market erected around the circus and the green countryside beyond. Passersby stopped, trying to glimpse him perform over the canvas wall. Below, the blonde rider stopped her horse and watched.

"Now," Drugho called. "I want you to jump, grab the trapeze, and swing to the other side."

The group of workers laughed, passing jokes and wagers between them. The lovely rider shot them a cold glare but said nothing. Ahren stared at the simple bar hanging ten feet ahead and slightly below him. He licked his lips, tensed his muscles into a small crouch, and leaped.

Stretching outward, he grabbed the bar. His fingers tightened under the sudden strain. He swung, nearly reaching the opposite platform before swinging back the other way. Ahren rocked his weight and pitched himself forward, bringing him closer. Throwing his legs back, he increased the back swing and then sped toward the wooden ledge. As he reached the end of the arc, he released and flew through the air. He cried out as his body hurled upward, missing the platform, then plummeted down into the net below to the cries and laughter of his onlookers.

"That's good enough for me," Fegmil said with a grin. "You'll start training immediately until you're ready to perform. Until then, find Otto; he'll find work for you."

Patrons trickled into the market grounds throughout the day, enjoying entertainment and food while perusing the many booths. As the sun began to wane, their numbers swelled to the hundreds. Music called from the multiple stages and vendor booths. By the light of colored lamps and bright explosions from the fire breathers' performance, customers wandered through the rows of tents and wagons, mesmerized by the intoxicating scent of oils and spiced foods lingering in the air.

Ahren found himself running back and forth between the enclosed circus arena and the performers' wagons with a seemingly endless list of tasks readying for the show. He hurried along the canvas outer wall, his arms loaded with colorful juggling rings, as hawkers and performers worked the mob. His gaze focused on a young girl deftly cutting the purse from a man enthralled in a harlequin's act.

Crime always rose when a circus descended on a city. Some by the workers themselves, most by the local thieves lured by the herds of easy targets with hefty purses. The Darclyian Circus however, brought more than just petty thefts.

"Hey!" Otto yelled, sticking his bald head out between the canvas flaps. "Hurry up."

Squeezing the rings, Ahren jogged to where the stage master waited and slipped inside.

"Stack those by the blue curtain," Otto barked. "Then we need to get the beasts inside."

Together with several of the other workers, Ahren wheeled the tiger pen behind the curtains and walked the Tzalkian elephants over from their corral. He lingered in the back as the show began, running props and keeping an eye out for anyone trying to sneak inside without paying. Felka, the blonde rider he had seen before, performed knife throwing with her father. The audience cheered as gypsy acrobats rode around the ring, doing incredible tricks atop their racing horses. Roaring tigers leaped through flaming hoops, and Drugho and his partner Jan amazed the crowd with aerial flips and balancing acts high above the ground. All the while, Fegmil worked the audience and orchestrated the show.

The Darclyian Circus held the reputation of being the greatest of its kind. Yet the masters of the Tyenee had discovered a pattern of elaborate heists wherever the performers played. Four weeks prior in the city of Stromfurt, the Vuschkuls Heart, a massive emerald, vanished during the circus's visit. Baron Czychlret awaited the gem in Frobinsky, and Ahren's orders were to intercept the stone before the thieves could deliver it. Finding it, however, would be the real feat. Until then, he had no choice but to play his part.

Two days later, the performers packed their tents into their brightly painted wagons and left the city behind. The caravan crawled along the muddy highway, stopping at the occasional village to give small shows and trading for fresh supplies. Most nights were spent on the road, circled in a ring where they rehearsed their acts, while trading stories and gossip.

Ahren plunged himself into their fold, helping fix wagon wheels, tending the horses, and practicing with anyone who would teach him. Some of the performers, like Drenryck, the tiger master, did little to welcome him. Drenryck spent most of his time with his wife Gerta and their son, who rarely left their wagon. However, many of the other workers welcomed Ahren's enthusiasm and encouraged his acceptance.

Slipping deeper into their circle of trust, he found himself invited into different wagons to enjoy games and gossip over drinks. They told him of dimwitted patrons buying counterfeit goods thought to be from distant lands, and laughed at the exploits of their pickpockets while their victims watched the shows. Yet none of the intoxicated workers ever alluded to the grander thefts Darclyian Circus was suspected of. Ahren simply laughed along with the tales, occasionally sharing stories of his own minor thefts and burglaries.

"You're doing much better," Drugho said patting Ahren on the back.

Ahren looked back at the taut ten-foot line he'd just walked stretched between the tree stumps. "Thanks."

"Once you can get that five times without falling, we'll put you up on the long one. Until then, keep practicing." The gypsy hopped off the stump and headed to the main fire ring, joining the group circled around the cooking supper while working on their costumes and goods to be sold in the fair.

Ahren started down the stretched rope once again when Felka strolled past. She stopped to watch. He smiled to her, but a faint breeze rushed past, causing the rope to wobble beneath him. Keeping his breathing steady, Ahren maintained his balance until it stilled, then continued to the other side.

Felka clapped her hands. "Magnificent."

Ahren leaped, somersaulting off the three-foot stump and landing with a dramatic bow. "I was about to say the same to you," he said, plucking a purple flower and holding it out.

"Now *that* is a performance," said Fegmil's voice behind him. Ahren turned to see the tiny circus master saunter over from beside his wagon. A ribbon of gray smoke trailed from his wooden pipe. "The dismount is essential. Just because your trick is done is never an excuse to stop entertaining." He drew a long pull from his pipe. "The flower is a nice touch. Danger and romance always draws a crowd."

Felka's pale cheeks reddened. She accepted the flower from Ahren's hand, nodded tersely, and hurried off.

The quellen sighed. "Love, my friend, like anything in a circus, is not without its own risks."

Ahren chuckled. "I mean no harm by it."

"I'm sure you don't. Just remember, she can cut that flower's stem with a knife at fifteen paces. Her father, Achim, can do the same while riding horseback." He puffed and blew a cloud of smoke into the breeze. "You should know; I've seen you practicing with them."

Ahren nodded.

"But I'm not here to father you. In fact, I wanted to say you're one of the fastest learners I've seen in years. So good, that I think you're ready to start."

"Thank you."

Fegmil smiled. "We'll reach Kiedow in a week's time. Some of our riders will go on ahead tomorrow to choose a site and hang posters. This'll be a real show. Not one of these little village acts we've been doing. So you better be ready."

"I will be," Ahren said. "I'll do whatever you need me to do."

The Gremiskian mountains loomed closer as the caravan continued south down the narrow highway. Small villages grew more frequent, and at each one, a group of performers would break off for a few hours to dazzle the peasants and spread word of the upcoming show.

The evening sun lay low, casting long shadows across the rocky peaks when they finally reached the city built up along a mountain's side. They turned off the road and stopped in a wide pasture just outside the main gates. Fegmil and Otto hopped from their wagons, immediately issuing orders. Ahren hurried through the shifting maze-work of carts and tents, carrying poles and equipment. Lanterns and torches bathed the scene in golden light as the sun set behind the city. Songs and laughter echoed through the chaotic grounds amongst shouts and the pounding of mallets. Ahren stretched colorful canvas between the wagons surrounding the miniature city. His stomach growled at the growing sweet aromas of food wafting between the lanes. Benches were set, banners raised, and corrals lashed. As dawn broke over the mountains, the Darclyian Circus was ready to begin.

Ahren spent the next several days working a mixture of various tasks. He cleaned all the animal pens save the tigers' cage, which Drenryck insisted on doing alone. Whenever his tigers were not on display, the tiger master lowered the wooden awning over the wheeled cage, preventing anyone from seeing inside.

While running errands or selling trinkets in the small booths took a large portion of Ahren's days, he spent just as much time performing. He worked the crowds with balancing acts throughout the day, and at night, in the large arena, he swung from the trapeze above the audience, warming them up before Drugho and Jan's spectacular act.

After the show, many of the performers ventured into the city at night. Ahren accompanied some of them the first two nights, but then elected to stay at camp. Once most of the workers had left or gone to their beds, he snuck from his tent and broke into the empty wagons. He searched Fegmil's first. The fastidious quellen kept detailed books and records amongst an impressive collection of trinkets and oddities from across the world. Ahren checked for hollow books, and secret compartments. A hidden cache built in the rear wall yielded several bags of silver, yet the emerald wasn't there. Cracking open the door, he confirmed no one was outside, then hurried from the wagon.

Otto's cramped wagon reeked of onions and mildew. Ahren quickly dug through the stage master's belongings but found nothing. Outside a group of drummers gathered around a campfire and began to play. Carefully, Ahren slipped out the back and crept away as others wandered to join in the revelry.

He meandered away from the commotion and snuck into one of the storage wagons forming the large performance ring. Its lack of windows left the interior dark, forcing him to slow his search. He'd just about finished when a muffled whimper came from outside.

"Where's Fegmil?" someone hissed.

"He's coming." Ahren recognized Otto's distinct graveled voice. "What happened?"

"Jan and Drugho had made it inside when I heard shouting," Bjornrek answered, his Larstlandic accent heightened with the excitement in his voice.

"Pl … please get it out," a man mumbled painfully.

"Don't touch it!" Otto snapped. "Someone get Yemda. She can help him. Tell me what happened."

"Saint Vishtin, he's bleeding all over the place!"

"I hurried back around," Bjornrek continued, "and saw a man running from the house screaming for guards. He had a bow in his hand."

"Bastard was in the house," Drugho growled. "We didn't even see him."

Torchlight moved outside and Ahren sank further back into the shadows inside the wagon.

"What happened?" Fegmil demanded.

"Jan was shot!" the gypsy answered.

"How?"

"There was an apprentice or someone inside. He shot him and fled, but Bjornrek got him as he ran for help."

"I don't … want to die," Jan sobbed. "Get it out of me."

"Don't worry. Help is coming."

"Did you get the eagle?" Fegmil asked.

"Yeah," Achim answered. "Then we broke off the arrow. Bjornrek put his cloak over him and carried him out the gates."

Jan's sobs grew more struggled. "Please. Please."

"Hold on, my boy," Fegmil soothed. "We'll fix you. Did anyone else see you?"

"I don't think so," Bjornrek said.

"Get something to stop the bleeding!" Drugho snapped.

Ahren's heart raced as footsteps hurried toward the wagon. He dove behind a long box and pulled a folded tarp halfway over him. Orange light flickered off the walls as someone stepped inside. A box of iron stakes crashed to the floor as they dug through one of the shelves and hurried out.

"Jan? Jan!" Drugho yelled.

"He's dead."

Ahren crouched lower during the long silence and pulled the rest of the heavy tarp over himself.

"Otto," Fegmil said. "You and Bjornrek bury him. Somewhere no one will find him until after we're gone. I'll hide the eagle before anyone comes looking for it."

"What about Kossintry?" Achim asked.

Drugho snorted. "What about it?"

"The tower. Who's going to replace Jan?"

"He's right," Fegmil mumbled. "Who else can do it?"

"Kerlen can."

"Are you sure?" the quellen asked. "What about Ahren?"

"Ahren's too new. Kerlen has proven himself."

"Fine. Tomorrow we'll say Jan got killed in a tavern brawl. Meanwhile, we'll tell Kerlen the plan. You've got six weeks to get him ready." He sighed. "Now go."

Ahren remained still while the men dispersed. He'd found the inner circle, but still didn't know where they hid their stolen treasure. Earning their trust would be a harder task. A plan began to form in his mind. Once everyone had left the performance ring outside, Ahren crept from the wagon and hurried back to his bed.

"Good," Drugho said, sitting on Kerlen's shoulders as the younger acrobat rose to his feet while standing on Bjornrek's. The gypsy stood and reached for the platform above him when Kerlen buckled, sending the tower of bodies to the ground.

"I'm sorry," Kerlen said leaping to his feet to help Drugho up.

"It's all right," Drugho replied, through a forced smile. "It's a difficult move. Are you all right Bjornrek?"

The muscled man brushed the blond hair from his eyes and staggered to his feet. "Fine." He returned to where he had been standing and lowered to his knees.

"Can I try that?" Ahren asked, walking from the wagon he'd been leaning against.

Drugho shook his head. "Maybe next time. This is something I want Kerlen to learn."

Ahren shrugged. "Then let me take *your* place. You can instruct us from the ground. Maybe get a different perspective on what we're doing wrong."

The gypsy stood silent for a moment, then gave an amused smirk and a sweeping gesture. "Go ahead."

"Thanks." Ahren waited while Kerlen crawled up onto the Larstlander's shoulders and then climbed up onto his. He swayed, trying to keep his balance

Kerlen slapped his leg twice, "Up."

Bjornrek slowly rose to his feet.

Ahren's muscles tensed as he tried to keep from falling off the acrobat's shoulders. Once the Northman reached his full height and planted his feet securely down, Ahren braced himself as Kerlen slowly moved his feet up onto Bjornrek's shoulders and stood. Their bodies trembled, struggling to keep balance.

"Keep your knees stiff," Drugho ordered. "Rise in one motion."

Once they had reached a precarious equilibrium, Ahren held his breath, and carefully rose. Kerlen held Ahren's feet firmly against his shoulders as Ahren reached out and took a firm grip on the rough-hewn platform above him.

"Perfect." Drugho hollered. "Now hold tight. Kerlen, climb up."

Ahren felt the man beneath him shift and grab hold of his hip and slide out from under Ahren's feet. A sudden jolt of weight hit as the young acrobat pulled himself up. Ahren's fingers dug into the planks. Kerlen's legs wrapped around Ahren's dangling feet as he adjusted his hold, then climbed up over Ahren's back and onto the platform, nearly kicking him in the face.

Drugho clapped his hands once. "Ahren, swing up."

Taking a quick breath, Ahren pulled himself up and threw

his legs over the lip of the creaking ledge. He looked back with an accomplished smile to see the dark-skinned gypsy man pursing his lips.

"Clumsy, but you did it. You must make it effortless. Fluid." He snapped his fingers five times in rhythmic succession. "It should take that long to begin and end the trick. Now climb down and start again."

Weeks passed as the caravan continued south, leaving Mordakland and passing into Rhomanny. Ahren's skills grew in great strides, then slowly honed as he religiously practiced with acrobats, trick riders, and knife throwers. By the time the circus reached Kossintry, his determination and persistence had earned him their respect and trust.

As usual, they made camp outside the city walls, allowing enough room for the fair-goers to gather. Ahren worked tirelessly, setting up everything he could outside the wood and canvas-walled performance ring. Otto tried to get him to help with the trapeze lines, but Ahren was busy with Felka, erecting smaller stages for the other acts.

The white moon glowed high in the night sky by the time the grounds were finished. Exhausted, the workers retired to their tents and wagons as soon as their chores were complete. Ahren lingered in the camp, finding menial tasks to do while everyone else went to bed. Once they were asleep, he circled around behind the performance ring and squeezed under one of the tight cloth panels.

Crickets sounded inside the circular arena, lit by only the frosty moonlight. Ahren wove between wooden benches, past the horse track, and up to one of the massive poles standing at its heart. Grabbing hold of the thick knotted rope, he quickly scaled up to the platform above. He looked out across the grounds visible over the arena wall, checking for anyone still lingering about, then climbed to the top platform.

The poles swayed gently under his weight, a sensation he barely noticed anymore. Ahren grabbed one of the thick, taut lines suspended between the mast-like posts, swung his legs up, and crawled upside down over the empty arena. Weaving past the hanging ropes connected to hoops and trapezes, he stopped at a dark rope securely knotted to the support line. The loose rope ended at a pair of swirl-painted bars hanging on a hook above the highest acrobat platform. Drugho used them for his grand trick that only he could do. Ahren locked his legs tight around the taut rope and let go. With his hands free, he hung upside down and worked the tight knot holding the trapeze. The gypsy acrobat always inspected the lines when setting up, but now that it was finished, no one would see the slipknot Ahren tied in its place. He cinched the knot tight; making sure it could support some weight, then crawled back to the creaking poles and climbed back down.

If blame for the knot's failure would be cast, it would fall only on those who set up the lines, leaving Ahren a solid alibi. With a smile, he hurried out of the arena and back to his bed.

Farmers and merchants poured in the next morning, erecting tents and pens. Ahren and the other acrobats watched from atop their platforms as the faire spread out around the multi-colored ring. The smells of cooked meats wafted through the air, making his stomach rumble as they neared the end of their pre-show practice.

Once his portion was complete, Ahren twirled from the trapeze and onto the net below. He took his time, helping set up the seats and moving props as Drugho began his crowning stunt. The gypsy leapt off the highest platform in a spinning flip and caught Kerlen's hands as he swung upside down off a trapeze. The two men sailed back and forth with increasing speed before Drugho flipped away, catching and spinning off the hanging bars. Ahren held his breath as the gypsy flew upward, catching the lowest bar on his personal trapeze. The knot held as Drugho swung out over where the crowd would sit, then back around. The dark-skinned acrobat flipped upside down as he flew past again. His legs opened, readying for the final trick when the rope popped free, sending Drugho hurling out into the air. His arms flailed, trying to correct his fall as he crashed into the hard wooden benches.

"Drugho!" Ahren yelled, racing to where his master had fallen. Blood ran down the gypsy's face as he lay across one of the tipped benches, an arm bent sharply just above the elbow. No telling how many other bones were broken.

"Is he all right?" Otto shouted as he and the other workers swarmed around them.

Ahren slid his fingers along Drugho's neck. "He's alive. Someone get Yemda!"

"Saint Vishtin," Fegmil muttered, stomping out of Drugho's green and purple wagon. "A catastrophe."

"How is he?" Ahren asked.

The small quellen looked up with a start to see Ahren sitting on a nearby barrel. "He'll heal. But it'll be months before he can perform."

Ahren sighed. "What do we do?"

"You and Kerlen will have to step in for him. The show can never stop. Just check the rest of those ropes before you go."

"Kerlen and Vifel already did."

"Good." Fegmil stood still, tugging his moustache. "You told me that you'd do anything I asked," he said, apprehension accenting his voice.

"Just tell me what you need done."

The circus master peered around them, then gestured Ahren to follow. They meandered through the narrow lanes and stopped between a pair of empty carts.

"As you've seen, some of our income isn't the honest type," Fegmil said.

"I've seen." Ahren shrugged.

Fegmil nodded. "A few cut purses help feed everyone, but that's not enough to keep this show going. Sometimes we have to do something a little more daring."

Ahren leaned closer. A shiver slithered up his spine despite his ignorant façade. "How do you mean?"

"By now you understand that we're all a family … at least, I *hope* you do."

"I do," Ahren assured.

"Good. We have a lot of mouths to feed and a lot of expenses to keep everything together. There's a good deal of talent in our family as well, talent that provides for everyone else."

"How?"

Scratching his chin, Fegmil scanned around. "Burglary," he

whispered. "There's but a few of us involved; the most trusted. Understand?"

"I do."

"Drugho is part of it. But with his arm …"

"What do you need me to do?" Ahren purred.

Fegmil's gray eyes twinkled. "After the show, we'll give you the details. You've got four nights to get ready." He patted Ahren on the leg. "Until then, get back to work."

Felka blew a wisp of golden hair from her eyes and hurled her leaf-bladed dagger at the target board a dozen paces in front of her. It spun through the air and stuck into the pine planks with a hard *thwack*, severing the red string pulled tightly across it.

"Wonderful," Ahren said, clapping his hands. Approaching the board, he surveyed his own three blades jutting from the knife-chewed planks, the furthest no more than two finger-widths from his own intact string. Frustrated, he ripped the daggers free.

"You're getting better," she said as Ahren handed her back her single blade. Hoots and cheers erupted outside the canvas-and-wagon wall circling the arena. Drenryck always drew applause from the mid-day crowd.

"So are you," he laughed. "Pretty soon, I'll have to blindfold you if I'm to stand much chance of winning."

Felka's sea-blue eyes mischievously winked. "That could be interesting."

Ahren swigged water from his clay tankard on the bench beside them, then threw his first dagger. It thudded into the board, just a hair below the mocking red string.

"Almost," she said.

Chewing his lip, Ahren readied his second dagger when Fegmil and Drugho strode through the flap into the ring.

"Ahren," the gypsy snapped. He carried his slung arm against his stomach like a tiresome burden. "Stop playing and get to your stretches. You have half an hour until your ale-stage performance." His swollen purple eye had barely healed since his fall three days prior.

"Right away," Ahren said, still miming his throw.

Fegmil gave a low cough as he sauntered over. "After the big show, change clothes and meet us in here. We'll get a good look at where we're going tomorrow night."

"Any hint as to what we're doing?" Ahren asked.

The little quellen shrugged. "Goldsmith."

Ahren hurled the dagger. The tip of the sharp blade buried into the plank and the cut string fluttered down. "I'll be there."

Weak applause celebrated Ahren's success as he stepped off the tightrope and onto the twelve-foot tripod across the stage. "Thank you, thank you," he said in Rhomanic. "If you enjoyed my act, the chink of coin is the best praise to hear. So enjoy the faire and the wonders from around the world, but don't forget to catch the main show this evening in the arena." A pair of young girls quickly circled around to the back of the crowd with open hats, begging for tips before the audience could easily escape.

Ahren slid down a rope onto the stage and ripped off his hat with a flourish. He managed to coax a few coppers from straggling patrons before enthusiastic, bell-ringing hawkers and the aroma of roasting lamb seduced them away.

"Very impressive," said a slender man, dropping a silver into Ahren's hat. A purple scar running from the corner of his lip was all that marred his unassuming demeanor.

"Thank you. I'm happy to have entertained you," Ahren said with a smile.

The gentleman scanned out over the fairgrounds. "Tell me. Would you mind showing me where to find the exotic birds? There's one specimen I very much wish to see."

"Of course." Ahren scooped the coins from his hat and pulled it back over his head. "Which one?"

"The Black Raven."

Ahren chuckled, hiding the sudden tightening in his chest. "But all ravens are black."

A half-smile drew across the man's thin lips as he pulled a bronze pendant partially out from under his open doublet. The Tyenee stamp marked the medallion's face. "Not all of them."

"Ah," he whispered, tension melting. "Let me take you there."

They slipped through the crowd beside one of the wheeled bird coops, halting where no one was. A group of young men stood cavorting at the neighboring tiger cage fifteen feet away.

"My name is Karrem," the man said, watching an icy-blue parrot chew seeds from a clay bowl. "I came to find out how everything was faring. I assume by your little show that you haven't found it yet."

"Not yet. But I'm close. I've infiltrated the thieves."

"Close isn't what we need." Karrem reached through the wire bars and stroked one of the bird's long tail feathers. The irritated parrot waddled away down its perch. "You'll be in Frobinsky in a just a few weeks. By then it'll be too late."

The boisterous boys wandered over to where Ahren and Karrem stood. The two men casually strolled over to the tiger cage. The two massive cats lay inside, silently watching the newcomers.

"We're breaking into a goldsmith's tonight," Ahren muttered.

"Luvrncheck's?" Karrem asked, amused.

He nodded. One of the tigers rolled to its feet and began pacing along the bars of its tiny cell.

"How?"

"It doesn't matter." Ahren glanced back over his shoulder for anyone nearby. "Once we get the goods, I'll see where they hide them. Then the Vuschkuls Heart is ours."

"You have until tomorrow night," Karrem growled. He cracked his knuckles slowly as a man and woman strolled past. "If you can't get it before the circus leaves, the Tyenee have other methods of getting it."

"Such as?"

"Highwaymen. It's messy, but effective in emergencies." Ahren swallowed at the thought of everyone being butchered over a single emerald. The green-eyed tiger stopped and stared at him, as if somehow understanding the possibility. "That won't be necessary," Ahren managed.

"I hope not. I have a cooper shop by the Narenset Oratory within the city. Come there if you have any problems or once you have the stone." Without another word, Karrem turned and walked away.

Shadows flickered across the nighttime arena, cast red under the light of lamps hanging along the inner walls. An orange half-moon peeked over the horizon. Tingles of excitement and anticipation ran across Ahren's skin as he stepped through the flap. Fegmil stood beside one of the rough-hewn benches speaking to Achim and Bjornrek, while Kerlen, Otto, and Drenryck quietly listened.

The circus master clapped his hands and smiled as he spied Ahren approaching. "There he is. Ready, my boy?"

"I am," Ahren said with a nod.

"Perfect. There's been a slight change."

Ahren's brow creased.

"What?"

"Nothing important," the quellen said with a dismissive wave. "Achim will accompany Drenryck on another errand, so Felka will be joining you as lookout. She's readying the cart outside."

"I see."

"Good." Fegmil tugged his graying moustache as he looked everyone over. "Make it fast. Good luck."

"We'll be back in two hours," Bjornrek said, rising to his feet. The massive Larstlander snapped his fingers. "Let's go."

Ahren and Kerlen hurried after the hulking strongman out the back to where Felka waited beside the horse corral with a wooden cart filled with straw. She smiled as Ahren approached, then took the handles and followed them toward the city.

"Are you ready for this?" she whispered over the squeaking wheels.

Ahren nodded. "Have you done this before?"

"Many times," she chuckled.

The city guards barely looked up from their posts as the four circus workers passed through the massive arched gates. Few travelers strolled the dark streets, gathering mostly at small pubs and taverns. The cartwheels bounced and shook down the winding, cobbled roads leading deeper into the city. A towering statue of a warrior, his sword raised to the heavens, stared silently down as the thieves passed through a square and followed a dark lane's gradual slope. Elaborate knockers of iron and bronze adorned the sturdy doors lining the streets. Birds erupted from a dark belfry as it chimed the hour. They swarmed around the onion-domed steeple until it fell silent, then returned to their roosts.

The road leveled out and turned. After several more empty blocks the street split around an island of stone before coming back together. A square tower jutted up from the small slice of land. Granite posts connected by a thick, twisted chain encircled the property, discouraging anyone from crossing the six-foot span between the street and the tower walls. Dark, narrow windows looked out from the second and third floors. Ironbound double-doors closed off the front of the fortress. Above them, a carved woman held a wooden sign by a golden chain.

Luvrncheck's held the reputation as the finest goldsmith in Kossintry if not all of Rhomanny. Its customers included nobles and kings, and it was said a wedding ring crafted by Luvrncheck's smiths would ensure happy marriage and strong sons. As its renown grew, so did the threat of thieves. To protect themselves, the owners erected the imposing tower capable of staving off armed invaders, let alone courageous burglars. In its four-century history, Luvrncheck's had yet to be robbed.

After checking that no one was on the streets, Felka stopped the cart along the curb beside the building. Stepping over the swinging chain, the three men hurried to the wall. Bjornrek dropped to his knees and Kerlen instantly mounted his shoulders. With a quick jump, Ahren hopped up onto the acrobat's back and held his breath as the three of them all stood at once. The slit-like window above flew closer and Ahren grabbed onto the stone windowsill and clicked his tongue, signaling Kerlen to go. The slender man quickly scaled up Ahren's body and slid through the narrow opening. His hand grabbed onto Ahren's wrist and helped him inside.

Blocky shapes loomed in the darkness. Allowing his eyes to adjust, Ahren slowly made out long tables strewn with braziers and unusual equipment mounted to the oaken planks. Rows of intricate tools lined the walls. He quietly wove his way through the workroom and listened at the door.

Hearing nothing, he signaled Kerlen, and the two men began rummaging through the workshop.

Ahren ignored the gold chains laid out across the table beside him and moved to a massive iron-bound oak cabinet bolted against the far wall. Kerlen stuffed half-finished rings and other baubles into an empty sack as Ahren removed the picks from his pouch and began working on one of the three huge locks on the armoire doors.

Kerlen had finished his looting and tossed the burlap sack out the narrow window by the time Ahren managed to pop open the difficult locks. The old hinges groaned as he pulled the heavy doors wide. Brass-handled drawers filled the interior. Ahren pulled one open and gasped to find it filled with small gold bars, not much larger than his thumb. Removing an empty bag from his belt, he scooped the heavy ingots and dropped them inside. He tied it shut and handed it to Kerlen before taking out the second empty sack. Ahren dumped the last of the gold bars into the bag and started on a drawer of silver ones as Kerlen barely glanced out the open window before dropping the treasure below.

"You!" someone shouted outside. "What are you doing?"

Ahren hurried to a narrow window to see a soldier racing to the cart where Felka and Bjornrek stood.

The soldier jabbed a gloved finger at the bulging sack in Felka's hands. "Thieves!"

"You're mistaken," Bjornrek laughed, taking a step closer. The muscles beneath his dun shirt flexed, readying to strike.

"Stop!" The soldier ripped his sword from its sheath. "Don't move!"

Biting her lip, Felka's hands traced closer to a bulge at her waist. Her hesitation only affirmed Ahren's suspicion she'd never used a blade for more than show. Ahren thought of the flat dagger hidden in his boot, but didn't have time. Swinging the half-empty bag in his hand he hurled it down at the soldier still advancing toward the Northman.

The heavy sack sailed down, smashing into the side of the guard's helmet, knocking it from his head. Gold and silver bars exploded out, glinting briefly in the air before scattering across the cobbles like tinkling hailstones. Dropping his sword, the stunned soldier staggered and fell.

"Quick," Ahren hissed, turning to Kerlen beside him. "Down!"

The two thieves slipped through the window, grabbed the bottom ledge, and dropped to the ground below. A sharp yelp came from behind. Ahren spun to see Bjornrek skewer the guard with his own sword.

"Let's go!" Ahren snapped at Kerlen, reaching for the small ingots scattered across the ground. Shouts of alarm came from the darkened streets behind them as the four thieves escaped up the road, hurrying for the city gates.

"Idiot," Bjornrek growled after passing through the gate. "You didn't see him walking down the street?"

Kerlen remained silent, his eyes downcast.

"We had to leave over half the gold, and could have been caught!" The Northman's hateful glare could have crushed stone.

Ahren held his tongue as he pulled the squeaking cart behind them. Kerlen's carelessness was inexcusable, but no more than murdering the guard. The penalty for being caught had raised tenfold with the soldier's death.

"I want to thank you," Felka whispered, jolting Ahren from his thoughts.

"For what?" he snorted. "Losing half the treasure?" They turned off the dirt road and into the empty fairgrounds. Fat pigs stirred in their filthy pen as the thieves passed.

"But I know why you did it," she said flatly. "And I'm grateful."

Ahren guiltily smiled. "Don't worry about it."

Felka licked her lips. "You need to leave."

"What?"

Felka swallowed. Her lip trembled as if struggling to speak. "Something bad is going to happen. You need to go."

Ahren's brow creased in confusion at the young woman's terrified expression.

"Here we are," Bjornrek said, stopping at the tigers' caged wagon. Heavy locks hung from the lowered wooden awning, preventing anyone from seeing inside.

"What do you mean?" Ahren asked.

The grinning Larstlander pulled a brass key from his purse. "This is where we keep the treasure." Hinges screeched as he opened the rear door. "Nice and safe."

Ahren backed away, waiting for one of the beasts to lunge from the shadows.

"It's safe," Bjornrek laughed. "See for yourself."

Cautiously, Ahren approached the open door and peeked into the dark wagon. Something moved in the back. Squinting, he made out the shape of a man lying inside on the straw-strewn floor. The figure rolled over, revealing Karrem's bloodied face staring back at him. Ahren's eyes widened in terror. Something hard smashed into the back of his head and everything went black.

A muted scream roused Ahren from unconsciousness. His skull throbbed in dull pulsing pain. He reached up to feel the swollen lump, but coarse rope bound his hands behind him. Filthy straw came into focus as he opened his eyes. A hard thud followed by another muffled cry came from behind him. Rolling over, he found himself locked in the tiger cage, now inside the performance arena.

A small crowd had gathered behind Achim. Karrem stood tied and gagged against a target board twenty feet before him. A dozen daggers protruded from his body. The curly haired knife-thrower twirled a slender blade in his hand before hurling it. The dagger whipped through the air and imbedded into oaken planks. Karrem's severed finger fell to the ground to the roar of cheers and laughter. Icy terror flooded Ahren's veins. He twisted against his tight bonds, trying to loosen them enough to reach the dagger he still felt hidden in his boot.

Gerta, the tiger tamer's wife, glanced away from the macabre entertainment and smiled as her gaze fell on Ahren. "He's awake!"

"There you are, my boy," Fegmil said. "Just in time to see your friend's finale."

"What is this?" Ahren demanded, twisting against the coarse rope.

"Don't you know?" the quellen laughed. "This is the final performance of the Black Raven." Fegmil lifted a bulging sack. "Isn't this what you were looking for, Black Raven?" He removed a sparkling green emerald the size of his small fist. The massive stone glittered in the orange lamplight. "We took you in, and you betrayed us."

"He saved me in the city," Felka shouted. Tears traced down her pale cheeks.

"No, child." Achim drew another blade. "A hunter will spare a wolf if he thinks it will lead him to the pack."

"Enough!" Fegmil yelled. "Achim, finish that one off. He bores me. It's time for Ahren to pay for his crime."

The knife thrower hurled his dagger into Karrem's throat. Blood burst from around the blade as the wounded man struggled against his bonds. Bjornrek yanked open the tiger cage door, grabbed Ahren's ankle, and dragged him out.

Ahren drew his legs tight, then kicked the strongman hard in the chest. Bjornrek's grip loosened and Ahren twisted from his grasp.

"Get him!" Fegmil screamed.

His hands still bound, Ahren rolled from the lunging Northman and scrambled to his feet. Achim readied his dagger. As Ahren passed one of the thick trapeze poles, he feigned a stumble, lifting his chin and exposing his throat. The sharp blade flew through the air and Ahren ducked just in time for it to hit the wood behind him. Dodging another of Bjornrek's swings, Ahren reached behind him, grabbed the dagger and cut his bonds.

An iron-like fist smashed into his jaw, sending him to the ground. Still holding the blade in one hand, he scooped up a fistful of dirt and lurched away before the Northman could grab hold. Leaping up, Ahren whirled around and threw the gritty dirt into Bjornrek's eyes. Ahren ducked to the side and hurled his blade into Achim's shoulder as the knife thrower prepared for another attack.

Furious cries filled the arena as the circus thieves charged. Shoving Kerlen aside, Ahren dove and tackled Fegmil to the ground. The heavy sack fell from the quellen's grasp, spilling treasure across the trampled, straw-strewn track. A gem-encrusted gold eagle bounced out beside the Vuschkuls Heart. Ahren scrambled for the massive emerald when he heard a terrible growl behind him. He spun around to see Gerta rip away her robe as she fell to her knees. Tiny pimples spread across her body, sprouting orange and black hairs. Frozen in horror, Ahren watched the woman's mouth split open, and her teeth elongate into dagger-like fangs. Behind her, her son Liebren roared as he finished the same transformation.

Fegmil rolled to his feet and drew a short knife from his belt. "Kill him," he ordered, kicking the gem from Ahren's reach.

Ahren sprang to his feet and ran as the half-formed tigress lunged. He punched Drenryck in the gut as he raced past and seized the knotted rope hanging from the acrobat platform above. Clambering up the line, Ahren drew up his legs just as one of the tiger's paws swiped past. Sweat beaded his brow and trickled into his eyes. The rope trembled and Ahren looked down to see Kerlen and one of the other acrobats climbing after him. Ahren reached the top and ripped the flat dagger from his boot. Fervently, he sawed the thick rope until it snapped under the two men's weight, sending them sprawling to the ground below.

Ahren spied the green gem lying before one of the vodka wagons forming the ring. Grabbing a trapeze bar beside him, he leaped to the other side. The rope pulled taut, nearly jerking from Ahren's sweating grasp. He swung wide out to the side and circled around, flying over the enraged mob, let go, and somersaulted through the air. Wood groaned and popped under his sudden weight as Ahren landed atop the wagon and rolled to his feet, almost sliding off the edge. The tigers charged toward him. Roaring and snapping, they clawed the wagon roof eaves. Bottles shattered inside as their heavy bodies knocked against the side, nearly tipping it over. Quickly, Ahren unhooked one of the lanterns hanging at his feet, barely avoiding one of the tigers blurring swipes. He hurled it down at the animals below him. Glass shattered and flaming oil exploded across the wagon, splattering into the beasts' fur. The howling tigers sprang away and rolled, igniting the dry, straw-laden ground.

Ahren jumped off the burning wagon and snatched the emerald before the spreading flames could reach it. He dropped to his knees as a wooden bench sailed past. It smashed into a cargo wagon, knocking its hanging lantern to the ground. Bjornrek grabbed another empty bench and charged, holding it like a ram. Springing to the side, Ahren rolled away as the screaming Northman plowed past. Bjornrek swung the bench like a great club. It whooshed inches from Ahren's head, fanning his hair. He dove forward, shouldering the strongman as Bjornrek awkwardly tried to correct the wild swing. Dropping the heavy bench, Bjornrek crashed backward into the burning oil-soaked hay.

A thunderous crack rang from Drenryck's leather whip. His face contorted in rage, the tiger tamer lashed it out. Ahren threw up his arm to shield himself and searing pain exploded as the whip split it open. Drenryck brought the whip back for another strike, but Ahren hurled his flat dagger into the beast master's gut.

Smoke flooded the arena as wind-fueled flames spread across the stretched canvas walls, igniting the other wagons. Shouts and cries came from both sides of the ring as circus workers struggled trying to contain the spreading blaze. Ahren's watering eyes burned under the thickening smoke. Coughing, he grabbed hold of a nearby wagon and pulled himself to the top. Orange fire sheeted along the wagon's outer side as the burning cloth-covered wall ignited the wooden eaves. Ahren jumped over the licking tongues of fire and rolled to his feet.

Horses whinnied inside their lashed corral as smoke and orange embers blew across the wide field. Ahren hopped the creaking fence and reached for one of the chestnut stallions when a voice screamed behind him.

"Son of a whore!" Otto marched toward him, clutching a rusty cleaver-like hatchet. He chopped the ropes binding the corral gate closed and threw it open. "I'll kill you!"

Ahren stepped back, scanning the ground for something to defend himself with. The bald man charged, holding the hideous weapon high. He reared back to swing but suddenly staggered. The cleaver fell from his fingers and Otto eyes went empty. He fell to the ground, twitching, a dagger handle jutting from the back of his skull. Ahren looked up to see Felka standing, silhouetted in the fiery glow, an unsheathed dagger in her hand. Their eyes met and they stood silently locked in each other's gaze as panicked screams for water echoed around them. She raised the dagger, ready to throw, but stopped.

Keeping his eyes on hers, Ahren grabbed the restless stallion and swung himself onto its back. She remained still. Glass shattered and flames plumed from one of the burning vodka wagons.

"Come with me," he said, extending his hand.

The uncertainty in her eyes melted and she lowered her blade.

Ahren edged the impatient steed closer. "Let's go."

She took his arm and he pulled her behind him. She held tight to Ahren's hips and he kicked his heels into the horse's sides. Thick smoke blanketed across the grassy fields. They rode from the city, the galloping hooves drowning out the cries. Her arms circled snugly around him as they crested a low hill, leaving the burning ruin of the Darclyian Circus behind.

Born of Darkness

The soft strum of the minstrel's dulcimer trickled through the dim tavern below the steady drone of voices and clinking tankards. Burning logs popped and crackled in the fireplace behind the bearded performer, casting long shadows across the room. Smoky tallow candles, mounted on unsanded columns flickered dimly. Dice clattered across a table, followed by hoots and laughter from the huddled audience.

Seated in a far corner, beneath the stairs to the second floor, Ahren sipped his lukewarm ale. Carelessly, he gazed over the decades of graffiti scratched across the weathered table. Shadows wormed across the booth's wall. Ahren pretended not to see them. He sighed, then finished his clay tankard and slid it to the table edge. After weeks aboard ship, sailing to the city of Destri to deliver a strongbox for the Tyenee, a solitary ride across the country to Ralkosty was just what he needed.

A beer maid set a tankard brimming with stale swill on the table. Ahren handed her a pair of coppers and the weary-eyed wench winked, snatched his empty cup, and hurried away with a swish of her blue skirts. Her shadow from the candles behind her seemed to hesitate for a brief instant before fleeing under the direct light. Ahren shook his head and swigged the tankard, dismissing the animated shades as the products of ale and exhaustion.

It wasn't the first time he had witnessed sentient shadows. He could still see Katze's soft face, framed between black curls. No woman had ever haunted his memories as she did. And no woman ever would again.

"Pardon me, good sir," said a boisterous voice.

Startled, Ahren turned to see a stout, square-bearded quellen standing beside the table. At almost four feet, he stood taller than most of his kind. Muscles bulged beneath the quellen's tan shirt and his short arms appeared even thicker than Ahren's.

"Yes?" Ahren said.

"My name is Wyrin." The sour reek of wine wafted from his mouth. He removed a bulging leather satchel from his shoulder and set it on the table with a metallic chink. "I'm a blacksmith and wanted to show you some of my wares."

Tradesmen moving from table to table in a tavern were hardly uncommon. Most peddled only small crafts or hocked their personal belongings trying to settle a gambling debt. A few attempted fencing stolen merchandise. But not once had a blacksmith ever approached him in an inn. Ahren gestured to the seat opposite him. "What do you have?"

The quellen hopped up into the seat and shifted nervously before untying the sturdy bag. "Something for everyone," he said, spilling the contents partially across the table. "Spring traps, buckles, ax heads, anything you want."

Ahren picked up a polished ring set in a crude wooden case. He ran his finger along the twisted woven design etched around the sides and the wide top. Ahren pressed a tiny nub on the side and a small hooked blade, no larger than a fingernail, sprung open.

"Ah, that." Wyrin chuckled, dabbing the beads of sweat from his face. "Not overly useful, but effective if needed."

"How much?" Ahren pushed the blade closed until the release button popped back into place.

"Two bishkas."

Ahren's brow rose. Any reasonable smith would demand at least twice that had they crafted it themselves. But the ring's true origin didn't concern him. He removed a pair of gold coins from his purse and handed them to the fidgety quellen.

Wyrin's gaze darted to the bar room and then back to Ahren. "If you liked that ring, you might find this interesting." He handed over a simple dagger sheathed in a dun leather scabbard.

Drawing the blade, Ahren rolled the checker-carved grip down his palm and held it tight. "Very nice." He slid his finger down the deep groove running along the blade. "Good balance."

"Not as flashy as some like, but that's the idea. Twist the pommel."

Ahren turned the mushroom-shaped knob capping the back

end and one half of the dagger's wooden handle opened, revealing a hollow cavity nestled inside. His eyes widened in impressed surprise. He felt along the inside of the smooth niche set through the tang and along the inside of the wood grip on the other side. Carefully, he closed the hinged door and twisted the pommel back into the original position, leaving no sign of the hidden compartment.

Wyrin held out his hand and accepted the dagger back. "I'll wager a man such as yourself might find use for something like that. You'll never find another like it."

"What do you want for it?"

Sucking his lip, the fidgety quellen opened and shut the handle several times before answering. "Eight bishkas."

Ahren set the coins on the table without a moment's hesitation.

Wryin snatched the gold up and handed Ahren the blade. "Thank you. It's been a pleasure doing business. If you are interested in any more of my goods, you should come to my shop." He quickly swept the other merchandise back into his satchel and hurried off. The shadows inside the booth seemed to slink away as the quellen left.

The shadowy image of a woman's soft face seemed to appear then vanish in the corner of Ahren's eye. He blinked and stared at the spot the apparition had been, but saw nothing. Grabbing his tankard, he gulped it empty, trying to wash away the already ale-fueled paranoia and bitter memories. Years before, when he had been an initiate into the Tyenee, he'd thwarted Dolch, a ruthless thief lord with the demon-possessed powers of darkness. Only a few months back they'd met again, the moving shadows returning after Dolch had tracked him to Lichthafen, killing his beloved Katze on a savage quest for vengeance.

Forcing his attention elsewhere, he picked up his newest purchase. The fine dagger itself would have fetched six bishkas in any city. The well-hidden compartment would double that. Ahren twirled it between his fingers, enjoying its exquisite balance. He twisted the pommel, opening the hidden compartment, and a folded scrap of parchment fell onto the table. Puzzled, he picked it up and read the two words written inside.

Help me.

A cool wind blew down the dirt road, fluttering Ahren's hair and rustling the leaves above, as he followed the lane to the blacksmith's shop. The shop itself appeared normal in the moonlight. Yet the round, two-story house against it stood so low that Ahren could touch the eaves with little effort. His fingers slid closer to the dagger at his belt as he stooped and knocked on the sturdy door. A small inset window squeaked open, spilling light across Ahren's face.

Wryin's gray eyes peered through the small portal. "Ah, you came!" A bolt clicked on the other side and the small door swung open. "Please, please. Come inside."

"I came to see your other wares," Ahren said as he ducked through the low doorway into a room a few inches lower than himself. The heavy smell of smoke filled the humble house, fed by the dozens of candles and oil lamps burning from every shelf and tabletop. Polished beaten plates rested beneath many of the burning tapers, collecting spilt wax and reflecting their light in every direction.

The quellen smiled nervously as if trying to play down the excessive décor. "Can I get you something to drink?" He picked up a pewter mug and filled it from an open clay bottle from his small dinner table.

Ahren held up the tiny folded note. "What is this about?"

Wryin's hand trembled as he set the bottle back down with a thud. "I'm damned. Cursed."

Ahren's brow rose. "Cursed?"

"Yes." He handed the drink to Ahren and sat in one of the simple chairs beside the table. "Citavnah, the witch, she's cursed me. Damned me to torment." He lifted the bottle to his lips and gulped two mouthfuls down.

Eager to leave the frustratingly small room, Ahren glanced at the door. Listening to the insane ramblings of a drunken quellen was not how he wished to spend his evening.

"Don't think me mad." Wryin leaned closer and whispered, "The shadows are watching me."

Ahren froze. His notion to leave now washed away in tingling fear. "The shadows?"

The blacksmith nodded. "They follow me. I see them creeping beneath trees, and in windows. They lurk everywhere, surrounding me, waiting for darkness to fall so they can swarm. Don't tell me you can't see them!"

Ahren lowered himself onto a small stool. "How did it happen?"

Wryin swigged the bottle again. "Taddia, my wife, she'd grown gravely ill. Priests, healers, no one could help her. She was dying. I couldn't just stand by, so I went to Citavnah. The villagers would ridicule me for it, but they didn't have to watch her suffer. If you love someone, truly love them, you'd do *anything* for them, wouldn't you?"

Ahren nodded. He lifted the tankard and sipped the bitter vodka.

"Citavnah said she'd help me. She said I'd never lose my Taddia if I followed her instructions. The witch gave me a black gem and told me to fashion it in a curved knife. I could only work on it at night and had to burn the bones of a dead man in my forge, then mix Taddia's blood in the water. So I did it." He ran his hand across his mouth. "I made her the best blade I'd ever forged and when I returned to the witch's house she told me to hurry home and my wife would be with me always."

"What happened?"

"She was dead in our bed when I returned. Gone." He drew a long breath as tears welled in his eyes. "That night, the shadows in our house began to move. Not much at first. I thought it was the ale, but then they became more. I saw Taddia's face in them, watching me from the ceiling beams and under the table. I can hear her voice at night calling for me. Cursing me. I've damned her," he sobbed.

"Have you told anyone about this?

"That I made a deal with a witch?" he laughed. "No. 'Wryin got what he deserved,' they'd say, right before they burned me. It's been three weeks. I can't work in my forge, there's shadows everywhere. So I decided to find someone from outside. Someone who won't think me mad. Someone who can kill that evil witch for what she's done."

"But why me?" Ahren leaned closer. "There were others in the bar. Three men were traveling to Ralkosty; surely they could help you."

"I thought about it," Wryin said, tears running down his leathery cheeks. "But then I saw the shadows. The shadows that follow you."

Ahren swallowed, icy fear creeping up his spine.

"No one sees the shadows following me. No one. But I know you did, and I can see yours. You're damned like me."

A dark tendril wove across the far wall as one of the sputtering candles dimmed. Tingles slithered along the nape of Ahren's neck, urging him to look behind him. Turning his head, he spied a flicker of movement in his own shadow cast from the lamp beside him. He jumped to his feet, nearly cracking his head against the low ceiling. Light spilled across the floorboards, sending the shades fleeing back to the corners and beneath the furniture.

Panting, Ahren gulped down the rest of the tankard. "Tell me where to find this Citavnah. I'll leave in the morning."

Small crimson birds chirped and fluttered in the treetops as Ahren rode down the narrow road the blacksmith had told him to follow. Beams of early sunlight shone through the branches, casting long shadows across the hard-packed trail. The peaceful morning did little to quell Ahren's foreboding dread. Whatever this witch was, Ahren couldn't help but doubt the mere circumstance of meeting Wryin in the tavern. *Where does chance and manipulation meet? Was it fate which gave me the desire to ride across the countryside instead of sailing around? Was the decision to stop in this particular village truly my own?*

An ancient moss-covered stone stood beside the road, its once elaborate carvings now faded and worn to little more than the vague face. Ahren steered his horse down a narrow path between the trees, heading deeper into the forest. Twisted branches hung low over the faint trail, snagging his clothes and forcing him to duck. The canopy above grew thicker, blocking out the sun's warm glow. An eerie silence enveloped the woods. No songbirds called from the trees. No squirrels leaped through the branches. Only the soft rustle of wind-stirred leaves accompanied the horse's slow clomps.

The path crested a low hill, slicking through the remains of a long-forgotten cemetery. Withered gravestones jutted like broken teeth or lay half buried in dirt and leaves. A broken statue watched Ahren ride slowly past, its stone face frozen in piety. Dark pits dotted the tiny graveyard beside mounds of loose soil sprinkled with bleached bones. Snorting, Ahren's horse tugged against its reins. He patted the animal's neck and urged it down the trail.

The agitated horse continued its protests, insistently trying to veer from the shadowy path. They reached a narrow brook softly trickling through a rocky ravine. A rickety bridge, completely hidden beneath an emerald blanket of thick moss, stretched across to the other side. With a loud snort, the horse stopped at the steep bank, refusing to go further. Ahren nudged with his heels and the horse reared up, nearly throwing him. Holding tight, he managed to calm the frightened animal long enough to dismount. It pulled against the reins, its eyes wide with fear. Ahren struggled to tie the leather cords around a slender tree.

Ignoring the horse's whinnies and stomping hooves, Ahren inspected the rotting bridge. Carefully he set his foot on the mossy wood and bounced. It creaked, but held. He drew a breath and hurried to the other side, then continued down the trail.

Thick trees rose like church columns, holding aloft a dark canopy of gnarled branches. Leaves crunched under Ahren's feet as he followed the twisting path over another hill and through a shallow valley. Tingles skittered along his neck. Something moved ahead.

Narrowing his eyes, Ahren peered through the woods to see a cloaked shape standing in the shadows crisscrossing the trail. It stood still, staring back at him with unseen eyes. Ahren stepped closer and the figure vanished.

Startled, he looked around, trying to see where the figure had gone. He spotted the stranger now to the left of him beside a broken tree trunk. A short, curved blade extended from its hand. Ahren reached for his own dagger, but the apparition disappeared.

He whirled around, his heartbeat hammering in his ears. It stood to his right, not twenty feet away. Her pallid, wrinkled face stared at him from beneath the frayed hood. She raised her empty palm and then vanished.

Movement flickered in the corner of his eye and Ahren turned to see the witch beside him, her filthy-nailed fingers reaching for him. He jumped back, but felt a hand on his shoulder. Ahren spun to see the hideous witch behind him. Her hand shot to his throat, then lifted him off the ground.

"Ah," she purred, ripping the dagger from his grip and dropping it to the ground. "Very nice." She slid her blade under the neck of his shirt and sliced it open with an effortless caress. Choking against the witch's iron grasp, Ahren managed to look down. Inhaling deeply, the witch licked her thin lips. Her cool breath wafted across his chest. Citavnah ran her fingers over his skin. Veiny tendrils of flesh had grown around the knife's bone handle, fusing it to her palm, thumb, and little finger.

"No wonder he likes you." Her jagged nails dug into his neck, forcing him to look away. She twisted her grasp to the back of his neck and slid her bladed hand up under his throat. "Let's go." With a hard squeeze to the base of his skull, she marched him through the valley to a gray yurta nestled in a rocky clearing.

She pushed him through the leather door flap into the dark tent. The stink of stale smoke and rotted meat hung in the air. Ahren's eyes adjusted to the darkness, making out the shapes of a small fire pit and several cluttered tables.

"He's here, as you said," she said.

Excellent. A hollow voice answered. *Put him in the box.*

Struggling against the witch's grasp, Ahren tried to glimpse who had spoken, but Citavnah lifted him up. A dirt-caked sarcophagus lay along the far wall beneath a dusty cloth. She yanked open the thick lid and pushed Ahren inside on top of the brittle remains of a skeleton wrapped in rotted rags. Bones crunched beneath him as he fought against her. Her grip tightened around his neck, choking him. Futilely gasping, his head swam and his thrashing legs lost their strength. Still squeezing, she set a polished obsidian mirror at his feet, then slid the lid closed, plunging him into blackness.

Panting, Ahren pushed against the lid. The dry bones cracked under him, stabbing into his back as he pressed, but the heavy stone didn't budge.

He drew a long breath, forcing panic aside. Slowly, he traced his fingers along the seam but found no gaps. He braced himself inside the narrow box and pushed his weight sideways against the lid, but it didn't slide. Something slithered up his leg.

Hello Ahren. The voice rasped from all around him. Airy tendrils, like darkness itself, wormed through his clothes and slid along his skin. *Do you know who I am?*

Clenching his jaw, Ahren suppressed a scream. The darkness stroked up his neck, brushing his ear, quickening his panicked breaths.

Yes, you remember me.

As long as he'd live, Ahren would never forget the demon he'd seen in Dolch's lair, the dark reflection of himself that smiled from inside a black mirror. The evil creature that had possessed the thief master, giving him terrifying powers, was now inside the stone coffin with him.

You're very clever. Strong, smart, passionate. I recognized it the first moment I ever saw you. I could make you powerful, Ahren. More than just human. More than anything that has ever lived. Its seductive voice whispered in his ears like a gentle lover and unseen fingers traced along his lips. *Just let me inside you. Take me in, and I'll give you everything you've ever wanted.*

"You took what I want, bastard!" Ahren spat through clenched teeth. He kicked and twisted, trying to fight the demon from him, but the narrow coffin held him in place.

Did I?

The blackness opened before him, revealing Katze's beautiful face. She stood on a rooftop, her cloak billowing in the night's breeze. The visage dissolved and reformed to her lying naked on his bed, her skin glistening in the candlelight just as it did the first night they had made love.

Is this what you want? Its amused voice continued. *Soft, vulnerable, adoring? I doubt it.*

Katze's image melted away, replaced by a slender, beautiful woman scaling a brick building along a watery canal. Her auburn hair whipped in the wind as she swung onto the roof and quickly dispatched a lax guard with a thrust of her glass stiletto. She turned toward Ahren, as if sensing his gaze, and smiled. She then ran and sprang through an open window and out of sight.

This is your desire. Your urges, your fantasies betray you.

Memories of Karolina played before Ahren's eyes. She writhed atop him, her tight muscular body moving with his. He smelled her sweat on his skin and her firm hands squeezed his as she held him down. The scene changed to him wrestling with her in a dark cellar, fighting for their lives while hidden urges welled within them both. No one had ever touched him as she had. And his desire swelled as if time had never passed since last they'd met. Twice the beautiful assassin has escaped him, the second by his own consent.

Cunning, lethal, strong. Don't deceive yourself, Ahren. You want her, you always have. And only I can give her to you. Let me inside you. Take me in.

"No!" he screamed, scrunching his eyes. The image continued to play before him. He twisted his head, trying to escape it, but to no avail.

You'll be strong. Stronger than Dolch, stronger than anyone alive. Oh how he'll envy your power.

"I killed him!" Ahren growled, still fighting the unseen tentacles prying between his teeth and worming inside his cheeks. "The bastard is dead!"

Is he? The demon laughed. *He'll find amusement in that claim. He loathes you, Ahren. How he wishes your blood on his hands. But no, I forbid him. And when he arrives he'll embrace you as his brother. His stronger, favored brother.*

Ahren's sharp breaths quickened. Living darkness pressed him down, seeping between his lips and up his flaring nostrils. He lashed, kicking against the lid and knocking his head back against the stone floor as he fought it.

Let me in you. Take me and we will be beautiful.

Bones slid and crunched beneath him as Ahren rolled over. Invisible fingers pulled his hair and squeezed his flesh. He struggled, banging himself harder against the stone walls.

You'll see darkness as you can't imagine. Power at your fingers. A god feasting on all your desires. Imagine it and it will be yours.

"No! No!" he screamed. He fought harder, driving bone splinters into his legs with each kick.

The darkness howled back. *Stop fighting! I will have you. What's yours shall be mine. Surrender yourself. Yield to me!*

"Submit, Ahren," Karolina soothed. The phantom image caressed his face. "Take me."

"Never," he cried, fighting away her hand.

Karolina's pale face scowled and her eyes blackened to dark orbs. *"I will have you,"* she wailed in the demon's voice. Inky tentacles writhed inside her mouth then cascaded out, splitting her face apart as they latched onto his.

Screaming in terror, Ahren bucked and fought, wracking his body against the stone prison. The slithering mass squeezed his jaw, prying it open, and hair-like tendrils poured into his mouth. Choking, and gagging, he threw his head back to escape, slamming it against the unyielding stone and knocking him unconscious.

Sweet fragrance and soft moans roused Ahren. Through blurred vision, he made out a pale slender form atop him. Copper hair cascaded over her shoulders. She slid up and down, grinding herself against him. His pulse strengthened and grew with her movements. She lowered her upturned face toward his. Strands of sweat-slicked hair hung across Karolina's cheeks.

"Good to see you again," she purred, her fierce eyes sparkling in the firelight.

He tried to touch her moist skin but couldn't. Tight bonds held his wrists above his head.

She slid her hands up his arms until her firm breasts pressed against his bare chest. "Going somewhere, lover?"

Ahren's breath quickened. Their bodies moved faster in their growing rhythm. He leaned up, running his tongue along her neck and kissing her jaw. A sour tinge of rot tickled his nose, but an intoxicating incense quickly washed it away. Pushing his arms back, he met her body with harder and faster thrusts. Moans of ecstasy, each one louder than before, escaped her lips.

Releasing her grip she sat higher, pressing down against him. He pulled against his bonds and kissed her rounded breasts. Their silky skin felt dry and spongy against his lips.

She bent down and kissed him, tugging his lips with hers. "I'm yours, Ahren. Tell me what you want." Her acrid breath flooded his senses.

Blinking, Ahren's vision cleared to see Citavnah grunting upon him. Folds of wrinkled flesh slid against his. Purple spider webs of dark veins ran through her sagging breasts.

"Tell me," she croaked through chipped yellow teeth. Dingy curls of gray hair hung across her hideous face.

Ahren screamed and struggled against the abrasive ropes at his wrists. The witch continued her movements, uncaring of Ahren's realization. His sharp, panicked breath drew in more of the sweet incense wafting over him, fueling the arousal despite his horror. Citavnah dipped her curved knife into a shallow clay bowl beside the bed, coating it with runny black fluid.

"No, no!" he shouted, still fighting the bonds. She sliced his upper arm and increased her thrusts. An icy heat shot through Ahren's body. Scrunching his face, he screamed and climaxed. Dizzying numbness swept over him and Ahren fell again into unconsciousness.

Ahren's eyes flickered open, followed by a whirling vertigo. He still lay naked, bound to the filthy bed. Shadows danced and swirled across the yurta's walls cast red in the light of dying embers. Drawing a long breath, he closed his eyes, forcing the dizziness to pass.

A pained groan gurgled beside him.

Breathe, child. Breathe.

Ahren craned his head to see Citavnah huddled near the wall, her wrinkled back toward him. She rocked back and forth with heavy breaths, then threw her head back with an agonized wail. The witch twisted her body, revealing a swollen belly. She maneuvered to her knees and dark blood exploded down her pale legs and pooled beneath her.

Terror seized Ahren's gut as he watched the foul witch giving birth to whatever had grown inside her. He twisted the ring on his finger and jammed the small button along the side. The tiny hooked blade sprang open and he began cutting at the coarse rope binding his right arm. Citavnah's loud breaths quickened. The fraying rope snagged the small blade. Steadying the ring with his thumb, Ahren furiously sawed faster.

Shadows writhed along the walls like hornets as the witch let out a shrill cry.

It's coming. Wonderful!

The rope snapped in two. Reaching up, Ahren worked the tight knot still holding his other hand above his head. The harsh bonds loosened. He gritted his teeth in pain and ripped his hand through the tight loop.

Citavnah screamed again, sending the animate shadows swarming toward her. They teemed through the air around her like whirling wisps of smoke.

Fervently, Ahren untied his ankles, chipping his nails until they bled. His pounding heartbeat hammered inside his ears as he tore the last of the knots free. Desperate, he scanned the dim room, searching for a weapon. His gaze narrowed on a crude cleaver lying on the table beside the bloodied remains of a plucked hen. He crawled to his feet. A sudden wooziness threatened to buckle his weak legs.

Citavnah cackled and a baby's shrill cry filled the dim tent.

Forcing himself forward, Ahren snatched the rusted cleaver and charged the sweat-drenched witch straddling a glistening black pool. She spun her head toward him, her cracked lips twisted into a perverse, evil grin, and Ahren hacked the wide blade into her neck. Blood burst across the room, splattering over his naked body. She erupted in maddening laughter that gurgled and bubbled out from the jagged wound. Ahren swung again, cleaving through the side of her face, but the witch continued her roaring cachinnations. She lunged, driving her grafted blade at his heart. Leaping to the side, Ahren chopped the cleaver down. The heavy blade hacked through her wrist, sending a spray of blood across the yurta. Her gnarled hand fell to the floor, still clutching its cursed blade. Citavnah screamed and Ahren buried the cleaver into her head. Rage bellowed inside him. He chopped again and again until the witch's still corpse lay silent at his feet.

Panting, he wiped the cold, splattered blood from his face. He caught his reflection in the black mirror propped against the wall the witch had been facing. The image stared back at him with a disparaging smile and holding a small bundle to its bare chest.

Too late, Ahren. Chuckling, it gazed down on the wrapped baby in its arms. *What is of you is now mine.*

Ahren swallowed the nauseating horror rising in his throat as a tiny hand reached up from the bundle toward the demon's face.

Our child may have been conceived in flesh, but it has been born in darkness, born of me. It laughed.

Shadows swirled through the air around Ahren like tattered translucent sheets. He squeezed the heavy cleaver in his hand.

The dark reflection rolled the newborn over and gently pulled the blanket away. Black eyes stared out from the baby's quivering face. *Say hello to your death, Ahren. Do you want to choose a name?*

The flying shadows danced with the demon's laughter. Ahren

hurled the heavy blade at the obsidian mirror, shattering it into hundreds of tiny shards. The swarming shades vanished, leaving him alone in the dim yurta as the laughter faded in the distance.

We'll meet again. I promise.

Ahren's overwhelming fear washed away, leaving a calm focus. His shredded clothes lay like useless rags beside the bed. He snatched the witch's threadbare cloak from the floor and threw it over his shoulders. He lifted a candle from a weathered table and held it against the yurta's felt walls. The orange flame caressed the gray fabric then caught. "I look forward to it."

About the Author

Raised in the swamps and pine forests of East Texas, Seth Skorkowsky gravitated to the darker sides of fantasy, preferring horror and pulp heroes over knights in shining armor.

His debut novel, Dämoren, was published in 2014 as book #1 in the Valducan series; it was followed by Hounacier in 2015, and Ibenus in 2016. Seth has also released two sword-and-sorcery rogue collections with his Tales of the Black Raven series.

When not writing, Seth enjoys cheesy movies, tabletop role-playing games, and traveling the world with his wife.

Visit Seth's website: http://skorkowsky.com/

Curious about other Crossroad Press books?
Stop by our site:
http://store.crossroadpress.com
We offer quality writing
in digital, audio, and print formats.

Enter the code FIRSTBOOK
to get 20% off your first order from our store!
Stop by today!

Printed in Great Britain
by Amazon